BEAUTY AND THE BOSS

Praise for Ali Vali

Balance of Forces: Toujours Ici

"A stunning addition to the vampire legend, *Balance of Forces: Toujour Ici* is one that stands apart from the rest."
—*Bibliophilic Book Blog*

Calling the Dead

"So many writers set stories in New Orleans, but Ali Vali's mystery novels have the authenticity that only a real Big Easy resident could bring...makes for a classic lesbian murder yarn."—***Curve Magazine***

Blue Skies

"Vali is skilled at building sexual tension, and the sex in this novel flies as high as Berkley's jets. Look for this fast-paced read."—*Just About Write*

Carly's Sound

"Vali paints vivid pictures with her words...*Carly's Sound* is a great romance, with some wonderfully hot sex."—*Midwest Book Review*

"It's no surprise that passion is indeed possible a second time around."—*Q Syndicate*

Acclaim for the Casey Cain Saga

The Devil Inside

"Vali's fluid writing style quickly puts the reader at ease, which makes the story and its characters equally easy to get to know and care about. When you find yourself talking out loud to the characters in a book, you know the work is polished and professional, as well as entertaining."—*Family and Friends Magazine*

"Not only is *The Devil Inside* a ripping mystery, it's also an intimate character study."—*L-Word Literature*

"*The Devil Inside* is the first of what promises to be a very exciting series…While telling an exciting story that grips the reader, Vali has also fully fleshed out her heroes and villains. *The Devil Inside* is that rarity: a fascinating crime novel which includes a tender love story and leaves the reader with a cliffhanger ending."—*MegaScene*

The Devil Unleashed

"Fast-paced action scenes, intriguing character revelations, and a refreshing approach to the romance thriller genre all make for an enjoyable reading experience in the Big Easy…*The Devil Unleashed* is an engrossing reading experience."—*Midwest Book Review*

Deal with the Devil

"Ali Vali has given her fans another thick, rich thriller…*Deal With the Devil* has wonderful love stories, great sex, and an ample supply of humor. It is an exciting, page-turning read that leaves her readers eagerly awaiting the next book in the series."—*Just About Write*

The Devil Be Damned

"Ali Vali excels at creating strong, romantic characters along with her fast-paced, sophisticated plots. Her setting, New Orleans, provides just the right blend of immigrants from Mexico, South America, and Cuba, along with a city steeped in traditions."—*Just About Write*

By the Author

Carly's Sound

Second Season

Calling the Dead

Blue Skies

Love Match

The Dragon Tree Legacy

The Romance Vote

Girls with Guns

Beneath the Waves

Beauty and the Boss

Forces Series

Balance of Forces: Toujours Ici

Battle of Forces: Sera Toujours

The Cain Casey Saga

The Devil Inside

The Devil Unleashed

Deal with the Devil

The Devil Be Damned

The Devil's Orchard

The Devil's Due

Visit us at www.boldstrokesbooks.com

BEAUTY
AND THE BOSS

by
Ali Vali

2017

ISBN 13: 978-1-62639-919-8

This Trade Paperback Original Is Published By
Bold Strokes Books, Inc.
P.O. Box 249
Valley Falls, NY 12185

First Edition: September 2017

CREDITS
Editor: Shelley Thrasher
Production Design: Stacia Seaman
Cover Design by Melody Pond

Acknowledgments

Every story might start with an idea that takes months to write, but no book is done without a great team. Thank you, Radclyffe, for your support from the beginning and for your friendship. Thanks to Sandy Lowe for the title—those are always the hardest, and this one's perfect.

Thank you to Shelley Thrasher, my editor. As always, you taught me something, and for that I'm always grateful.

Thank you to my fantastic first readers Kim Rieff, Cris Perez-Soria, and Connie Ward. You guys rock and always have great suggestions, so I appreciate the input. It's nice to know, though, that I can surprise you with a good plot twist.

A big thank you to the BSB team, my fellow authors, and Melody Pond for a great cover. Life at times knocks you flat with surprises you never see coming, so I thank my BSB family for not only helping me get up, but for letting me lean on you. I love you guys.

Thank you to all the readers for your unwavering support and for your many emails. As always, every word is written with you in mind.

It's amazing how life can change in such a short time and how much pain you can endure without breaking from the weight of so much loss. The only way to survive is to be lucky enough to have friends and someone who loves you shoulder the burden with you. Thank you to my big brother for all the memories and for your unwavering support for all of my fifty-three years. I hope your eternity is only smooth waters, big fish, and a cup that never goes empty.

Thank you, C, for making me laugh when I didn't think I could, for simply holding my hand when words weren't necessary or possible, and for thirty-two years full of joy. I love you. *Verdad!*

For C
A lifetime will never be enough.

For my big brother
Rest easy, brother, and know you are missed.

CHAPTER ONE

Fashion designer Ellis Renois used the back door of her main studio in the Garment District, wanting to avoid anyone vying for the summer internship from trying to make an impression before it was their turn. The large open space on the top floor was where her team took her sketches and transformed them into the reality of the runway. She'd always felt alive in here, and she used these interviews to find the person who felt the same way. The only thing was, it had to be someone who would put in the work and not want to just show up for the accolades of Fashion Week.

Her best friend and business partner Rueben Maddox was waiting just inside. "Take the sofa," he said of the spot they used when they had guests for previews. The space was eerily quiet since the staff was on holiday for a few weeks and would return when she started sending sketches from her own vacation to add to the ones already in the finishing stages. A skeleton crew would follow her out of town, and one of the head seamstresses would fly back and forth to make sure everything stayed on track for the fall.

"It's not too late to change your mind," Rueben said.

Ellis was growing tired of this same damn conversation they'd had in the last couple of years. "This will go much faster if you leave out the lecture, Ruby."

"You can't blame me for trying."

"True, but don't push it by driving it in the ground. You'll break a nail, or worse yet, you'll ruin your outfit by breaking a sweat."

She smiled at Rueben and moved to her assigned seat, stopping to put her hands on her hips when she spotted a kid walking slowly in the back corner of the room. Whoever she was, she was moving her head like she was trying to commit every inch of the space to memory.

"Hold up, Ruby. Hi," Ellis said, stopping in front of the big leather chesterfield. "Are you here for the internship? Not that I'd turn you down, but you look a little young to be in the workforce." She unbuttoned her jacket and held her hand out after spotting the book in the girl's hand. "Let's see your sketches."

"How come you don't think it's my diary?"

The kid, who appeared barely ten, had moxie, and her slightly long, dark hair falling in her face made Ellis think she was ready for a photo shoot. She sat and patted the spot next to her. "If it's your diary, you must have a lot of emotion in those pages."

The kid had a good laugh, but she hesitated before taking a seat. "Why'd you say that?" The girl had obviously thought about joining her and chose to stay on her feet.

"You've got an awful lot of colored pencils for the average diary. Can I see, or is it too personal?" She stood and waved the kid to the table against the wall of glass as a way to put her more at ease. The view from here was shit, but the light was phenomenal, so she coped. Staring at something beautiful all day would definitely blow her work-life concentration right out the window. Not that it didn't anyway.

"How about I go first." She moved some of the work-related sketchbooks to the side and reached for one from the bottom shelf of the long table, opening it to the first page. "Put your book down," she said, pointing to the space she'd made. "Or not," she said when the kid pressed it closer against her chest.

The first sketch in her book was of her and her mother Amis, when she was about the same age as this kid. Back then, Amis had been one of the seamstresses in a place very much like this. They always spent their Sundays, Amis's only real day off, at the center of some beautiful place, and her mother had done a masterful job of choosing locations that built the artist in her soul one stunning landscape after another.

"This is my mother, Amis," she said of the sketch she'd done a few years back. The finished product hung over her fireplace at home.

The kid opened her book and handed it over like it was her heart on a plate. "Here," she said, making eye contact only for a moment.

"I'm Ellis," she said, placing the sketchbook next to hers. "What's your name?" She held her hand out where the kid would see it. "How it works is, you tell me your name to introduce yourself, and then you shake my hand firmly but not painfully."

"I'm Sawyer. My mom wants to meet you." Sawyer shook her hand a little too long with a slightly sweaty palm, but she didn't mind since the kid was obviously nervous.

After Sawyer finally let her hand go, Ellis flipped through the pages of really good sketches. Sawyer wasn't Monet yet, but the raw talent was there. At times, no matter how much the person wanted it, you couldn't build on faulty ground. Sawyer had the kind of talent that would blossom only under the right care. "How'd you get back here?"

"Everyone out there has like a major case of the willies, so I went exploring. One of the doors led back here." Sawyer shrugged and still wouldn't make eye contact. "Did this mess my mom up?"

She finished going through the book. "Did she help you with these?"

"No. She tells me all the time to follow my heart."

Ellis had to smile when Sawyer rolled her eyes. "Do you know what that means?"

Sawyer cocked her head to the side before shaking it. "Not really, no."

She flipped through her own sketchbook to the few she'd done when she'd visited Monet's gardens in France and then opened her book of his work. "These are of the same place." She pointed between the two. "This is the way he saw it, and this is the way I did. One's more literal than the other, don't you think?"

"They're both nice," Sawyer said, putting her hands on the table and standing on her toes to see better. "You're really good."

"Thank you, and we were both doing what your mom told you, so she's right about following your heart. Eventually you'll see how important that is." She handed the book back, and Sawyer immediately held it against her chest.

"But what's it really mean?"

"Everyone has their own interpretation, but here's my take. The world and how we see it is like loving a certain kind of flower over another. I might look at daisies and see weeds, but you might love daisies so you see something beautiful. You don't want someone telling you how to think about the flowers—you know it's a completely personal thing. Art's all about the eye of the person with the brush in their hand, and what you put on the page or canvas is what's in here," she said, tapping the side of Sawyer's head, "and in here," she said tapping over her heart.

"Thanks...I guess." Sawyer seemed hesitant to leave.

"You want to hang out here until we're done?" Sawyer smiled slightly and sat on the stool she'd pointed to and waved Rueben off when he stared at the girl. "Come on, Ruby. Let's get started. What's your mom's name?" she asked Sawyer.

"Charlotte."

"Should she go first or last?" Ellis asked, immediately putting a stunned almost pained expression on Sawyer's face.

Actually, Sawyer looked at her as if her answer would totally mess her mother up if she were wrong. "If it was you, would you go first or last?" Sawyer finally said.

"Smart kid," Rueben said.

"I'd say first," Ellis said seriously. "First impressions make their mark for either good or bad, so they save time either way."

❖

Charlotte Hamner glanced around while massaging her abdomen, trying to relax the crampy ache that was growing since Sawyer hadn't come back from her exploring. Her daughter's curiosity made it impossible for her to behave all the time, but she kept her promises, so panic hadn't set in since Sawyer had sworn she wouldn't leave the building. She didn't know where she was at that exact moment, but she was sure Sawyer was still in the building and not kidnapped in the back of a van somewhere.

"Ms. Hamner," the man who'd introduced himself as Rueben Maddox said, holding the door open. "If you're ready, Ms. Renois will see you now."

"Thank you, and I'm sure this will completely torpedo my chances, but if my daughter comes back, could you tell her where I am and that I won't be long?"

"I'd be happy to, but I think you have nothing to worry about," Rueben said with a genuinely warm smile.

Charlotte smiled back, even though she had no idea what he was talking about, but she was as thrilled to meet him as she was Ellis

Renois. Rueben Maddox knew a lot about what women really wanted in evening wear, if they could actually afford his stuff. She'd copied one of his designs and made her own for an event at school.

"Thanks, but you have to know Sawyer. She's a free spirit, so I hope she doesn't get into trouble before we're booted out of here." She tried to juggle her bag and portfolio to be able to shake his hand, and Rueben had to take the large sketch case from her. "It's an honor to meet you, and thank you."

"It's an honor to meet you, and you don't have to worry since Sawyer and I have already met," he said, pointing to her daughter, who was sitting and sketching in her book at a large table by the windows. "She might be a free spirit, but she's a polite, well-behaved one."

Charlotte was somewhat shocked to see Ellis Renois standing behind Sawyer, seemingly giving her pointers as Sawyer drew something. She wasn't surprised that Sawyer was drawing, but that she was actually smiling was something new. Usually Sawyer was shy around new people, and she was super-secretive about her art with everyone, even though her talent was extraordinary for someone her age. Not even Sawyer's deadbeat dad Kyle or anyone in his family had ever seen this side of their daughter.

"I'm so sorry," she said softly, not wanting to break Ellis and Sawyer apart.

"Whatever for?" Rueben said, carrying her bag to where Ellis was standing. "I think the boss is more impressed with Sawyer's book than that of any candidate we had last year."

"Ms. Hamner, welcome," Ellis said after placing her hands on Sawyer's shoulders. "Keep going, kid," she said to Sawyer. "Let's see your stuff."

"Thanks for inviting me, and I hope we haven't been a bother," Charlotte said as she glanced back at Sawyer as she opened her portfolio and grabbed her designs.

"Listening to Sawyer give me advice was no bother."

Ellis quickly spread Charlotte's designs out over the table, and both Ellis and Rueben studied them as if they would be tested for every detail when the interview was over. Of the twenty she'd brought, Ellis set five aside and stacked the rest. These showed a casual outfit, two business suits, and two dresses for informal evening wear. All of them were variations of something Ellis had put out during her career but incorporated the minor changes Charlotte would've made to appeal to a wider audience.

"I don't necessarily think you're mocking me, but you don't seem to like my stuff either," Ellis said, still flipping through the other sketches again. This time she set three aside. "No one has ever taken this exact approach, so I'm curious as to why you did."

"I'd never mock you or anyone, but not everyone is a supermodel, Ms. Renois." She held up the sketch closest to her and started talking before Ellis fired her without even considering her for the job. "Flaring the skirt on the suit will flatter a wider hip," she said, pointing to the change and moving on to the next one. "Adding straps and a little length to the dresses will encourage more women to try them, and casual doesn't mean you can't accessorize a little." The outfit now had a wide belt and slits in the three-quarter-length sleeves.

Ellis held up two of her originals. "Tell me about these."

"My mother and I share a love of vintage clothes, but not everyone loves the hunt, so I tried to design with that in mind." The dress that resembled some from the forties would've been sold in that era as everyday wear, but hers were tighter through the hips and leg, with a slight slit, all in linen. The top wasn't as buttoned-up modest as the style back then, and she'd done away with the collar. "Most dresses from this period had a blouse-and-skirt look about them, but I moved the buttons from the waist to the hem of the slit to draw your eye to the legs. To highlight the buttons, I'd go with something like an onyx material for the white and bone for the black."

"These could go from the office to an evening dinner?"

"I'm motivated by what would be a good investment for anyone on a budget. Something like this would be versatile for a number of occasions and could be changed easily with some basic accessories so it wouldn't appear like you're wearing the same thing over and over again. I think of it as couture for the everyday woman."

"What about red?"

"I didn't think that would be a good choice since that'd be definitely memorable. Red would be good as a once-in-a-while dress, so it'd get more time in the closet instead of wear time."

"Thanks for coming in," Ellis said, not asking another thing and handing over all her work.

"Is red your favorite color?" she asked, not believing that color, of all things, would be the reason she wouldn't be considered.

"You mean you don't know what my favorite color is? You researched enough to change my designs, but you skimped on something so crucial?" Ellis spoke in a tone that signaled she was done. In that one instant, every moment Charlotte had spent agonizing over this meeting seemed like such a waste. Ellis Renois was tall and incredibly good-looking, but she was kind of an asshole. "Maybe you should've considered that and a few other things, Mrs. Hamner."

"It's Ms. Hamner, and it shouldn't matter what your favorite color is. Not everyone looks good in red."

"Thank you for the lesson in fashion, *Ms.* Hamner. I don't know how in the world I've gotten along without it this long."

"Sawyer, get your things." She zipped up her bag and waited for Sawyer to put her pencils away before leaving without another word. Maybe it wasn't too late to hire on with someone else, even if all she did the entire summer was sew.

"You should've shaken her hand, Mama. She's big on that," Sawyer said as they rode the elevator down.

"You're right. I'll remember that for next time," she said, thinking Ellis was lucky she didn't punch her in the throat for being such an ass.

CHAPTER TWO

D o you have everything set?" Jennifer Eymard asked Dalton Burton as they had lunch at the Clocktower restaurant. "I haven't heard from the dragon lady, so I'm curious," she said, laughing at their nickname for Ellis's mother Amis.

Once the business had ballooned to the point where Amis couldn't handle all of the everyday items, Ellis had hired Dalton as a manager to take on part of the workload. He'd helped the Renois House expand to where they now had thousands on the payroll. Once they'd reached that size, Jennifer had become the CFO, at Dalton's suggestion, and as usual, Ellis agreed, not wanting to be bothered by what she thought was the minutiae of the business.

"I've just got to get Ellis to sign the paperwork before she leaves, and no one's picked up on it yet. You did a good job of burying the most important section in all that legalese," Dalton said. They needed to get back, but he really wanted to stop at his place to release some of the pressure Jennifer had built up with her foot pressed against his crotch. "She's hot to get out of town, so this might actually work. We couldn't have timed this more perfectly."

"Then get the bill, lover, and let's do a little celebrating." Jennifer pressed harder with her foot, making him have to take a deep breath. "I told you this would be easy."

"Don't gloat until she signs."

The waiter rushed away with his card, and he had to push Jennifer off before he came in his pants. That hadn't happened to him since high school, and he wasn't about to regress.

"You want me there so you don't mess this up?" she asked, which instantly turned him off.

Condescending and sarcastic commentary he got plenty of at home. "I think I can handle it since I've gotten us this far, haven't I?"

"Darling, you know I meant for moral support. Of course you've done great so far, but we're so close." Her tone had become syrupy sweet.

Dalton couldn't wait for the bill to come so they could get the hell out of there.

"Just take a cab back, and I'll meet you at the office. No sense in whipping up suspicion now," Dalton said.

He stared at her when she ran her foot up his leg. "Jennifer, I'll meet you back at the office."

"Don't be mad," she said with a slight pout.

Fuck, he thought, knowing what the next couple of hours would be like. Jennifer was good in bed. That alone had made his wife repulsive to him now, but she could also be a pain in the ass when she wanted to be. "Like I said, Ellis hasn't signed it yet, so let's wait on the party."

"But you're mad," she whined.

"I'm being cautious. There's a difference. Go ahead and take off."

He came close to sighing in relief when she stood up but didn't make that mistake until she was out the door. The moment alone gave him time to reflect on what he was getting ready to do. Ellis and he had been friends for years, and she'd given him the opportunity of a lifetime, but Jennifer had made him want more than Ellis was willing to give. Hell, if Ellis was honest, she'd admit the business wouldn't be where it was without him, so if she wouldn't reward him, he'd just take it.

"After tonight I'll lock you on the hamster wheel of life like you did to me," he said and tried to calm the nerves that were upsetting his stomach. "It's my turn to be the top guy."

The last candidate was the best flirt in the bunch, and she reminded Ellis of the woman from last summer. It was a shame her designs didn't match her talent in the come-on arena. "Thank you for coming in. Rueben will be in touch." The woman took her hand and held it as she looked into her eyes, as if trying to hypnotize her into giving her the job. "Take care now," she said, prying her hand loose.

It took Rueben ten minutes to get back, giving her enough time to find the original sketches Charlotte Hamner had shown her. Design, she'd learned quickly, was always a compromise, from the original idea to the final product, and that compromise usually came down to one simple thing…money. Only a very few could afford what the final outfit would cost if it was produced with every specification she envisioned initially.

"Have you made up your mind?" Rueben asked when he returned. "Or do you need more time?"

"Considering we're on a time crunch, and I'm also late for lunch with my mother, it's now or never. Have you made up your mind?" She held up the sketch of the casual outfit, which wasn't much different from what Charlotte had showed her, but definitely different than what the final product had turned out to be.

"There's no way she would've had access to that since we never release those until the show and subsequent launch to the market. And even then, we only show the final sketches and not the first draft. That went into production without the belt and the sleeve design. If you remember, the version Ms. Hamner liked couldn't be brought to market because it would've been either too pricey or too cheesy if they downgraded the belt to something other than leather."

"That doesn't answer my question," Ellis said as she returned to the designs.

"She thinks like you, but she hasn't found her edge yet. Her original designs are good, but they're missing the 'it' factor that would make a woman carry the dress to the register and hand over her credit card."

"I know that about *Ms*. Hamner, and she's closer than you think to the 'it' factor. What about the rest of them?" she said as she put the sketches back into the book from a few years back and shelved it. The only book out was for this year's show, but Ruby had just taken it from the safe. It was complete as far as the initial sketches. They'd spend the next few months finalizing what the crew was already physically putting together, and only then would she make changes to the pages. Art was one thing, but she needed to see something on a woman before she even contemplated redesign.

"Do you really want to waste time talking about the others?" Rueben said as he locked the cabinet that held all her original books. "Or is this about the fact that Charlotte Hamner isn't going to fall into your bed with a few well-placed moves and pretty words on your part?"

"You don't know me that well, Ruby. It's not always about the ass factor. She's got a kid to consider, so she might not want to uproot her life to follow us home."

"She's blond and beautiful, so the ass factor always comes up, my friend. Why not ask her what she's willing to do about the moving part before you make the decision for her? This one isn't your typical summer-fling material, and maybe that's a good thing for you."

"Don't push it, Ruby. I'm not in the mood. I like women, and I'm not going to apologize for it."

"Seriously? Come on. You know I'm right. This has been an unmitigated disaster from the beginning."

"I think unmitigated is a little extreme, drama queen, and I'm not changing my mind. Just give me a rundown on everything else, and I'll think about *Ms*. Hamner. She was the only one in the bunch with a fresh idea."

"Everything's packed, and since this was the last thing on your list before we fly out in the morning, we're ready to go," Rueben said in a flat tone, never glancing up from his black leather folio.

Ellis was sure Rueben slept, bathed, had sex, and ate without ever putting the damn thing down. It was still in one piece and not in tatters only because Ellis had purchased one with the finest leather she could get. Rueben deserved nothing but the best, since he was her best friend and his designs for the Renois Fashion House were inspirational.

He was talented in design and keeping her life on track, so he was always close by with his folio full of appointments and what he liked to call the blueprint to beauty. She was also sure he had enough ideas folded away in that book to keep them going for the next three years.

"Look, I know this isn't your thing, but it's important to me. I refuse to let a few setbacks change my mind about going forward."

When they'd started together, they'd agreed to always help someone get their start in the business, and nothing would make her stop wanting to find talent. Fashion designers, successful ones anyway, she'd discovered through the years, very seldom liked to share the limelight, but she figured karma would only help if she continued her quest to find new talent and help grow it.

"I'm not lecturing, so stop saying that, but you've paid enough dues and kept your promise enough years. Why not skip the intern this time and save yourself a lot of heartache? We've got enough to do without having all the problems some of these people come with." He cut his eyes up at her without lifting his head, as if to see if she'd bite on what he'd been asking for three years in a row.

"Come on, Ruby. Don't you remember being that baby-faced hopeful looking for one big break?" Their relationship had actually begun earlier than that, since Ellis had been the only one who'd talked to the then-wallflower Rueben.

They'd started small with a loan from Amis, never skimping on quality, which had paid off when they landed two up-and-coming actresses for the Golden Globes. They were surprise winners and had returned to see if they could find Oscar magic with a Renois design. Business had picked up after that and had skyrocketed when they'd landed two of the three dresses the first lady had worn a year after that to the inaugural balls.

"You can't drag me that far back in time, thank you. God, I was such a dork back then," Rueben said, snapping the book closed.

Rueben had wanted to stay in the background, which had surprised her, but he'd never been able to shed his Midwestern farm-boy shyness. Then again, most boys from the Midwest didn't know what taffeta was and why it should be used sparingly, if at all, so that had explained his quiet nature. She loved him enough that she seldom said anything about Rueben's list of quirks. He didn't complain, though, when she launched Renois's Maddox line of evening wear. It was an offshoot of the Renois line, and his creativity had made it a success.

"A dork who owned three hundred and fifty-two scarves," she said, combing back her dark-brown hair that was longer than she usually kept it.

"Don't remind me." He pointed his pen at her. "And I'll never forgive you for not telling me how much those things upped my dork factor."

"It was all part of your charm." She gazed out to the nondescript building next door. This view and the one from her apartment that overlooked Central Park were the only two she saw when she was working. The stories the tabloids loved to print about the women in her life never mentioned her long hours. Granted, she'd had plenty of women, but nowhere near the number the news rags liked to write about. Right now there were no women, plenty of work, and an apathy that was starting to swamp her. She was anxious to get out of town, hoping the change of scenery would get her back in the groove of loving all this again.

New York was the center of the universe when it came to fashion, but she'd never been able to really think in this city. Her mother, Amis, said it was because of her ADHD, but in her own defense, it was hard to concentrate in a city that never really slept. The studio and the apartment she owned off the park at Fifth and East 72nd Street were tastefully decorated, a prime location, and the site of countless parties whenever she was in the city—but it wasn't home, and it was more of a trophy than anything else. A big bank account, a perfect home, and fame weren't the basis for happiness, no matter what other people thought.

"And it was your charm that almost wrecked our show this year, so why don't you think of some other way to pay the universe back for our good fortune? You could donate to badly dressed children maybe," Rueben suggested.

"Why does the word *no* unlock the crazy, gouge-your-eyes-out, witch factor in some women?"

Rueben stood next to her and held her hand. It was the same comfort she'd provided him when her intern/entry-level designer from the previous year had caused a scene by stripping naked at her show, screaming obscenities the entire time as she walked the runway.

The hysteria had started when Ellis told her they wouldn't be sleeping together anymore and she wasn't getting her own line. Ellis still hadn't figured out which of the options had caused the childish behavior. No matter. The tantrum had gotten a lot of press, most of it good, so she couldn't complain. She figured it was the young woman's perky tits and great ass that the press had fallen in love with that had saved them.

"Isn't that a rather sexist statement?" Rueben said sarcastically.

"You act like that at times, but I already know the list of what drives you down Main Street of crazy town."

"Oh yeah, what?"

"Hunger and heat, and add a broken heel or a run in someone's stocking before going on, and you've hit the trifecta. I have yet to make you insane enough to strip in front of a large crowd though." They both laughed before she leaned over and kissed him on the cheek. "I promise to behave this year, Ruby, but I'm not breaking our pledge."

"I want that in writing, preferably in blood, so you'll remember it when your brain goes to mush when they show you their tits."

"You've got that all wrong." She stood and grabbed her jacket. "The last thing in the world that happens to me is turning to mush when someone shows me their tits, as you so elegantly put it. Trust me on that. It's the complete opposite of mush."

"You're disgusting and a bit touched in the head."

"But you love me anyway." She blew him a kiss on her way out the door.

CHAPTER THREE

Y ou need to eat more," Amis Renois said to Ellis before she sat next to her at Carnegie Deli.

"If any model on our payroll heard you say that, they'd hire a hit man to take you out." Ellis always tried to get a corned-beef sandwich and an order of chopped liver before leaving the city. She kissed her mother's cheek and took her hand. Aside from Rueben, her mother never held her tongue, even when it was necessary to hurt her feelings by disagreeing, but her brutal honesty had taught Ellis never to fear the truth. It was a blessing in an industry often full of petty, jealous backstabbers.

"You're one of the only designers who admits to the world a woman has curves and, God forbid, breasts, and the sky has yet to fall." Amis made the universal hand motion for a woman with both breast and hips as she laughed. "It's why places like Macy's and Target, as well as the high-end boutiques, are banging on your door, and you never lack dates on any night of the week. Women love you, chéri, and you make them look good. It's a powerful combination."

"I'll stick to the casual date and making them look good. Any longer than that and my luck runs aground on the rocky shoals of life."

"I really should've limited your reading as a child," Amis said, laughing again. "Such gloom for so few years on this earth. You need to find someone who makes you see and appreciate the goodness in life. It's the only way to truly experience its beauty."

"I have you for that, so my life's full."

The waiter set down the assortment of food Amis had ordered and hesitated when he took a long look at Ellis. Damn Ruby and his insistence on putting her picture on their latest marketing campaign. Hoping he'd move on, she said, "Thank you."

"Kiss Ruby for me when you see him again. The expression on your face whenever anyone does that is priceless."

"The two of you are a laugh riot. Next time, your picture is going on the campaign, so you can be the center of attention."

Ellis tried her best to get through at least half of the enormous sandwich, but her appetite didn't hold out that long. After a few bites of cheesecake she was done and ready to finish her list of errands before she left for home.

"Are you coming down South with us?" Ellis asked as she paid the bill.

"I'll be there in a few weeks. The dynamic duo is having problems, and I want to oversee their solutions. That should give me plenty of time."

"What kind of problems?" Ellis smiled at her mother's nickname for Dalton and Jennifer.

Dalton and Jennifer had been key employees for a time, but Ellis hadn't anticipated that the people she trusted with her business would become lovers and somewhat secretive. That was one reason she was glad her mother was president and still enjoyed overseeing most of the business end of things. Amis was the only person she truly trusted, and since the contracts Dalton and Jennifer had signed would be expensive to break, Amis was the one person who kept the two in check.

"According to Dalton, the contracts with Saks had some glitches in them," Amis said. "I went over everything with legal, so I'm not sure what he's talking about. If this is just more bullshit to waste my time, I hope you're okay with me firing him the second I find any irregularity on anything remotely fishy. I keep trying to find a cause to cut them both, but they have a talent for slithering along without crossing the line that would get them fired."

"You get a raise if you find that, and call Josh at Saks and see what the deal is." Ellis took her mother's hand and helped her outside. "I'll see you tonight for dinner."

"What's your next stop?"

"I finished the interviews this morning, so I have to make a decision. After that I'm ready to go."

Amis stared at her but kept her mouth shut.

"What?" Ellis laughed when her mother shook her head but smiled. "I promised Ruby I'd behave, so you can stop worrying."

"Ah, chéri. You are the most talented person I know, but behaving isn't in your repertoire of gifts. I have no one to blame but myself, though, so who am I to tell you anything? I taught you that life is a buffet to be enjoyed, but who knew you'd be so drawn only to the dessert section." Amis kissed both her cheeks and hugged her as if using all her strength. "Try to at least pick one who'll keep her clothes on during fashion week, hopefully during the show anyway. The rest is up to you."

Ellis smiled as her mother grabbed both her ears and gently shook her head. "Let me know if you need any help at the office or with Saks."

"Good luck, and I'll handle those two, no problem." Amis kissed her cheeks again. "The most important thing, chéri, is to pick one who'll make you happy. After all, isn't that the most any of us can hope for?"

"I'll try my best, Mama. I'll try my best."

❖

Charlotte pinched the bridge of her nose, trying to forget the blossoming headache the present phone call was causing. "You already flaked out on me this morning, and you haven't seen Sawyer in three months. If you come get her until I get off tonight, you'll get the chance to spend time with her."

"What can I tell you, babe? Boss said to show up or forget about showing up at all." Kyle Snyder laughed in a way that made Charlotte want the magical power to crawl through the phone connection and strangle him when she reached the other side. "The way you harp about money, you'd think this was a good thing."

"I don't harp about money to lavish on myself, Kyle. It's to help take care of Sawyer. I have to work a double shift tonight and my sitter's sick. I hate having her sitting there for so long. Do you think your mom could watch Sawyer for a few hours? Once you're finished at work you can pick her up." She couldn't believe the words had come out of her mouth, but desperate times and measures made even the devil look good. She still cursed her sixteen-year-old self for actually believing the bullshit Kyle had been peddling way back then. That she was ever that naive was stunning. "I don't ask you for much." And you don't give much, she thought but didn't add, on the chance Kyle would actually come through this one time.

"You know Mom loves the brat, but she's not feeling good."

That meant she was so hung over she could barely remember Kyle's sorry ass, much less her granddaughter. Charlotte hung up. Kyle and his entire family were total assholes and losers, but he'd given her one thing she wouldn't trade for anything in the world. Sawyer was a bright, enthusiastic kid who'd made life a juggling act from the day she was born, but she was the greatest gift the universe had ever given Charlotte. It was like the powers that be had taken a day off from fucking her over to give her a perfect daughter.

Charlotte set her phone aside and didn't feel the same satisfaction as slamming it down. She didn't have time to brood about it, so she started walking around the apartment, getting ready for work.

"Mama, you okay?" Sawyer asked as she pulled on Charlotte's shirttails. She was stretched out on the sofa watching TV, her hair going in all directions. Eight and a half years of trying to tame it had been in vain.

"How'd you like to work with me today?" Charlotte tried her best to make her voice light. "You can bring your books and read or draw."

"Really, I can?" Sawyer cocked her head back as far as it'd go to look up at her. The crooked smile made Sawyer all that more adorable.

"You bet."

"Is it my fault you still have to work there? I know you don't like it," Sawyer said, following her to the one bedroom they shared.

Their apartment wasn't great, but you'd never realize that by the monthly rent. The only way to pay for it was the waitress job she didn't care for at all, yet the hours were flexible. When she was struggling to make it through school, it had been a godsend.

"It's not your fault, and I'm going to get a much better job, so don't worry about it." Charlotte kissed the top of Sawyer's head and hugged her. "Mrs. Cleaver's sick, so I'm sorry you'll be stuck watching me all night. I'll buy you a burger and a chocolate shake to make up for boring you to death until ten."

"Make it strawberry, and you can stay late," Sawyer said with a laugh.

She put on the polyester outfit from hell and carried Sawyer's bag for her so she could easily hold her hand on the subway. The diner was a block off Times Square and usually packed with tourists and theatergoers, but her boss didn't mind her bringing Sawyer since she sat and either sketched or read.

"How'd it go?" Serena, her fellow waitress, asked as Charlotte punched in. "If you get the job, is there any chance of free clothes for all your closest friends?"

"Ellis Renois is an ass, so I doubt I'll be getting more than the five minutes she blessed me with today. As for free clothes, I seriously don't think even her mother gets that."

"Sorry," Serena said as she put her hand on Charlotte's shoulder. "I know how much you were looking forward to this chance."

"I guess I've got more dues to pay, so do you mind keeping an eye on Sawyer when it gets crazy tonight and pass the word?"

"We'll keep her in fries and pie," Serena said, waving over her shoulder as she headed out with a fresh order book.

Six hours later Charlotte was sure that selling herself on the street would be better than this job. The tables she was responsible for had won the prize for the troubled section that night, and it seemed like every other table had sent at least half of their orders back. The only thing all of the rejected food had in common was that it was her fault it was bad.

Charlotte waved and smiled at Sawyer as she headed to the single the hostess had just put by the glass wall. "What can I get you to drink?" she asked, holding her finger up to the people three tables over screaming about wedges of lemon, which made no sense considering they were all drinking lemonade. She had a feeling that this menu peruser would be the next in line to complain, since the menu had a lot on it, but it wasn't exactly *War and Peace*. She needed to get going.

"Do you recommend the coffee or the hot chocolate?"

"Somehow, I don't think you need any more caffeine, so how about a lemonade that may or may not have enough lemon in it?" she said, figuring she didn't have anything to lose.

"Uh-huh, and would you recommend the burger or the hot dog?" Ellis finally put her oversized menu down completely and smiled at her. "Which do you think would be easier for you to tell me to shove up my—"

"Hey, I thought no such thing." She pointed at Ellis with her pen.

"If you didn't, you're kinder than I would've ever been in the same situation."

"I was hoping more like you'd choke on the burger, even if it is really good."

"Spunk," Ellis said and slapped the table with her open palm. "You'll need plenty of it in life. Do you have a break coming up or something? I'd like to talk to you."

"I get fifteen minutes in an hour, so I doubt you want to wait that long." Damn all these people in here and their pettiness tonight. If it was slower she could've had one of the girls cover for her, but not in this madhouse.

"I've got nothing going on except the need for a good burger cooked medium with mayo, one piece of lettuce, and grilled onions."

"How about pickles and tomato?"

"Put that on it, and I'll be happy to send it back like those idiots over there, though I doubt I can get that loud." Ellis pointed to the man holding up his plate and screaming for Charlotte. "How about some company though?"

"I'm sure one of the girls would love to sit with you, but that's an invitation to get fired on a night like this, so don't tempt anyone over here to amuse yourself."

"Ouch." Ellis put her hands over her chest as if she'd stabbed her. "I meant the lonely-looking kid in the corner over there."

"I'm sorry," she said, blinking rapidly while staring up at the ceiling, trying not to look Ellis in the eye. After a few deep breaths, she left before she could screw up anymore.

She couldn't have imagined Ellis's being here, so treating her like shit wasn't perhaps the way to handle the situation. But it was like she couldn't help being overly sarcastic. She headed over to the agitated man and listened to his grievance about the lack of crispy fries on his plate, giving her an excuse to head back into the kitchen.

"Is that who I think it is?" Serena asked as she waited for burnt fries.

"She's here to see me," she said, biting her bottom lip as to why Ellis was here at all.

"And you're in the kitchen? Are you insane?"

"I can't lose this job on the hope she's here to talk to me about another one."

"I bought you some time by seating Sawyer with her, since they seemed to know each other, but I'll check with the others and see if we can give you a few minutes. If I can pull it off, I expect you to get me some new clothes," Serena said as she slapped her ass. "I don't care if you have to do a little shoplifting."

"I'll see what I can do."

The plate of overdone potatoes seemed to take the irritation out of the guy, so she quickly stopped by every one of her tables, trying to curb any more complaining. When she glanced at Ellis's table, she noticed how animated Sawyer appeared. Something about Ellis brought that out in her child, since Sawyer tended to live in her head and only interacted so openly with her.

"Your burger isn't ready yet, but I've got a few minutes," she said, once Serena and one of the other servers waved her over to sit. "Do you mind if I stand so the whole section doesn't think I'm abandoning ship?"

"I'll go back," Sawyer said, but Ellis shook her head.

"What I wanted to talk to you about has to do with both of you, so stay." Ellis gazed up at her with the same smile Charlotte had seen on numerous buses and billboards. She couldn't help but question if the expression was genuine. "I'm not sure what you're thinking about, but you need a better poker face."

Crap, she yelled in her head as she did her best to relax. "Sorry. That's my 'I'm concentrating' look."

"It sort of resembles my 'this person is full of something not good' face."

She laughed at Sawyer's snort and decided to chance every possible tip she had coming by sitting down. "I was thinking of all those billboards and other things you're on these days."

"Then your expression makes sense because it's the same face I make whenever I see one." Serena set three plates down and put her hand briefly on Ellis's shoulder.

"Why?" Her first impression of shallow and egotistical might be right, but Ellis had a way of torpedoing holes of doubt into her gut intuition.

"Why what?" Ellis cut her burger into four very equal-appearing pieces and squirted a mound of ketchup in a spot on her plate well away from her fries.

The anal display wasn't something Charlotte ever associated with any type of artist of Ellis's success, so it was rather humorous. "Why does being the face of your brand bother you? Ralph Lauren's done it for years."

"Does seeing Mr. Lauren with his arms crossed wearing a usually preppy outfit make you want to buy something from his women's line?" Ellis picked up one of her quarter pieces of burger and finally made eye contact. "And I'm not trying to be sarcastic."

Charlotte tried to relax her face, again resolved to keep it that way no matter what Ellis said. "Not really, but it makes me think he's proud of what he does and isn't afraid to show it."

Ellis nodded as she took a bite, but her gesture didn't have the conviction of agreement. "Ms. Hamner, can I ask why you want to work with me?"

"Not to get my face on a bus, but if that's a serious question—"

"I'm being serious, and it's something I should've asked you earlier." Ellis went back to eating.

"I think every little girl dreams of working in fashion, or at least I did. It started as that fantasy dream, but eventually it morphed into the only thing I wanted to do. Once that came into focus, I put in the work to try to make it a reality."

"I started on a different track but arrived at the same place eventually. So now my reality is that I may dress like Ralph, but I love making women look and feel beautiful—all women."

"So it wasn't to get your face on a billboard in Times Square?"

"It's not a bucket-list item, no," Ellis said with what appeared to her as a mock shiver. "If it ever was, it's got a check next to it now. If you have time, I'd like to talk to you about a job."

"Really?" What Ellis had offered was the answer to every prayer she'd ever said, but her head seized with fear.

"I'm sure Rueben went over everything with you, but I want you to be sure. Accepting means you'll be moving to New Orleans for at least the next couple of months and maybe longer. We'll take care of the lodging for you and Sawyer, but the days are long. Being absolutely ready for Fashion Week isn't easy." Ellis then hunted through the fries as if in search of the perfect one and dragged it through her mound of ketchup before salting it.

There was, she was sure, some reason for her strange eating behavior, but now wasn't the time to investigate it. "What happens after that?"

"I'm sure you keep up with the gossip, so you might have some clue as to what might happen." Another hunt through her fries with no choice obviously meant she didn't see any other worthy potatoes.

"It's why I'm asking. Leaving is a gamble, and I'm not the only player at the table."

"Safe and sure never launched anyone's career, and I'm leaving tomorrow."

"Sawyer," she said, and Sawyer left them alone. "Did you wait until the last minute as some kind of sick test?"

"You knew the possibilities going in because Rueben is good at his job, and part of his job is disclosure. He showed all our cards before you came for that interview, and the interviews are flexible to accommodate my schedule. When you're in the position to hire, feel free to change the rules." Ellis glanced around the area before pulling out her wallet. "I'll need an answer tonight." She placed three hundred dollars and a business card next to her plate. "For all the tips I cost you," Ellis said before walking out.

"Was that Ellis Renois?" her supervisor asked when she bussed the table and brought the plates back.

"Yeah, and I'm sorry I took a break without asking."

"Did you get it?"

"She offered, but I didn't know what to say." She stuck her hand in her apron and touched the card Ellis had left. The chance had probably passed her by, but she'd wait until she was alone to beat herself up about it.

"You're a good employee, but I doubt you'll ever convince anyone to buy anything you design wearing that." He pulled on her collar before tapping his finger against her temple. "What are you afraid of?"

He didn't give any advice, so she took a deep breath and took the money and card out. All that was on it was a number and the name of the business. "I'm afraid of losing everything I've got, but fear never was the basis for success, I guess."

She walked outside with Sawyer and called.

"Rueben Maddox. Can I help you?"

"I'm sorry to bother you, Mr. Maddox, but Ms. Renois gave me this number."

Sawyer held her hand and crossed her fingers with the other.

"Are you joining us, Ms. Hamner?" The question was to the point, but Rueben sounded warm and approachable.

"I am, so I need the where and when." Those words ripped through her, but instead of gutting her, they made her lighter. "I'll be there, and thanks for the opportunity."

"We're looking forward to it."

"Please let Ms. Renois know how much I appreciate this."

"It's just Rueben and Ellis, and I'll have a courier drop off everything you'll need if you give me your address. The return is open-ended, depending on the amount of work to be done, and the hours are long since you'll find Ellis isn't your typical nine-to-five worker." He paused, and she could almost guess that some kind of warning was coming. "Think you can handle that?"

"I'm not going to let you down."

The call ended, and she hoped to hell that would be true. "You ready for this?" she asked Sawyer, but the question might as well be part of an internal dialogue to psych herself up for what was coming.

"Mama, you made it—smile."

That Sawyer understood and appreciated the moment better than she did made her laugh. "We're going to be okay." She said it out loud but figured it'd be her new mantra because all she really felt was off balance.

CHAPTER FOUR

The office was quiet since it was late, but it never seemed to be empty, and while Ellis understood the concept of long hours, she encouraged the people that worked for her to leave the building at a reasonable hour. This place was like her apartment, in that she didn't feel at home here either.

"Some psychiatrist would probably make a fortune off me," she mumbled as she entered her office, not bothering with the overhead lights but opting for the lamp on the sterile, neat desk. Three folders lay on the usually spotless top.

She sat and opened the first one and shook her head at the amount they'd stand to make stated on the sticky note Dalton had put on the first page. The word *COPY* instead of *FINAL* surprised her, since Dalton kept insisting that the contracts were ready to go.

No matter the level of success she achieved, that much money never failed to make that young kid still alive in her heart take a deep breath in awe. She hoped it would always do that. Losing the part of herself that still saw the wonder in what she'd built would mean she'd lost the drive that got her here.

"Oh, good," Jennifer said, leaning against her doorjamb. "Those need your signature before you leave. We were afraid we'd missed you."

"We? Did I miss a call or anything else? Besides, these aren't the final contracts, according to Dalton's note." She flipped through the pages as if she understood the convoluted language lawyers put in these things like their fee depended on word count.

Jennifer laughed like a date who wanted her to know how much she appreciated Ellis's wittiness. "He must've forgotten to make it clear that those are the final contracts. Since you're here, you saved him a trip south. You know how much Dalton detests New Orleans this time of year, so you rescued him from a heat rash."

Something about Jennifer made her want to walk away or order her to leave. She tried to ignore her feeling, willing herself not to cling to something imaginary that'd make this relationship any harder than it already was. The whim of handing over something she wasn't interested in doing had blinded her to how much she really didn't like Dalton as a person and, by extension, his good friend Jennifer.

"Actually, he's never mentioned his dislike of New Orleans. Whenever he's there he seems to enjoy the nightlife enough." She turned to the view and smiled at the crack she'd put in Jennifer's smug façade. "Whatever happens in the South stays there, but it's a big enough playground if you're into that."

"Good thing for his wife you're still here to sign these then." Jennifer had used her attention break to move closer. Actually, she'd moved too close, and that feeling to take flight came back.

"Is there anything else, Jennifer?" It occurred to Ellis then that in all the time Jennifer had worked for her, aside from that night that Jennifer had blamed on too much to drink, this was the first time they'd been truly alone. Her drunken escapade had been something both of them had tried to pretend never happened. "I've got an early flight and have all this to get through, so if you'll excuse me."

"Do *you* enjoy the nightlife down there? Those interns must cream their pants when you show them the town. Must be all that heat, booze, and depravity that makes them go crazy."

"Ms. Eymard, I'm sure you and Dalton are good friends, right?" She cocked her head slightly and kept her seat, even though she really wanted to physically throw this bitch out.

"What are you insinuating?" Jennifer's tone was harsh and fast.

It was like a spider who had spun such an elaborate web that she'd entrapped herself. "I'm not insinuating anything, just asking a question," she said, trying to do her best to act the part of the fly. "It's not a complicated question, so answer it."

"We're good friends—nothing more."

"Then your friend must've given you the employee manual, so your comments were way out of line. Consider yourself warned."

"Consider this." Jennifer moved faster than she expected, and she spread her hands in shock when she landed on top of her. Being this close made it easy for Jennifer to bite her top lip hard enough to break the skin.

"What the hell?" Dalton asked as he flipped the lights on.

The sudden brightness made Ellis blink repeatedly and finally push Jennifer away. "He's right. What the hell was that?" The coppery taste in her mouth could only mean that Jennifer's bite had also drawn blood.

"I said I wasn't interested, and she tried to force me." Jennifer obviously had a talent for starting her tear ducts on demand, making her performance all that more believable as she ran into Dalton's embrace.

"Come on, Ellis. Didn't you learn anything from what happened last year?"

"If this is the shakedown you two have been working on, let's hear it. Only the punch line had better include an exit clause for both of you."

"No, this is someone finally telling you that not everyone's for the taking." Dalton put his arm around Jennifer's shoulders and led her out after the admonishment. It hadn't taken much time for Jennifer's face to become red and blotchy from the hysterical crying.

"I believe it's time for both of you to go." She pressed a tissue to her lip and texted her mother to get to the office, and to call Rueben to meet them.

"You can't sweep this one away so easily, you pig." Jennifer screamed, and this time, she sounded unhinged, as if Dalton had just saved her from a horrific rape. "Dalton, call the police. I want to file a report."

"Are you sure?" Dalton asked with sympathy so contrived that Ellis figured he'd choke on the words. "There's no other way you want to handle this?"

"Would this other way maybe involve my checkbook?"

"I'm your CFO, so believe me. You don't have enough money to make this go away." Jennifer wrenched herself away from Dalton and ripped her blouse so that buttons flew around the room.

Ellis watched the sad attempt to add to her story and could only think of one strange thing, considering what was going on. She wondered what brand of blouse would've come apart so easily. Laughing now would only make things worse, so she turned her attention to the two security guards who had arrived fast enough that they were out of breath. They no doubt were gifts from her mother.

"Dalton, do you want to call the police, or should I?" She had to replace the tissue against her lip after she asked.

"You're taking this too lightly, considering what's at stake," Dalton said, placing his hands on Jennifer's waist. "Do you know how hard it is to defend yourself against harassment and creating a hostile work environment?"

"I guess I'm making the call then, and I'll be happy to add battery to that since I'm the one bleeding." She picked up the phone, and Jennifer screamed again.

"No, I'm calling," she said, having to tone down her behavior, Ellis figured, because of the new witness. "Can I go to my office? I'm too traumatized to stay here."

"Yes, ma'am, but let me and Mr. Burton escort you," the taller guard said. "I don't want anything else happening to you tonight. My partner will stay with Ms. Renois until the officers get here."

"Thank you." Jennifer held her clothes together, appearing as if she really had been mauled.

"Dalton, take good care of your girl," Ellis said. "And make sure neither of you leaves until this is taken care of."

"Ellis, you do realize fame doesn't get you out of everything," he said, his menace finally seeping out a little. "No one gets to live a charmed life from beginning to end."

"You're right, but to tell you the truth, charm had never been a talent of mine."

He laughed and slammed his fist into his hand. "What is it then?"

"Shredding things that…what's the best way to put it?" She wished he'd come after her to give her an excuse to put her hands on him with justification. "The things that don't fit into my life for any reason, even if I thought them worthy in the beginning."

"Did you read my note?" Amis asked as she cleaned the cut on Ellis's lip.

"I didn't while that bitch was in here. What's going on?"

"Take a look before we deal with whatever the hell this was."

Ellis's antique desk had a hidden drawer, and Amis used it when there was something she wanted only Ellis to see. But this time the note led to the wall safe. Amis handed her the contract Dalton had asked her to sign, backed up by the viper who'd literally taken a bite out of her. Her supposed old friend Dalton had to know that her attorneys were more sophisticated than that.

"Ellis," the security guard said softly. "They sent two detectives, so I thought you'd want them to start in here."

She told her story, and the detectives took notes and asked good questions, but perception was always everything in every situation. Once they saw Jennifer, compared their sizes, took into account their positions, and factored in her history—she'd put herself in handcuffs.

"So she just bit you for no reason?" The detective that'd obviously drawn the bad-cop straw asked. "Sounds a little out there."

"Maybe the smell of silk made her crazy, but you might want to ask for some clarity on her motive. I don't have a clue, except that maybe she thought it was the easiest way to a big settlement." She waved her guard closer, and the man handed over a CD. The two detectives stood shoulder to shoulder in front of her computer screen and watched. "But like in all things, we don't always get what we want."

"You want to press charges?" the detective said after watching the CD.

The way out of Jennifer's contract had come wrapped neatly by Jennifer herself, so she nodded. "Whatever I can file, go ahead and do it, but I need to talk to her first."

"You can't threaten her," the good cop said.

"I'm going to fire her, Detective. I'll leave the threats up to you."

Dalton was sitting next to Jennifer with his arms wrapped around her, seemingly doing his best to console her.

"Ms. Eymard, please stand up and turn around," one detective said while the other guy moved closer to Dalton. "You're under arrest for battery."

"*I* was the one attacked," Jennifer screamed, becoming totally hysterical again.

"The security system shows otherwise, ma'am." Jennifer glared at Ellis as the cuffs clicked into place.

"Where do you want your personal items sent?" Ellis asked. "Your services are no longer required, and after tonight you'll no longer be allowed in the building, especially with the accessorizing you're doing these days," she said, pointing to the handcuffs.

"You bitch." Jennifer lunged at her as if she'd come unscrewed from the professional woman Ellis had known.

"We're done, but, Dalton, you're not."

Jennifer yelled Dalton's name until the elevator door closed. It had surprised Ellis that Dalton had stayed, but all his plans were not coming anywhere near fruition. That she finally had the means to fire him without having to honor his contract didn't make her happy. For all his shortcomings, Dalton had helped her build this empire.

"You didn't have to do that," Dalton said, facing off against her and Amis.

She dropped the contract on her desk and tapped the thick wad of paper with her finger. "And you didn't have to do this. What the hell were you thinking?"

"If there's a mistake, it's not mine."

"Dalton, you don't for one minute think I didn't run down where the changes came from, did you?" Amis shook her head as if completely disbelieving his answer to her question. "You made the changes and rushed them by legal. A mistake I could've forgiven, but theft of something I worked so hard for isn't. You're fired, Dalton, and my parting gift is to advise you to hire an attorney," Ellis said softly, wanting him out of her life as soon as humanly possible.

"You owe me, so this isn't over." The security guard pointed to the door, and Dalton waved him off. "You're going to wish you'd just signed that."

"Make sure to lock him out of everything. If he tries to come back, call our NYPD friends and have him arrested. Get out of my sight, Dalton, and next time, try to come up with threats that actually mean something."

❖

Charlotte repacked for both her and Sawyer for the fifth time. It didn't help to look at the clock and see the minutes after three in the morning tick by, but she couldn't unwind. The nerves that had started when she'd accepted the job had made sleep impossible, but she had to figure out a way to calm down, or she'd look like someone had beaten her by the time she got to New Orleans.

Her boss at the restaurant had guaranteed her job would be waiting for her, but maybe that wasn't the best thing. Fear was at times a good motivating force that caused you to find the creativity to make it. She glanced at the clock again and zipped her bag when she saw it was a quarter to four. The alarm was set to go off in two hours, so if she had a chance of falling asleep, now was the time.

She heard the ding of her phone alerting her to a message, but who the hell was up besides her?

I'm looking forward to working with you.

"If anything, I could sell her number," she said as she stared at the message she assumed was from Ellis. "I'm sure plenty of women out there are just dying to talk to her."

Why are you awake? And thank you.

She typed out the answer, not expecting a response.

Same reason you're still up. Dial the number. There's only so much typing I can do this early, or late. Depends on how you see it.

She called and smiled when Ellis answered immediately.

"Thank you for picking me."

"In a week you'll be cursing my name, but it was an easy choice. You have talent, Charlotte. I did want to apologize for the short notice. Usually I'm not so tyrannical."

"You really don't mind that Sawyer's coming with me?"

"It's a new year, so I'm looking forward to trying new things. Sawyer will be fine."

Charlotte heard Ellis yawn, and she couldn't help but do the same.

"Take a short nap, and I'll see you soon."

This was like a surreal dream in that she'd gone from fantasizing about a career in fashion to talking to Ellis Renois in the middle of the night. The job she'd landed wasn't where she thought she'd start when she was working her ass off in school. She felt like a high school player starting in the World Series. The rest of her life would never be the same.

She held her phone against her chin and looked around her crappy apartment. "If that's true, I hope it doesn't land me back here, but a taste of success is better than no taste at all, I guess."

❖

"You stupid little bitch." Dalton squeezed the heavy crystal tumbler and thought about chunking it at Jennifer's head. He'd had to call in more than a few favors to get her bailed out of jail before the morning arraignment, and he'd followed her back to her apartment. He wasn't ready to face his wife and confess he'd lost his seven-figure salary and the perks that came with it. "If you'd left it alone, we could've pled ignorance if that fucking old bitch had found the change."

"You can stand there and seriously call me stupid? Do you honestly think any attorney, even the most incompetent one, would make a mistake that gives us more than fifty percent of the company? No, moron, this was a gamble you concocted that'd only pay off if she'd signed. She didn't, so like we talked about, we've only got a few plays left."

Jennifer combed her hair back and twisted it into a messy ponytail. She'd changed as soon as they'd arrived and appeared comfortable in her jeans and man-styled shirt. That sexy all-American look had reeled him in, but his drive to fuck her had completely fucked him over. All those luxuries in his life were gone, and he didn't have it in him to start again.

"You think we have any plays left? That's a joke because she'll see them coming a million miles away."

Jennifer glared at him so he stared at the scotch in his glass. "Your problem is, and always has been, that you consider yourself a player, but you're terrified to color outside the lines. Only good boys paint inside the lines even if you think the painting is risqué."

"So you're going to go all Jackson Pollock on me and hire someone to kill Ellis? If that's your plan, count me out." He poured himself another drink and wanted to sleep and wake up to his life before Jennifer came into it. If he had a do-over, he was sure he'd make better choices. "I'd rather be poor than locked up like an animal."

The box she brought from the bedroom made him curious, but not enough to move. Somehow it seemed like a bad idea to put his prints on whatever was inside. Of all the stupid shit moves he'd make in his life, lying down with this viper overshadowed everything even remotely close.

"There's a way to kill Ellis, and then there's a way to kill Ellis." Jennifer laughed as she opened the box and presented it to him.

"Good God." This had the potential to carry more time than murder. "How? Wait. I don't want to know."

"This time you either do it my way or get out."

He slammed the glass down, clenching his fist when the liquid sloshed over his hand. "I'm not some punk with no brains."

"No. You're something much worse. You're a middle-aged guy with no guts or imagination. This is how we get it all back and then some."

"Look. Let's calm down before this gets out of hand. We talked about this, but we're sailing into waters that could land us someplace like where I just got you out of." He stared at the book that Ellis really did treat like the bible and felt a pain go through his chest at the implications of it being here and not locked up in the office. The box was the physical evidence that he was fucked because Ellis would never be that forgiving if Jennifer did anything stupid with what was inside.

"We found the information, and we're going to use it to get what we deserve, so choose, Dalton. You can either walk out and go back to that bitch you're married to, or grow a pair and cut your own path. No matter what, we have to go ahead and cut her off at the knees, and enjoy that she'll never have seen it coming."

He nodded but couldn't take his eyes off the book. "What choice do I have now but to stay?"

CHAPTER FIVE

Charlotte followed Ellis and Rueben off the plane, still surprised that they'd all traveled together, but Ellis had even picked them up. Her new boss wasn't the most talkative person, but Charlotte sensed something wrong over and above Ellis's mangled top lip she didn't have when she'd come to the restaurant. It actually appeared as if someone had taken a bite out of Ellis, with intent to harm her. That wasn't the issue, she guessed, since Rueben had made quite a few frantic calls, so whatever it was must be bad.

"How'd you manage to forget that?" Ellis's teeth never seemed to come apart as she spoke.

"It was in my office locked in the credenza. After everything that happened last night, it slipped my mind. I'll call Amis, and she'll have a reason to get here earlier. She can hand-deliver it."

"Call her," Ellis said as she flagged down a porter.

The tension in the large SUV rose to an awkward high by the time they reached the French Quarter, and Charlotte was afraid Ellis would end up strangling Rueben. She wanted to take in the sights, but she was too busy trying to decipher what the hell was going on.

"Can I help with anything?" She spoke to Ellis since Rueben was on the phone again. "What's wrong?"

"Ruby forgot his book." Ellis took a deep breath and seemed to force herself to smile. "Sorry about my mood, but we really don't have that much time to finish our line. Having the only other copy of the bible out of my sight freaks me out, especially since it has all the changes I've made in it. After the experience I had last night, this isn't the time to get sloppy."

"Wow," Sawyer said when the car stopped so a gate could open. The house certainly deserved a wow.

"I love this place." Ellis got out and entered a code into the keypad located on the large stone wall that encircled the property.

The courtyard was completely paved with ancient-appearing bricks, the only greenery coming from the multitude of potted plants dispersed through the area. Charlotte glanced around, but it was hard to take her eyes off the large Spanish-style house that seemed to span the entire block. The colors were muted, drawing her attention to the bright-red front door. It reminded her of their first conversation about color. Maybe red really was Ellis's favorite hue.

"It's beautiful," Charlotte said as she took Sawyer's hand.

"I'll be happy to give you a tour in a little while, but I have to make a few calls first." The door opened and an older man came out, his appearance the only thing that had made Ellis smile since they'd landed. "Hey there." Ellis opened her arms, and the hug she gave him seemed heartfelt. "How are you, Uncle Malcom?"

"Lonely roaming around here alone, but not anymore."

Whoever he was, Charlotte could tell he really cared about Ellis, and the feeling was mutual. "Wait, Sawyer," she said as Sawyer tried to break free.

"Let me introduce you." Ellis let the man go but kept her arm around his shoulders. "Charlotte and Sawyer, this is my Uncle Malcom. He'll show you out back to where you're staying." The short introduction was all they got before Ellis disappeared.

"She's usually not that obnoxious," Malcom said, shaking his head. "God knows I love her, but sometimes she acts like she was raised by wolves."

"You'd better not let Amis hear you say that. She'll tear your throat out with her fangs," Rueben said as he took his turn hugging Malcom.

"My sister only scares me when she's standing right next to me."

Charlotte laughed and stuck her hand out, only to be pulled into a hug as tight as the one he'd given Ellis. "It's nice to meet you, sir."

"Please, call me Malcom, and welcome." Malcom held both her and Sawyer's hand as they walked inside. Another younger guy and woman passed them smiling, and Charlotte guessed they were the staff.

Charlotte stopped right inside and just stared at the paintings. The massive pieces that lined the grand staircases were stunning. Every one of them featured faceless women, since the subject of the art was actually the clothes. She recognized every single piece going up those stairs, but they appeared different painted in oil.

"She did these?" Sawyer asked, finally wrangling free of her. "I'm not good at faces either."

Malcom laughed, which made Charlotte relax her cringe a bit. "I don't think that's why she did it like that, sweetheart."

"This is Ellis's trophy wall," Malcom said, the pride in his tone hard to miss. "The clothes were the winners, and everything else was never important enough to keep her interest."

"Is that a warning, Malcom?" The clothes were evidence of Ellis's genius, but sometimes whatever higher power bestowed such talent demanded something in return. Ellis's obvious heartlessness for anything else seemed to be the price in this case. Charlotte needed to remember that fact and concentrate on getting her start, yet keeping her distance.

"What an interesting thing to say. Everyone seems to know that Ellis has a reputation—that's not something I'm going to waste my breath defending. She is, though, my family, so I'll tell you that no reporter or rumormonger ever concentrates on the positive. It's not a warning at all. The next few months will go better if you open your mind and leave your preconceived notions at the curb outside."

"We're staying here?"

"Ellis figures you and Sawyer will want some space that's your own, so you'll be right out back." He led the way to the other side of the good-sized pool. "We're lucky in that it's one of the only houses in the quarter with a pool and more than one building on the grounds."

The building close to the pool surprisingly wasn't the pool house. It had a big common area and a nice kitchen, and according to Malcom, it also had two bedrooms. "What is this place?" she asked, dropping her purse on the brown leather sofa.

"A long time ago, when the house was built, it was the caretaker's shack. It's been upgraded through the years to become a guest cottage. Everything you need is here, but you have an open invitation to eat at the house with us. It's not mandatory, though, so do what's comfortable for you and Sawyer."

"It's beautiful, thank you. Will we start work tomorrow?"

"I'm sure Ellis will be down here once her calls are done, so why don't you unpack and wander back in an hour for lunch. Sawyer, your room is the one on the right."

"Mom, look," Sawyer said, making Malcom smile before he waved and left.

The corner of the room was filled with blank canvases, an easel, and all the supplies Sawyer would need to make art. Now Charlotte understood Ellis's allure. She certainly had the ability to zero in on what made people happy and had the resources to deliver it. She also had the looks and the kind of personality that made you want to be close to her—the kind of allure that made you want to be the center of Ellis's attention even if only for a brief second.

"I see," Charlotte said, and the display of generosity made her think of Kyle. What a difference from one human being to another when it came to Ellis and Kyle. Ellis realized not only that Sawyer was alive but had figured out what made the kid tick after spending less than an hour with her, total. The only downside would be that, in a couple of months, Ellis probably wouldn't remember who they were.

"I see," she said, more softly, trying to think of a way to let Sawyer down easy when that came to pass.

❖

"And how do I know this is legit?" Benson Norwood asked as he eyed Jennifer and the book she was holding. As a reporter for the monthly *Styles and Trends*, he was familiar with both Jennifer and the pet she'd dragged along, Dalton.

If Jennifer's claim was right, he'd talk his boss into running a special issue as payback for the lawsuit Ellis had slammed him with a couple of years prior. The exposé he'd written about Ellis's sexual exploits for once wasn't true, and she'd had plenty of ways to prove every word was fiction. It was a miracle he'd been able to keep his job, but he owed that to Dalton. When the judgment that would've shut the magazine's doors came down, Dalton had talked Ellis into a token settlement. He knew he'd have to return the favor one day, and this was the price, he guessed.

"Since when do you ask if something's legit?" Dalton turned from staring out into the alley, and Benson figured the man had been hitting the bottle pretty hard, judging by his haggard appearance and swollen features. "You owe me."

"Hey, I appreciate what you did, but we both now know the consequences of printing something that's not true." The urge to open the book was making his hands itch, but he had to cover his ass first. "I hear even *Vogue* is writing about you two getting fired yesterday. Any comment on that? If it's true, then we both know you didn't get that as a parting gift from Ellis."

"You little son of a bitch." Dalton crossed the room quicker than Benson thought possible, and he was even more shocked when he couldn't break Dalton's hold on his lapels. "You think you get to walk away for free after I saved your ass?"

"Owing someone something is one thing, Dalton, but getting sued for theft of intellectual property is some other colored donkey altogether. Hell, the court wouldn't even buy a confidential informant the last time around. I print this, and it'll be a fucking disaster—a fucking disaster that I could end up doing jail time for." He couldn't get Dalton off him, so he stood up in case he had to defend himself.

"You're going to print this or I hand these over to the cops and then to every rag like yours that's interested." Jennifer dropped a large envelope on his desk with no explanation—he didn't really need one, and it was like Dalton could read his mind. "She was only fourteen, Benson, and it was just two years ago. Still enough time for the cops to be interested in your little hobbies."

"You were there, you bastard, and not as a bystander," he said to Dalton.

"I'm not in the picture though. You can look if you don't believe me." Dalton shoved him toward the envelope.

"I believe you, since I figured you'd fuck me over eventually." He tossed the envelope into the trash since Dalton and Jennifer weren't about to hand over the file the pictures were stored in. "So how does printing these help you?"

"You let me worry about that, but they've got to hit within the week. It won't do me any good if you sit on them forever."

"I'll print them, but I can't say when. If you want fast, I hope you've got glossy prints of my boss doing something *he* doesn't want published."

"We don't need that, honey." Jennifer laughed and dropped another big envelope on Benson's desk. "We've got glossies of you doing something colossally stupid that *you* don't want printed."

Benson's glare only made her laugh harder as she picked up her box and waved over her shoulder on the way out. The magazine's offices weren't in the best neighborhood, so Dalton was glad they had a car with a driver running and waiting. Wherever they were going, though, wouldn't keep them safe from Ellis's wrath—that he was sure of.

In all of Jennifer's calculations and scheming, that was the only thing she hadn't factored in. Ellis Renois wasn't some trust-fund spoiled brat doing this out of boredom. No, Ellis was street-smart and vicious when she needed to be.

"Now what?" His phone rang again and he silenced it, but really wanted to throw the damn thing out the window. Since the night before, his wife had called him every ten minutes, it seemed.

"Now we go home to really get the rumor mill going, and then we renegotiate new contracts."

Despite his urge to run away, damn if Jennifer still didn't have an effect on him as her hand slid up his thigh. "You think Ellis is seriously going to offer us another job?"

"Lover, in about a week no one will remember who Ellis is. No, we're going somewhere that'll appreciate us. It's time to hook up with someone who'll see how valuable we can be, and we start over." She squeezed him so hard he thought of begging her to go down on him, but he didn't want to give the driver a show. "It's time for you to start fresh all the way around."

"That's not as easy as it sounds."

"It's exactly that easy, if you want it enough."

❖

"It's not there," Amis said calmly.

The second time she said it, Ellis closed her eyes and rested her head on the edge of her desk. The second time was a necessary confirmation since the first time Amis had said it, she'd thought she misunderstood. Every year, for security reasons, she made two copies of the upcoming line. She kept one and Rueben the other, and she'd thought to question Rueben about it only after they'd landed. During the trip to the house he'd simply thought he'd forgotten it. "It can't be gone. Did you go through his desk?"

"Chéri, aside from a large number of ketchup packets, there's nothing else in Rueben's desk—nothing. The bible is gone."

"That bitch had to have taken it, and if she did, we're totally screwed."

"Before we panic, let's make sure that's the case. Don't jump off the ledge just yet."

At first she wanted to fly back to New York and beat the crap out of Dalton and Jennifer for sheer satisfaction. She was stupid to think this situation would end so easily and neatly by simply firing them. "Keep looking and keep me posted. If I'm right, working to finish this show is a complete waste of time."

"Did Rueben's book have all the latest changes?"

"For once they were both up to date." She raised her head when she heard the door open but kept her eyes closed. "Whoever has it can share our entire line for the upcoming year with the world."

"Let's hope it doesn't come to that, so let me organize my search party."

"It's gone?" Rueben asked, his expression a perfect example of horror. "Ellis, you have to believe that I locked it up. I would've never just left it out."

"I'm not blaming you, and there's only one viable explanation for all this." She relaxed her expression when Rueben's eyes grew glassy, and she would've ignored the phone to comfort him, but that wasn't an option. Sigrid Nymand, the former Swedish model, was still beautiful, but now she was the grand dame of *Vogue*. Her influence was legendary, but her friendship was one of Ellis's most prized assets.

"Sigrid, how are you?"

"Right now I'm guessing I'm doing a hell of a lot better than you, darling." Sigrid's accent was one Ellis could listen to all day, but her comment was the first nail in her coffin. "Do you have time to talk?"

"For you, always. You know that." A long conversation initiated by Sigrid and not one of her minions meant the nails would keep coming until Ellis was buried.

"What the hell happened last night?"

Ellis couldn't lie or try to evade the facts—Sigrid wasn't asking to fill in the gaps. She was calling to confirm *all* the facts. "Are you asking out of curiosity, or in a more official capacity?"

"Ellis, drop the stoic act and don't bullshit me. I'm calling because one of my people got an anonymous call from someone who claims you did plenty of naughty things." Sigrid laughed, and Ellis put her head down again. "I wish I were a little younger so you'd be interested in doing naughty things to me, so that I don't give a damn about."

Sigrid had been married to the same man for close to thirty-five years, but Ellis always enjoyed her flirtatious personality. "Don't count yourself out of that game, Sigrid. I'm one of the teenage boys at heart, with your swimsuit picture on my wall. But it's been a while since I've been either naughty or nice to anyone." She told Sigrid what had happened and heard the sigh when she was done.

"The caller also said they had your bible. Please tell me that part of all this nonsense isn't true."

"My mother's looking, but I think it's gone. Considering what happened last night, we both know where it is, but unless I can prove it, I can't legally accuse them." She took a deep breath and glanced up at Rueben, who was now crying. "Did they offer to sell it to you, or are they giving it away?"

"Actually, neither. They were being nice by sharing the news, but before you celebrate, it is going to be published, and soon, from what they said. If I knew who and when I'd move mountains for you, but they didn't want to ruin the surprise."

"Thanks for the call then."

"What are you going to do?"

The question made her want to laugh at the sheer absurdity of it. "I'm going to have a drink and think about it. We both know the likelihood of mounting a successful show with all the time in the world, much less when there's no time at all."

"My darling, don't disappoint an old woman who has a crush on you. Amis is one of my oldest friends, and that's whose blood runs through your heart. She gave you more backbone than that, so skip the booze and concentrate on what you do best. Success is and always will be the best and most satisfying revenge."

"Thanks, my friend, and you're right."

She hung up and walked around her desk to hug Rueben. "Never underestimate a bitch in heat, Ruby. That's what Jennifer was from the beginning, and I should've paid closer attention. This isn't your fault, so let's see what we can do about it."

❖

"Mom, do you think Ellis will show me how to use all this stuff?" Sawyer had opened every package in her room and set up her easel.

"Maybe, but don't bug her about it, okay?" The hands on Charlotte's watch hadn't inched forward all that much, but she was determined to wait out the hour before moving.

"You want me to go?" Sawyer said.

"What? Sorry. I was thinking." The knock was probably what Sawyer meant. "And I'll go. Keep unwrapping."

She opened the door and stepped back when Ellis leaned against the frame. "I apologize for dumping you on my very nosy uncle when we got here."

"No need for apologies."

"I know, but Malcom will accuse me of being obnoxiously rude if I don't," Ellis said and smiled. "Since I have got a mountain of problems, I don't need to add to that. Do you have a minute?"

"You're the boss, so sure."

"I know we just got here today, but I'm not holding you to the job if you don't want to stay. Let's start there," Ellis said, and pointed to the table and chairs by the pool.

"You're firing me?" She didn't want to go back to waiting tables and chasing Kyle for support. "Why?"

"I'm not firing you." Ellis put her hands up and shook them. "I'm giving you an option. You can stay, or you can go back to a paid internship in New York with Michelle Yuki."

"Why would I want to leave, even if it's for another dream job?"

"I can't force you to keep quiet, but I'd appreciate if you didn't share what I'm about to tell you with anyone."

Charlotte nodded, and Ellis started talking. Once she finished, Charlotte couldn't help but stare at Ellis's swollen lip. She'd of course noticed it on the flight down but figured Ellis's love life wasn't any of her business.

"She bit you?"

"As unbelievable as that story sounds, she did bite me, then ripped her shirt open. I'm having a hard time understanding that level of bat-shit crazy, but then I've got bigger problems." Ellis's smile wasn't too wide, probably because of the cut. "All the work that started the second last year's line came out is gone—I take that back. The work is somewhere, but it's getting ready to become public. It might as well be gone."

"So you're not mounting a show?"

Ellis's expression made Charlotte want to point in a direction that would lead Ellis out of the fog she seemed utterly lost in. "I'll try to answer that, but not right now, so give me a day."

"I appreciate you getting all that stuff for Sawyer. She's in heaven in there, and it feels like another Christmas. At least that's how she's acting."

"Sawyer seems like a special kid." Ellis glanced away from her and fell silent for a while, as if thinking about something. "I'm not keeping you from anyone, am I?"

"What do you mean?" It was almost funny that Ellis would've thought of this only now, so she asked simply to give her a hard time.

"I doubt the kid hatched from an egg. If you're here for a couple of months, won't her dad miss her?"

She did laugh at that notion. "Sawyer's dad misses her all the time, but it's mostly voluntary. He misses visits, support payments, and just mainly misses the boat on all things Sawyer. Don't worry about us."

"I didn't mean to pry." For once Ellis looked uncomfortable. "I need to think, and sometimes that's easier to do with a sketchpad in my hand. Maybe Sawyer and you would like to come on a walk with me?"

"We'd love to, and I want to stay. I thought we should settle that now."

"Are you sure? You could learn plenty from Michelle."

She nodded and grinned, wanting for some reason to make Ellis feel better. "That's probably true, but I'm staying."

"Might be a boring summer."

"You really think that?"

Ellis finally let loose a big belly laugh. "Not if you believe the *National Enquirer*."

CHAPTER SIX

S o this book," the detective from the night before said as he took copious notes. "It's important?"

"Do you like football, Detective?" Amis asked, making him look up at her.

"I happen to be a big fan, why?"

"Imagine you design all your plays. Actually, you spend all year designing something no one who's ever played has ever seen before. You do that, and then someone comes along and steals all your hard work and shares it with the world. That's exactly what happened here, so yes, it's an important book. We actually call it the bible for a reason." Amis spoke slowly, trying to get this guy to understand, but she doubted she was getting through, considering he was dressed like he was allergic to starch and an iron.

"So, intellectual theft?" he said, winking at her. "I'm smarter than my pay grade, ma'am."

"My apologies. I'm trying to keep my daughter from either jumping off the roof or committing murder, but I'm having a hard time not doing either myself." She tapped her pen on her desk and had to drop it to stop. "Our attorneys said we needed to report it before we go forward."

"I'll rush the report and check with my federal contacts to see if they need to be brought in. Do you have any clue as to who has it?"

"I have our security people going through footage to see if I'm right, but Ellis's office is the only private office that has security cameras."

He pocketed his notebook and offered her his hand. "I promise we'll give this our attention, but I need a hint where to start. Maybe with someone here in the office before we move on to your number-one suspect."

She wrote a few names and slid the paper across the desk. "Sorry again about my assumptions, and this list is something you found in the trash, right? I don't want to be sued if someone gets insulted."

"I have got a feeling that I have a clue where to start and who to talk to without this. We'll be in touch."

She walked him to the door, where the head of their in-house production team was waiting. "Ruby called me," Opal Steele said, her hands pressed to her chest. "If I didn't believe him, your expression confirms this cluster fuck. How in the hell did someone walk out with that, of all things?"

"It's not something I want or have time to rehash." She waved Opal in and dropped into her desk chair. "What I need to know is the viability of a show. Can we pull it off?"

"Ellis has to come up with a completely new line, and if she does, we'll work our asses off to get it done."

"I'll need you in New Orleans if she gets over the shock of it." The door opened and her assistant held up a folder. "Now what?"

"This just arrived by private courier."

The copies Amis found inside confirmed the theft. It was, from first glance, half of the designs in their lineup. "This must be the fuck-you to top off what happened. Was there anything else with these?"

"No, ma'am. Well, only this." The young woman handed over a yellow sticky note with a simple smiley face on it.

"Get Jennifer and Dalton's team in the conference room. I'll be there in a few minutes." She waited until she was alone with Opal again before she started trying to take the steps necessary to overcome this situation. "Get on the next flight to New Orleans and tell Ellis to get to work. When I get there, I'd better have something to see."

"You got it."

"Where are you?" Amis asked Ellis when she answered the phone. She heard a lot of traffic noise in the background, so at least Ellis wasn't at home having some sort of breakdown.

"At Café du Monde. It was either here or a bar, so I'm playing tour guide."

"I'm sending Opal, and the rest of the team should arrive soon. Obviously, you're past me grounding you, but I want you to not let these people beat you. You need to embrace the passion inside you."

"Like I told Charlotte, I need a day."

"I'll save my pep talk until then, but I know you well enough to realize I won't have to give one. You should know that someone delivered half the designs in the book with a smiley-face note."

"No other hint as to what their plans are?"

"I think they plan to destroy us, so I beg you not to let them do this to you." She put her finger up when her assistant reappeared. "I love you, chéri, and I'll be there soon but I have to run."

"Love you too, Mama."

Amis smiled briefly but not for long. It was time to make sure their house was in order. "Hello, everyone," she said to the accounting team. "Until further notice you're going to answer to me. If anyone here is still loyal to Jennifer Eymard, I'll need to meet with you after this, but before you make that appointment, you should know Ms. Eymard is no longer with the company." She stared down everyone in the room. "I doubt anyone will take me up on that offer, but let me warn you. Anyone I can prove is sharing company information will not only be terminated but prosecuted."

After the first group left quietly, Amis repeated the exercise with Dalton's people. "Now to find that damn book before my hair turns any grayer."

❖

Ellis relaxed after dinner with everyone, trying her best to not telegraph how pissed she was. She was in a world of shit, but it was of her own making, so she couldn't lash out lest she hit herself. No way would she be able to sleep, so she put on a pair of sweatpants and a T-shirt and went down to what was originally the ballroom.

She often wondered what the parties in this room were like when the place was built. A large room with tall ceilings, wood floor, and silk wallpaper must have been something, but for now she used it as a workroom. She made the last-minute adjustments in here before all the pieces were packed and sent back for Fashion Week.

"Do you want me to go back and try to fix this?" Rueben said, startling her.

"Ruby, unless you gift-wrapped that thing for those bastards, get off your sword. I'm not blaming you, and I still love you." She walked to the long table and pulled out a few sheets of sketch paper. "I'm pissed, but not with you."

"Are you planning to start over?" Rueben came closer, his kimono dragging behind him.

"That's the million-dollar question of the day, isn't it? My plan for now is to run you ragged, so go to bed and let me see if there's any magic left in here." She tapped the side of her head. "Even if we show only two things, we're not going down without a fight."

"We can still get it back."

"Tomorrow might bring a miracle, but tonight I'm going to indulge the pessimist in me. That ship has sailed, and considering who's probably steering that pirated vessel, there's no way we'll see its return. Hell, they've already sent some of the designs to the office as a taunt. Jennifer won't give it back with a big apology. She wants to fuck me over, and she has page after page of ways to do it. All I've got to figure out is how to block her from doing that." She snapped her fingers after kissing his cheeks. "Do you mind babysitting for a little while?"

Charlotte didn't seem to mind being dragged out of bed or leaving Rueben on her sofa in case Sawyer woke up. "Bring your book."

Charlotte looked around the ballroom as she held her book under her arm. "Can I see what you had for this year?"

Ellis indulged her by taking all her sketches out and taping them along the wall. When she stepped back and studied the swatch of paper, she came close to crying at the thought of all the hours that had gone into creating them. Usually, she was always happy with what she put out, but this year was different.

"This year we're closing Fashion Week. We finally got that spot, so I was inspired to take it up a notch. Of all my stuff, I think these were my best."

"They are beautiful," Charlotte said as she touched each sheet. "I want to help you however I can."

"How about a blow to the head that'll get my creativity going?" She took Charlotte's book and flipped through it again. "Every year my interns usually get one piece in the show, but this might be your breakout year. If you end up with a couple or more, you have to start thinking about a style that's yours alone."

"That's my safe I'm-going-on-an-interview set of sketches." Charlotte spoke like a four-year-old caught with both hands in the cookie jar.

"So you don't think I'm edgy enough to appreciate that in a designer and you didn't share?"

"No," Charlotte said loudly, bringing her head up. She relaxed visibly when Ellis winked at her. "That's not what most people want to see. Most people go for the safe."

"You're right about that, but I'm not most people." The blank page usually was a kind of ticket to a new adventure she always was ready to take. Sometimes, though, it symbolized the door to everything that terrified her. "Let's forget all that tonight and do something else."

"I'm not interested in anything but work." The way Charlotte put her hands up made Ellis want to laugh.

"I'm crushed, but I totally understand. Go to bed, and we'll start again in the morning." She turned off the lights and walked Charlotte to the door.

"You're mad?" Charlotte asked incredulously.

"I'm amused that you think that's the effort I put into someone I'm interested in. That makes me sound like either I'm a rapist or I have magical powers. In case you didn't understand the sarcasm, I've got neither." She opened the door since Charlotte wasn't leaving. "And it sounds like you've already got an asshole in your life—you don't need another one."

"I'm sorry I hurt your feelings."

Charlotte had an obvious problem looking at her, but she was in no mood to let her off the hook. "You've got to have feelings to incur damage, right? I'm sure you've heard the rumor about how I'm sorely lacking in that department." She stepped back when Charlotte moved to touch her arm.

"I don't usually believe in rumors, and I'm not usually this rude." Charlotte moved fast enough to wrap her fingers around Ellis's wrist. "What did you have in mind?"

"Put your jeans back on and I'll meet you outside," Ellis said.

She'd had every intention of ditching Charlotte once she left to change, but something about her expression changed her mind. This would only be a little outing and nothing more. If they couldn't make it through that, she'd have to ask Michelle Yuki for another big favor once she shipped Charlotte and Sawyer out at first light.

"This summer should be hard enough without all this other shit."

❖

The night was hot, and the humidity was something Ellis thought was unique to New Orleans. It was like walking in a big open sauna that never let up and took some time to get used to—well, it was something you could try to get used to, but you'd be lying if you said you'd mastered it. Ellis took the keys to the small coupe she kept in the city and let Charlotte get her own door.

They headed out of the French Quarter to the business district and the Lowe Hotel. It was a few blocks from the Mississippi River, and while the hotel was nice, she was here for the restaurant and bar off the lobby. It was owned by an old friend whose family was food royalty in the city, and this was their newest jewel.

Ellis handed over the keys and opened the front door for Charlotte, having only so much capacity for rudeness. It was late, and they were out of the "party" area, but both the restaurant and the bar were still full. Everyone was drinking and seemingly enjoying the small band in the corner. No matter the night, all the articles written about the spot said the new owners tried for a fun atmosphere as an homage to the woman it was named for.

"I was wondering how long it'd take you to get here." The tall, gorgeous woman combed her hair back with a flick of her head.

Ellis opened her arms and accepted the kiss Jacqueline Blanchard delivered. If it were possible, she guessed that when Jacqueline's aunt Coco had passed away, the old partier had surrendered her throne to her niece. "I'm here to collect my free bread pudding for that." She pointed to the large painting over the bar. Della Blanchard, Jacqueline's grandmother and head of the Blanchard family and their businesses, had wanted her sister memorialized in the bar and restaurant that carried her name. Ellis had been surprised when Della had handed over her favorite picture of Coco as the one she wanted hanging in the bar, but having met Coco, it did in a way sum up her personality.

The painting of the redheaded Coco showed her at her makeup

table with her head thrown back in laughter. She was wearing a slip, red high heels, and for some strange reason a mink stole. It had been a fun piece to paint and gift to the Blanchard family.

"Do you like it?"

"With or without the beautiful artwork, your money's never been good here, you fraud. And I love it." Jacqueline lifted her hand before she slipped it into the crook of Ellis's arm. Magically a table with three chairs was set up, so they could sit down. "Come on, introduce me."

"Jacqueline Blanchard, this is Charlotte Hamner." She waited until they'd both shook hands before ordering a beer. "Do you want something to drink?" she asked Charlotte.

The waiter took their order, and Jacqueline pinched her forearm. "I'll trade you a dessert for my Fashion Week tickets."

"We'll get to that, but first, how's your sister?"

"Keegan is on top of the world, or should I say ruling the world from her kitchen uptown. The spot at Blanchard's became permanent a year ago, even though I was getting this place ready for her." A waiter came with their drinks and two beignet bread puddings. Every Blanchard restaurant was known for some variation of the classic dessert.

"She sounds happy," Ellis said, taking a bite and closing her eyes because it tasted so good.

"Keegan's happiness isn't centered on cooking anymore, sexy. She's found that Holy Grail of relationships we're all supposed to be searching for. The excellent side benefit is that I haven't had to pay for a parking ticket ever since because of the gorgeous cop she hooked up with." Two guys came in and stopped to kiss Jacqueline on the cheek.

"I'm sure that's why she sacrificed herself to monogamy."

Jacqueline shook her finger at her and laughed. "Are you sure you want to spend your time with this corrupting influence?" Jacqueline asked Charlotte.

Charlotte was caught with a mouthful of bread pudding but nodded to give herself a chance to swallow. "If you ask everyone who interviewed for the job, I'm the lucky one."

"I've known Ellis for a long time, so I can confidently say, they're partly right. She has her moments, but then, don't we all?" A waiter came by and whispered something that made Jacqueline sigh. "We're all set up to start delivering food, so just have someone call with the numbers. But right now, enjoy your prize and don't be a stranger. Thank you again for your gift. You made Della smile, so that alone makes you as close to perfect as they come." Jacqueline kissed her again and placed her hand on Charlotte's shoulder. "It was nice meeting you, and please come by for dinner some time. Don't let her keep you locked up, even if the house is beautiful."

"She's funny," Charlotte said before taking another bite of bread pudding.

"She is, and like the house she's a part of why I love this city so much. It's home and not full of people who want something from me other than to be my friend."

"Where'd you meet her?"

Getting to know someone was always such an interesting dance, but sometimes it involved a completely tedious list of things you had to get through whether you wanted to or not. Everyone seemed to ask those probing questions disguised as shyness that in a way drove Ellis mad. The next thing would be a walk through her childhood, she was sure, which she assumed, if she answered those questions, Charlotte would use as a stepping stone to lay bare all her secrets.

"Like Jacqueline said, years ago I was in school, and my mother was working for Lagerfeld. What are now trendy apartments in the Warehouse District used to be sweatshops and design centers sewing for big department stores like Saks and Macy's. A few designers like Lagerfeld had a setup like I do now, finishing the pieces here and shipping them for Fashion Week. Jacqueline's grandmother, Della, her mom, and her sister were all taking some time off from all this to enjoy one of the fashion shows in New York." Her beer was cold enough to make her want to order six more, but everything in moderation, Amis always said. "Jacqueline snuck in the back to see behind the scenes instead of the catwalk."

"She was memorable then?"

"That she was and is, but Jacqueline falls for charm of a different type. In her opinion I'll never be that charming. You both have that in common."

Charlotte dropped her spoon and grimaced like she'd bitten into something sour. "What's that mean?"

"You have an ex that's not me, and it never will be," she said, and laughed.

Charlotte didn't join her. "If you need to know, I got pregnant in high school. That wasn't the kind of news my parents wanted to hear, and Kyle—my ex—didn't want to hear it at all. From that moment on, it's been Sawyer and me." Charlotte was almost talking through her clenched teeth by the end of her confession. She was not only adamant but passionate—the perfect recipe for a great artist.

"My mother was in that same place you are, so I understand. My father wasn't an in-it-for-the-long-haul kind of guy. By society's microscope, I grew up poor, but Amis laid the world at my feet." She took some money out, despite Jacqueline's insistence on treating. "You'll either work it out with Kyle or you won't. Either way, Sawyer will be fine because she has you."

"Um...thanks," Charlotte said, as if not expecting her to be so nice. "Why'd you say that?" The question proved her right.

"Sometimes recognition gets us through the day, doesn't it?" She smiled, knowing she'd had such a steady diet of recognition it was an effort sometimes to keep herself in check. The work brought fame, fame brought money, and money with fame brought more yeses than nos. Then again, fate or karma brought people like Charlotte as well. They were fixated on the work, hoping the rest of the dominos would fall, and because they were desperate you could spot it instantly. For someone like that, the word *no* came easily from everyone around them.

"Is that what makes you happy?"

She shook her head as she glanced around the room. "See the couple by the glass over there?" She pointed discreetly to the woman in the black minidress with her hand over her mouth because she was laughing so hard. "That dress was in our line two years ago. She's not standing so I'm guessing either a twelve or fourteen. If she'd worn it on the runway, no one would've glanced up twice because she's not a stick, but look at her. Unless she's faking it, she feels beautiful in that outfit, and it's making her confidence show."

"I remember it, since the remake of the little black dress has been reworked for years, but you managed to make it one of the stars of the season."

"True, but that woman has no idea who I am. I doubt she's obsessed with keeping up with the trends or the gossip that fuels our industry. All she knows is she tried that on and she liked it. Making a woman feel like that makes me happy."

"Okay, but what does that have to do with me?"

"You're a good mom, you work hard at it, but I doubt very many people tell you that. Sawyer, though, will be a confident woman because of the foundation and the love you've given her. If you're anything like my mother, it's such a gradual teaching and pushing her in the right direction that she'll never figure out that's what's happening, but it's visceral enough that it'll be the centerpiece of her life. Her touchstone, if you will."

"Thank you, and I'm looking forward to meeting your mother. She's certainly raised an interesting person."

"That's hilarious, but Amis is my hero and the most important person in my life. I hope you like her, but enough of trying to find things to make me forget what happened. It's time to go to work, and when I'm done I want to feel like the woman in that painting."

CHAPTER SEVEN

The next morning Charlotte woke and used the kitchen to make breakfast for Sawyer, making enough in hopes Ellis would join them. After their night, she had to admit that she might've been wrong about her new boss, or she was still under the influence of all the compliments.

"Mom, can we go out today?" Sawyer had dragged herself into the room, acting like she could easily sleep another ten hours.

She combed Sawyer's hair back and kissed her forehead. "I'm working today, or I think I am. Let me find out what my schedule is, and we'll plan something. How about that?"

"Sounds good. What can I do while you're working?"

The knock made her jump but smile, until she saw it wasn't Ellis. "I'm sorry to bother you so early," the woman said with a slight French accent. "I'm Amis Renois."

Charlotte took her hand and studied the woman's face, finding only the shade of Amis's eyes familiar. Ellis had definitely taken after the man who had abandoned them. "I'm Charlotte and this is Sawyer."

"Ah, the artist," Amis said, smiling at Sawyer. "Ellis bragged about your work, so I'm looking forward to a showing soon."

"Can I get you some coffee or something?"

"Actually, I have a load of calls this morning, so I have a quick question." Amis waved her outside. "Have you seen Ellis this morning?"

"No, not since last night. Is she all right?"

"I'm sure she's fine and I'm just being overprotective. Where did she take you?"

She gave Amis an itinerary of their night and figured Ellis hadn't spent the night alone. Maybe Jacqueline Blanchard wasn't immune to Ellis's charm after all, and if that's what had happened, all that stuff Ellis had told her was probably bullshit as well. "Can Rueben tell me what to do?"

"This is an unusual year, so for today, why not go out and explore a little? New Orleans is a wonderful place, so enjoy yourself."

The opportunity that Ellis had found her back in New York with the Yuki house seemed like the best option for her. If she took it, she could also return Sawyer to familiar surroundings. "Can you be honest with me and tell me if she's even going to try? I really need to know so I can make other plans if that's not the case."

"My, my," Amis said, her face seemingly closing to a cold mask. "I'm so sorry we haven't fulfilled every one of your expectations in the mere hellish day you've been here. Have you ever had something precious stolen from you, Ms. Hamner? Think carefully before you answer, because I doubt you've faced even a small bit of what happened."

"I'm sorry I haven't suffered on the same grand scale, but don't pretend to know me." She tried to never let her temper get out of control, but this woman and her daughter had bent that rule all to hell. "I need to take care of my daughter and myself, so I'm not sitting around here wasting my time."

"Did you ever stop to think of the great number of people who are depending on the same exact thing? This isn't about Ellis's ego, you twit. It's about a company full of employees who'll get robbed too if this doesn't turn out well."

"I told you there was a job waiting for you if you didn't or couldn't stay," Ellis said with a flat tone. She stood in the doorway from the house to the courtyard with a sketchbook under her arm, appearing tired. "Just let Rueben know when you're ready, and we'll get you home."

"Just…just—" Charlotte couldn't finish what she wanted to say so she went back inside, slamming the door and startling Sawyer. She wanted to stay and get to know Ellis since she found she liked her even though she aggravated her to distraction, but she also had to find a way to get experience. She couldn't move forward with anyone else without that one little thing everyone wanted to see on her resume. She wanted to learn from one of the best in the business, but she hadn't planned on being part of all this drama.

"Mom, look." Sawyer pointed to the television.

The national morning show was reporting on the story that had broken late the night before. It was sad to watch five of what she knew were some of Ellis's pieces flash across the screen. The reporter obviously had only those, but it was the lead story for the day, so it wasn't the end of this for Ellis. She figured it'd be a slow drip until whoever was behind all this had buried Ellis, for this season at least.

"Is this bad?" Sawyer asked.

"Wait here, and I'll be right back."

The pool area was empty when she went back out, so she headed for the ballroom where Ellis worked. All the sketches Ellis had put up from the night before were still there, and Ellis was sitting on the table staring at them in a way that made Charlotte think they'd magically change.

"If you're all set already, I'll have Ruby get you a flight and the information you'll need to start with Michelle." Ellis shook her head as if to clear it. "You'll have a good story out of all this, if nothing else."

"I thought last night we agreed I'd stay."

Ellis jumped down and handed over her book that'd she'd left the night before. "I'm the first person to admit that some things look different in the light of day. You…today it sounds like you're not in the same frame of mind, and I can't really blame you, so don't worry about it. Good luck with the new gig."

"Okay, listen to me," she said, having lost all patience. "You don't get to read my mind to make wrong assumptions, you don't get to guess anything to do with me, and you don't get to talk or think for me."

"I'm not doing any of those things," Ellis snapped, as if having lost her own patience. "This fucking happened to me, and I'm mad as hell, but it's my problem. Some bitch and her gutless boyfriend who I thought was my friend stole hours and hours of my life, and now I'm expected to pull some miracle out of my ass." Ellis's volume rose as she spoke, and she grabbed her hair like she was getting ready to rip it out. "It's not that easy, and it's not helping that you think I'm some egotistical, rude, womanizing hack. If this isn't going like you planned, get out. It's not like I didn't find a place for you. Once you're out of my obviously bad company, you can laugh about how I probably more than deserved this."

"Hey, calm down," she said to Ellis's back, but that didn't keep her in the room. Ellis kept walking until she'd disappeared into the house. "What in the hell was that?"

"It's the meltdown I've been waiting for since she found out what happened, only usually it's some inanimate object that gets the brunt of the steam once the kettle boils over. The potted plant in her office gave its life for the last disaster, but it was really minor compared to this," Rueben said, directing his attention to the door Ellis had gone out of. "It's not my place, nor does it carry the weight coming from her, but I'm sorry that happened."

She lifted her arms and let them drop. "You may not believe me, but I really do understand."

"And I don't mean to insult you, but no, you don't. These lines aren't for Ellis's vanity or for the fawning rich crowds during fall Fashion Week. Do you realize how many people work for the Renois House? No new lines means no new orders, and no new orders means the entire structure collapses. She's not pissed with you, Ms. Hamner. She's pissed with you and everyone else on the planet at the moment. And the number-one person on that list is her."

"So what happens now? Does she want me gone?" The room seemed large and intimidating now that she sensed she was no longer welcome here.

"What happens now is totally up to you, and whatever you decide won't be held against you." Rueben finally turned and faced her with an almost melancholy smile, something she didn't think possible.

"Why say that? It makes me think me leaving will in fact be held against me."

"I'll get you a flight, and here's what you'll need." He ripped a sheet from the large black folio and handed it over.

"So I'm right."

"No, ma'am. I said it because it's true. You leave now and she won't hold it against you." He snapped his book closed hard enough to ruffle his hair. "She won't because in a way she expects it. You climb to the top, and people expect you to fall. It's the nature of our business. It's just that some people take real pleasure when it happens."

"I came here because I wanted to work with her, not be insulted or shipped anywhere else. If I've got no other option, I'll go home and appreciate her help getting me another spot, but that's not what I want."

Rueben laughed, which only made her angrier. "For once she might be right about this internship she's so fixated on continuing. If it'd been up to me or Amis, we'd have done away with it a long time ago."

"Why?" She leaned against the table, tired from all the turmoil. The only arguing she usually did revolved around Kyle and his lack of concern for Sawyer.

"Interns haven't exactly been Ellis's strong suit, and any one of your predecessors would've been back in the city by now. You're not afraid to stand up for yourself, so I think that'll be good for Ellis." Rueben jotted a few things on a blank page as he spoke, handing it over. "Do you cook?"

"I'm not great at it, but I try." She glanced over what he'd written.

"Good. You've got a choice. Either let me know when you want to go home, or you can help me now, and later when you get everything on that list." He gave her a wad of cash from his wallet and added one more thing to her list. "This isn't too demeaning for you, is it?"

"Will you put in a good word for me?"

"Not necessary, and take Sawyer with you. If you follow the order, it'll give you a good tour of the area so you'll get the lay of the land."

"Will she be okay?"

"In every way, Ms. Hamner. By choosing to stay, you'll see, more than anyone else outside her family, who Ellis truly is, and what built her empire."

"So the suffering will make her better, huh?" His laughter lifted a weight off her, and she laughed as well. "It'll be an interesting two months anyway."

"You have no idea."

❖

Ellis stopped with her hand on the newel post and considered going back and apologizing. The last person in the universe she should be blaming for all this was Charlotte, but unfortunately she had been standing in front of her at the one moment she couldn't hold everything in.

If she'd alienated Charlotte, she'd eventually make it up to her, but right now she needed to go somewhere that didn't require a whole lot of thinking, but she'd stay sober. She considered leaving the completely blank pad but grabbed it on impulse as she walked out the door.

She didn't have any one destination in mind, so she wandered through the neighborhood enjoying the glimpses of gardens she'd see if someone had left a gate open. New Orleans to her was like a woman with multiple but always fascinating personalities. Each area had a different look, a different vibe, but throughout, it was like what you wanted the love of your life to be—sexy, edgy, sophisticated, charming, and a little slutty when the occasion called for it.

"If I could find someone with all that, I'd pop the question," she said out loud. "Right now, though, you have to think about women's clothes and leave the woman out of it."

"Ellis Renois, you keep talking to yourself like that, and the only fashion you'll have to worry about is men in white coats." She recognized the voice, and only one person ever greeted her by grabbing her ass. "And white's way too drab for you to be looking at all day."

"Ms. Parrish, you're a beautiful sight on a pretty sucky day."

Brandi Parrish was a well-known pseudo celebrity of the French Quarter, since most locals had heard of her, but most also thought she was a myth. No one really ran a high-priced brothel anymore, most people thought, but the famous Red Door was indeed no myth. Brandi's girls had a substantial list of exclusive clients, including a number of heavy hitters that kept her candy-apple-red door open.

"And you, Ms. Renois, are as full of shit as ever," Brandi said as she moved to hug her. If she'd passed Brandi on the street she doubted she'd recognize her in her jeans, oversized man's white shirt, and large sunglasses. "But I happen to love that in a woman."

Brandi's kiss was hard and demanding, and despite Ellis's state of mind, it swept everything out of her head and focused her attention farther south. Her reaction must've been painfully clear, since Brandi pulled her head away and flicked Ellis's nipple. "You do realize there's more to life than clothes, right?"

Brandi's actions were new, but she wasn't complaining. "It's been a rough couple of months, but not anything like the last few days. All that tends to kill my sex drive."

Brandi pinched the other nipple hard enough to make her hiss. "Are you absolutely sure about that?"

"I'm stressed, not dead, darling." She took Brandi's hand and grocery bag before they attracted some lurking wannabe paparazzi. "Come on. Let me be chivalrous and walk you home."

"Such kindness needs to be rewarded." Brandi smiled in a way that made Ellis wish for a certain type of reward. "How about pancakes?"

The question was fairly in line with her luck lately, but it wasn't a surprise. Brandi had become more of a mentor and boss for some time to the girls in her house, so Ellis figured that whoever saw the inside of her bedroom these days was there simply for Brandi's pleasure and nothing to do with business. "I'd love some."

They weren't far from Brandi's place, but they entered through the back and well-maintained extensive garden around the patio and small pool. The house itself was old, traditionally grand, and in pristine condition. In the corners of the yard were two smaller structures, and the one on the left Ellis knew was Wilson Delacour's residence. Wilson had worked for Brandi since the beginning and considered his boss his only family.

"Come on." Brandi tugged her by the front of her pants to the other building in the far-right corner.

What Ellis had assumed was a gardening shed was actually a small but tastefully decorated apartment with a small galley kitchen. "Did you run away from home?" Ellis asked as she continued to look around the room. The decor consisted of high-end antiques, but the whole space had an airy feel from the large windows and open concept.

"Every once in a while, a girl needs some peace and quiet, so I converted the old maid's quarters a few years ago." Brandi took her bag back and started putting her groceries away after she'd kicked her sandals off. "Goes to show how often you visit."

"I came by for coffee last year, and you know it. You never mentioned this."

"I'm just giving you a hard time, handsome. Actually, aside from Wilson, you're the first person I've let in here. I'm semi-retired, so this little spot allows me to catch up on my reading while still keeping an eye on the business."

"Good for you." Ellis dropped onto the comfortable velvet couch and threw the prop under her arm onto the coffee table. For now, the sketchpad was all for show since the entire damn thing was empty. "So, no more dates?"

"I'm a whore, Ellis, so there's still a few."

"Believe me, honey, in my business I've met a few whores, and you in no way qualify."

"Obviously, you're not part of the church league here." Brandi finished her chore and came and sat next to her. "I've got more money than I'll ever think of spending, but it seems I can't give it away to what I think are worthy causes."

"Jesus, between the two of us we could have a pity party." She ran her finger along Brandi's jaw. They'd met a few years before, and she enjoyed Brandi's company. They didn't see each other often, but some good friendships didn't need massive amounts of time to flourish. Yet while they were good friends, Brandi teased her only to a point. Sex had never been in their equation.

"The charities around town are turning you down too?"

"Funny." She pinched Brandi's cheek and then shared her set of problems. "So save your money. I might end up needing a loan."

"Let's forget our problems for a little while altogether." Brandi moved into the circle of her arm after she lifted it. "If we do that, can I ask you a question?"

"Nothing too complicated, I hope."

"Do you find me attractive?"

Ellis almost laughed, but it didn't sound like a joke. "You're one of the most beautiful women I know. Why would you ask that? You have to know the answer, right?"

"Because you never seemed interested."

"I'm going to need to hire a PR firm just for my reputation," she said softly but kept Brandi next to her when she started to move away. "You're my friend, so I'll tell you the absolute truth if you want me to."

"Let's hear it."

"The thing is, no matter what the relationship, women turn me on."

"I know that, Ellis. It's why I'm asking the question."

"When it's a good friend, I try not to let my clit overrule my good sense, so with you it's not a question of attraction. It's more respect that keeps it in my pants."

"You do realize how the whole prostitute thing works, right?" Brandi laughed as she placed her hand on her abdomen.

"I guess I've never really thought of you like that."

"Calm down. I'm just kidding, but thank you." Brandi's hand moved under her shirt, and her touch was electric. "So at the moment we've both got some problems. Do you know what always makes me feel better?"

"Knitting?" She clenched her entire body when Brandi spoke softly right into her ear.

"So close." Brandi stood between her legs and slowly started unbuttoning her shirt. The white lace bra was simple, so she could see the dark-pink nipples it covered, and the sight made her wet. "Don't move. Just watch."

Brandi unbuttoned her jeans with the same patience she'd given the shirt. She shimmied them down her legs when she was done, and the bikini underwear she wore made Ellis want to act, but she followed orders. "Do you remember the day we met?" Brandi kicked her jeans aside and undid Ellis's belt.

"During the preview show here four years ago, and you invited me over for a drink. I'm sure you've heard how thrilling it is to get invited through that red door of yours. It was the highlight of my trip that year." She lifted her ass when Brandi prompted her, leaving her in very plain white boxers.

"I saw you, and I have to say, I haven't wanted to fuck someone that badly in a long time." Brandi tugged at her T-shirt next, so she leaned forward. "I'm glad as hell we became friends, but that first urge never goes away, does it?"

Brandi was a few years older than her, but she was gorgeous. "No. It doesn't." She closed her eyes when Brandi straddled her and kissed her like a woman who wanted to be touched. It wasn't until that moment that she realized how long it'd been that she wanted to be intimate with someone. For a womanizing asshole, she'd really stepped back from pretty much everything. Sometimes when you had everything, life lost the shine you were always working hard to achieve.

"Look at me." She opened her eyes when Brandi spoke and lifted her hands to Brandi's hips when Brandi reached behind her and removed her bra.

"So beautiful," she said as Brandi lowered it slowly, exposing perfect breasts. "You're truly beautiful."

"Thank you." Brandi moved off her and knelt between her legs. "Does *Vogue* know you wear these?" She laughed as Brandi popped the top of her boxers. "The only thing more traditional than this would be tighty whities."

"I don't know—I happen to think white is pretty sexy." She touched the side of Brandi's panties. "It's all in the cut, I guess."

"Enough shop talk."

She raised her hips again so Brandi could get her completely naked, then knelt between her legs. Brandi spread her open and teased her clit with just the tip of her tongue, which started a fire in her that she was suddenly in a hurry to put out, but Brandi obviously had other plans because she stopped. She put her hands in Brandi's hair and moved her head closer so she could kiss her. When Brandi pressed against her, she picked her up.

The bed in the one bedroom was an old beautifully restored four-poster, but right now she was only interested that it had a mattress. She put Brandi down gently and took her underwear off. Brandi was absolute perfection, and she spared a moment to admire her body before pulling her toward her until her ass was on the edge of the bed.

"Are you sure you don't want me to finish?" Brandi asked, but she didn't sound like she was upset with the situation.

She sucked Brandi in as she reached up and squeezed a breast. Brandi bucked her hips up and moaned loud enough that she felt the sound in her chest. This she was familiar with, had earned a reputation on, but Brandi was no casual conquest. Brandi was a professional, but her wetness encouraged Ellis to slide two fingers in.

Brandi came off the bed when Ellis's fingers were completely buried inside her, but Ellis quickly pulled out and slammed them back in. She sucked Brandi's clit in hard, sensing this was no time for gentle and romantic. The way Brandi was moaning made her think she was close, but then suddenly Brandi's sex relaxed before clenching her fingers inside.

"Fuck me," Brandi said when she fell back on the bed and her legs came apart as if she didn't have the strength to keep them together. "You could be a pro."

She chuckled at the compliment. "I could, but I'm more the charitable type."

"Then your kindness should be rewarded." It was the last thing Brandi said as she moved down her body and put her mouth on her. The way Brandi used her tongue was exquisite. It was the only word she could think of before she could concentrate on nothing but her clit. The more Brandi traced around it with the tip of her tongue before flattening it and applying pressure was maddening.

Ellis gripped the sheets with one hand and wrapped the other one in Brandi's hair. The orgasm took over in a way that untethered her from reality for a moment before it burned right through her, leaving her spent.

"Jesus," she said as Brandi moved to lie beside her. She put her arm around Brandi and smiled when Brandi draped her leg over her.

"Hmm. Maybe I should tell the nuns running the children's home down the street that I can prompt people to call out for the Lord."

"What you should do is thank God you're no hypocrite. You've lived on your own terms, and you made a success at it. To hell with anyone who can't accept that."

"You're good for my ego, Ellis."

"Likewise."

They didn't talk much after that, and when Ellis opened her eyes again, she was surprised to find three hours had gone by. She'd relaxed enough not only to sleep, but she had slept hard enough to not hear Brandi get up and make lunch.

"I'm no chef, but pancakes are my specialty."

Ellis got up and put on her boxers and T-shirt before joining Brandi at the table. "Thanks for today. You have a unique way of putting things into perspective."

"That's a new way to describe it." Brandi offered a bite of pancake drenched in Steen's cane syrup, and Ellis opened her mouth.

"The way I see it, no matter how much ugliness there is in the world, you can always find that one bit of beauty that balances it out."

"Thank you, and I have to say, you're as beautiful as all those clothes you create."

"It's time to get back to it, and I'm finally in the frame of mind to do just that."

CHAPTER EIGHT

"Then what happened, Mr. Rueben?" Everyone in the house except for the paid staff was in the kitchen making the simplest dish Charlotte could think of. Rueben had been entertaining them with stories of previous show catastrophes. Sawyer had asked a lot of follow-up questions, which only led to more stories.

"I rushed the poor girl out onstage, and it wasn't until she was four feet away that I realized her skirt was tucked into her pantyhose in the back."

Amis shook her head but laughed when he imitated the model's walk. "It's not a Renois show unless someone shows their butt," Amis said as she shredded lettuce for the huge salad she was working on.

"Don't mess with something that works, sister," Malcom said, throwing some peas at Amis. "A little behind never hurt anyone."

"I guess so," Sawyer said, sounding like she didn't know exactly what was happening but wanted to fit in.

"Sometimes it's a good thing, sweetie," Charlotte said, throwing a pea at Malcom when he laughed. The front door shutting made everyone quiet down. "I'm sure everyone wants to talk to her, but do you mind if I go first?"

Amis wiped her hands before waving Sawyer closer. "Come help me while your mama goes to work."

It was all the permission she needed to go in search of Ellis. The ballroom was empty, so she was about to head back to the kitchen when she ran into Rueben. "Turn right at the top of the steps, and it's the last room on the end. Remember to not take no for an answer."

"What exactly is the question?"

"It's not a question, but more your future relationship with her."

"Got it."

She climbed the stairs and knocked on the door Rueben had directed her to and got no response. Ellis might've been highly successful but had the temperament of a two-year-old not getting their way. For all Ellis knew, it could've been Amis knocking, and she'd ignore her as well? "This is ridiculous." She tried the knob and opened the unlocked door.

The room was large, or so she thought from the brief glimpse she got before slapping her hand over her eyes when Ellis came in from another room naked. Good Lord. Who the hell didn't lock their door if they were getting undressed?

"Can I help you with something?" The somewhat teasing tone reassured her that Ellis wasn't pissed.

"I knocked. I swear."

"Sorry. I was getting ready for a shower. You can open your eyes now."

Charlotte peeked through her fingers, making Ellis laugh as she tied her robe. "Take a seat if it's something important, or meet me downstairs if it can wait. I won't be long."

Ellis disappeared into the bathroom, so she closed the bedroom door and looked at all the beautifully framed pictures that lined the built-in shelves on both sides of the fireplace. The majority of them were of Ellis and her mother from childhood to now, but some showed Ellis and Rueben in the early years. Ellis hadn't had any great love except for her family, it seemed, so she sat in the old leather club chair by the window. The chair appeared fairly well used, and the book next to it was a collection of romantic poems.

The room had nice furniture, but like the rest of the place, it wasn't overdone or ostentatious. Ellis seemed to be a creature of comfort and simplicity when she was out of the limelight. She certainly was different from anyone in Charlotte's world, even though they seemed to come from the same place.

When the door opened, Ellis emerged wearing linen drawstring pants and a T-shirt, with bare feet and wet hair slicked back. "What can I do for you, Ms. Hamner?"

"You could call me Charlotte for one, and you could also give me a job." She stood up, but Ellis waved her back down.

"I thought you already had a job? Isn't this the part where you wave good-bye?"

"Well, I had a job, but I might've screwed it up by being too judgmental. Do you think we could reset and start over? I really want to stay and help you."

"There's nothing to reset, and I'm sorry for earlier. I'm, by rule, not usually such an asshole."

"You've been nothing but nice, so let's agree to start over." She held her hand out to Ellis and smiled when Ellis delivered a very businesslike shake. "Now that we've agreed to that, how about some meat loaf?"

"Best offer I've had in the last hour, so lead the way."

Their meal was as pleasant as the time they'd spent making it, only better since Ellis added some twists to the stories. Charlotte felt very included by the time they cleared the dishes, only to be chased from the kitchen by Malcom and his two assistants.

"How about coffee and beignets for dessert?" Ellis slipped on a pair of loafers and grabbed a small pad and pencil. "You two can help me walk off the tremendous amount of meat loaf I just ate."

"Sure, but I have to admit I pegged you for more of a foodie." Charlotte put her arm around Sawyer to follow Ellis out. The front drive was full of people, and Charlotte got introduced to the staff that had followed Opal Steele south. After the brief niceties, Ellis didn't keep them from heading to the hotel close by so they could rest.

"Now I believe you called me a simple eater," she said, teasing Charlotte. "Meat loaf isn't glamorous, but it's not easy to do well. I order it often, so trust me on that, but I love *it* because it reminds me of how much my mother loves *me*. It's the one meal that always cheers me up."

"Good to know if I'm ever in the doghouse again."

The three of them sat in the center of Café du Monde and ordered. Ellis glanced around as they waited and opened her pad. "Doghouses aren't my style. I punish all transgressions with either complicated stitching or ripping."

"Ripping seams is cruel and unusual punishment." Charlotte and Sawyer held their cups the same way—with both hands—which made Ellis smile when she considered how hot New Orleans was in the summer.

"That's the point, Ms. Hamner." She picked up a beignet and promised herself to start running in the morning. New Orleans was home, but it was murder on your waistline if you indulged every *envie*, as her mother referred to desire. Running beat the hell out of deprivation though. "Did you come up with any ideas, or did you spend the day making simplistic foods?"

"I actually spent the day bonding with Rueben and your mother so you wouldn't get rid of me. Tomorrow, though, I promise to try to put something together for you."

"We've got exactly ten weeks to do this. That's design, refinement, and making every piece." Saying it out loud for the first time cemented the feeling of just how impossible the task was, and she dropped the beignet. If she could kill Jennifer and get away with it, she'd take the time out of her tight schedule to do it.

"You know what they say about impossible tasks, right?" Charlotte picked up her discarded beignet and held it up next to her mouth. "You eat an elephant one bite at a time."

"One elephant, yeah, but we have a herd to get through in very short order."

"What's first then?" Charlotte shoved the piece into her mouth, giving her no choice but to take a bite.

"Tomorrow, get to know Opal. I'm sure my mom will help you with that, but I'll need you to put some designs together for me, and we'll see if they fit into the direction I'm not at all sure we're headed." She started to pick up another beignet, but the old saying Charlotte had mentioned sparked something in the middle of her chest. "Damn... come on."

"Where are we going?" Sawyer asked, slipping her hand into Ellis's.

"We're going to work."

❖

"I told you it's your job to convince him," Jennifer said so loudly into the phone that Dalton came running into the room. "I wasn't kidding about what I'll do if you fuck this up."

"Look, I gave him the entire book, and he's more afraid of Ellis's legal team than he is of what'll happen to me. Her team, led by Amis, has already put out feelers, along with a good dose of threats. Whatever she told my publisher made him break a sweat."

"Goddamn, listen to what I'm saying and cut out your pathetic whining."

"No, you listen, Jennifer. He's not going to publish any of it. If you need to burn me to make yourself feel better about that, then go ahead."

"Let me think." She wanted to throw something or hit something to alleviate the building pressure in her head. She'd had no way to know how badly this would backfire on her, and the aftermath it had left was an abyss she'd never really escape. "I'll call you back in an hour, so make sure you answer."

"Now what?" Dalton asked as he poured himself a healthy amount of scotch, even though it was eight in the morning.

"That fucker is going to renege on printing the book, so we need a plan B before the end of the week. All those designs need to be in some publication before Ellis has a chance to show them herself."

Dalton downed the drink in one gulp and sighed. "Maybe it's time to move on and start over. I'll file for divorce, and we'll be together as we find our next spot. Isn't that what you wanted?"

"Dalton, get serious here." She grabbed the bottle when he started to pour more. "We need to finish this."

"For what? The more you push and the more ground you scorch, the more impossible it'll be for us to get another job." He forcefully took the bottle back and poured more. "We went for it and we lost. If we cut out now, no one can prove anything, so we're in the clear."

"We won't get anything done if all you do is drink yourself into a slob. If you won't help me bring Ellis down, then run back to that fat bitch you're married to." She left him to his self-pity to get ready. She usually loved her condo, but these days it was like a stylish prison she had to escape if only to get the hell away from her cell mate Dalton.

"There has to be a way," she said as she stepped under the hot spray of her shower. The answer would have to come because she refused to give up. Dalton didn't understand that, for as much as Ellis had given them, her hatred for their former boss trumped all that. Ellis had a lot to answer for and even more to pay.

"What are you going to do?" Dalton stood outside the shower, slightly swaying.

"I'm going to save our asses with or without you. If I continue to be the one doing all the work, then you really do need to move on." She finished her shower, not wanting his eyes on her any longer, so she wrapped a towel around herself before shutting him out. "The only way forward is alone," she whispered to her reflection.

Dalton, like everyone in her life, didn't deserve her loyalty, so it was up to her to give Ellis what she had coming to her.

CHAPTER NINE

Y ou want what?" Opal asked the next morning. Only a few people were up, but Ellis wasn't surprised that Opal and her mother were already on their second cup of coffee when she came down.

"Try Epstein's uptown and see what he has got in stock. If not, we need an order out of New York as soon as tomorrow. My goal for today is for you to have something to work with by then." She glanced out the window at Charlotte, who had her face turned upward as if enjoying the warm weather. This early, the yard was in complete shadow, but the space had a clear shot to the sky. "I'm headed to the zoo, so call me if you need anything."

"What's at the zoo?" Amis asked.

"Animals, I guess, but I had an idea last night when we went out for coffee. I'd explain, but I don't want to jinx myself."

Amis handed her a cup and kissed her cheeks. "Are you taking Charlotte?"

"Charlotte's going with you and Opal, and Sawyer, if she wants, is coming with me. And before you say anything, if Charlotte wants to learn the business, she should learn all of it."

"I'm going to say whatever comes into my head, ma chéri. You know this. What that girl wants is to be with you, so why send her out with two old but beautiful women?"

"You're completely wrong about that, but she'll eventually get all she wants of me. Right now, though, ease her into the game before she has to spend time with the beast."

"What's that supposed to mean?" Opal asked.

"Charlotte's heard a few horror stories about me, so it should be easy to keep my promise to be good. That's a good thing, because I sure as hell don't have time to be bad." She finished her coffee and headed to the ballroom with Amis. "When you get a chance, I need you to set up something for me. Only I need it to stay between us." She laid out her plan as Amis nodded. "If you call Sigrid, she can probably help with all that. She can't show bias, but she said she'd do what she could."

"Don't underestimate your sway, my love."

She hugged her mother before kissing her forehead. "It's no wonder I'm an egomaniac. I've got sway, but Sigrid has the throne and the crown. Very few souls are brave enough to tell the queen of fashion no."

Charlotte came in as she let Amis go, and she waved her over. "Is Sawyer up yet?"

"She's getting dressed."

"Good." She packed a bag with what she'd need and put an old pair of sandals on. "Think she'd enjoy a trip to the zoo while you go shopping?"

"Sure, but what am I shopping for?"

"Material and everything we'll need to create a new line. It'll give you a chance to get to know the people you'll be working with."

"You sure you don't need me to go with you?" Charlotte seemed to study everything she was putting in the bag.

"I promise not to lose the kid, if that's what you're worried about."

"No, that's not it. I just want to help if you're going to work."

"I am, but I need to start by myself. Besides, the process is more than putting the designs on paper. You're going to get the well-rounded education everyone else missed out on."

"Lucky me."

"It's shopping or ripping—your choice."

Charlotte waved to her and Sawyer as they pulled out with the top down. The expression on Sawyer's face when she'd asked her to join her made it easy to understand why people had children. She perhaps would've considered it if they came like this, already a small person with a personality and the ability to feed herself.

"Did you bring your book and colored pencils?" They crossed over Canal Street, the wide boulevard that divided the French Quarter from the Warehouse District, Uptown, and the Garden District neighborhoods. When Ellis was Sawyer's age, the stores along this street had been high-end clothing places with phenomenal window displays. A few were left, but now the chic spots were located in the mall close to the river.

"Got everything you said."

Ellis enjoyed watching how Sawyer's head was never still as she took in the scenery they were driving by. The kid was as curious as she was, but she always considered that a good trait in anyone. Curiosity was the most important building block of learning, as far as she was concerned.

"Good. You're going to help me put my show together." She took a left onto the street by the river to avoid traffic.

"Really?"

"It's only fair since you and your mom gave me the idea last night."

The Audubon Zoo had once upon a time been the place of nightmares if you were an animal lover. It'd contained all small cages that only made you feel sorry for the unlucky animals trapped inside. Finally, the outcry gave way to the large, more natural enclosures that provided them more room to roam. It was still cruel to keep them locked up, but most of the animals now had been born in captivity, so this was the only place they'd survive.

"Let's start with the big cats while they're still moving around. Once it gets steaming hot, we'll lose our window."

The black leopard lay in a tree stretched out with what appeared to be a piece of raw meat. He was a beautiful animal that stopped tearing at his breakfast to stare down at them. Ellis unfolded the portable chairs she'd brought and took her sketchbook out.

"When I first started," she flipped to an empty page and tapped on Sawyer's book so she'd do the same, "I was a lot like your mom in that I was hungry to make it. Does that make sense?"

"Yeah. She works real hard, so thanks for giving her a shot."

"This year it's a lot like that."

"Why did those people steal from you?"

She glanced at Sawyer and really couldn't think of a good answer. There really wasn't one that made any sense to her. "I'm not sure, but they've done their best to ruin my business. Without a line, it's going to be that much harder to get things going again if we fail."

"What do you want me to do?"

"Start drawing what you see, and use your imagination to put him somewhere that's not a cage."

They sat together, and she glanced over every so often to see what Sawyer was doing. Since the last few days had been all about honesty, she realized that her true passion had dimmed. The line they'd finished was good, but it lacked the creativity that had driven her when the whole world wasn't watching. Success had dimmed the edgy for the safe and acceptable. In other words—mainstream and homogenous.

She looked at the cat and started sketching a black dress with straight lines and black-stone embellishments. The just-under-knee length would be good for the big date, making it practical for everyone who didn't attend the opera or any type of ball. The stole over the shoulder would be black as well and be made of short-hair faux fur that resembled this guy. She added an oversimplified cat face in hot-pink rhinestones to provide color and drew a mask on the model's face.

The show would reflect every animal here, and she'd donate some of the proceeds from every fake fur to the animal-rescue shelter Sigrid and her husband owned in Africa. Everyone would assume it was her way of sucking up, but she knew it was Sigrid's passion.

"Wow," Sawyer said when she held up the sketch a few hours later. "That's awesome."

"Let's hope the world is as nice as you are." She'd finished preliminary sketches for three different cuts that the accessories would work with. "Want to try one more before we get some lunch?"

"Can I take some pictures first?"

They got back to the house around four, and Sawyer joined her as she called the team together. As everyone filed in, she wrote the number seventy-three in bright red on a dry-erase board.

"I'm sure Opal and my mother filled you all in on what happened. All your hard work on that," she pointed to the racks of almost finished pieces Opal had brought in, "is not exactly for nothing. I have plans for it, but whoever stole the book will most probably publish the designs to make the most of the theft. If not in print, through some media like the morning show yesterday."

A young seamstress raised her hand as she spoke. "What happens to our show?"

"We're going to start over, and we have seventy-three days to finish it."

"You're kidding, right?" another guy said.

"If we all want to be employed, then no, it's not a joke." She clipped the first sketch to the board on the wall and waited for them to look at it. She put Sawyer's sketch next to it. "Did Epstein have most of what I included on that list?"

"He had black velvet, for sure, but the stole material might be a problem," Opal said.

"I have an idea for that, but we need to start first thing tomorrow."

"Tomorrow? Hell, we're starting right now," Amis said. "You know Harold and I go way back. He'll unlock the store if I promise to pay retail, but just today." Everyone laughed since Amis's love of negotiating was legendary. "Ladies and gentlemen, grab your scissors and pile into the van."

"Do you want me to go?" Charlotte asked.

"You can go if you want to, but I had another idea."

"Lead the way."

❖

"Thanks." Ellis paid the delivery guy from her favorite Chinese place and put the bag on the counter of Charlotte's kitchen. They loaded their plates before sitting on the sofa to review the pictures Sawyer had taken. "The fall show I'd planned had fifty-two pieces, so even if I could come up with that many designs, it would be a stretch to finish."

"Are you planning to whittle down?" Charlotte sat with her legs folded under her.

"No way. I'm going to have fifty-two and a few extra if it kills me, you, and everyone in that room. We can make it if you take on a few."

Charlotte stopped right before biting into her eggroll. "A few? What's a few?"

"Let's shoot for five, or more if you can handle it. We'll look through these pictures, and some of them might inspire you toward something new. Or you might tweak something you already have."

"Okay." Charlotte lengthened the word, appearing to be in shock. "Have anything in particular in mind?"

"Since you inspired the idea, Sawyer and I picked something for you." Sawyer flipped through the pictures until the elephants appeared. "Think of it as one sketch at a time."

"Uh-huh, so you get all the sleek, sexy animals, and I get these guys?"

"Such a lack of faith," she said and clicked her tongue. "Eat, and I'll help you with the first one."

"If I haven't mentioned it lately—thanks." Charlotte smiled and glanced back at the screen and her selfie with Sawyer. The handler had let them come to the door of the enclosure since they were the only ones out there that early.

"You're welcome, and I should've asked first, but I signed Sawyer to a contract for some artwork."

"Yeah, Mom. Cool, huh?"

"Yeah, it really is." Charlotte started eating with an expression that Ellis took to mean she had something on her mind. If it was wariness or alarm, they were right back at square one.

"I'm getting in on the ground floor while I can still afford her stuff."

❖

Ellis gave Sawyer a quick lesson on how to put the sketch in her book on the blank canvas before she told her good night. The budding artist was hard at it, so Charlotte followed Ellis out.

"I'm sorry if I overstepped by offering her a job." The quiet meant the gang wasn't back yet.

"I'm not upset at all. You in a very short time have validated Sawyer's talent to Sawyer. She thinks I'm just being a mom when I tell her she's good, and since I'm the only one she's ever shown her stuff to, I don't think she believed me."

"She's really good, and if you don't mind, I'm going to prove it to her."

Charlotte crossed her arms and shook her head. "However you do it, I'll be grateful."

"It's not exactly a sacrifice. She's a good kid. Go get some sleep while you can."

"Are you working tonight?"

"Just finishing a few things, so I'll see you in the morning."

The ballroom would be a zoo for the rest of the summer, so Ellis headed to the study. It didn't really lend itself to being an art studio, but she didn't want to move the original furniture out of the space it fit so well. The successful farmer who'd built the house had made a true man cave for himself, and every owner since had enjoyed the things he'd found comfort in, since the room had stayed intact throughout the small number of owners.

She sat at the desk and started working on the next set of designs centered on the spotted leopard. The ease with which the work came was exhilarating. For once in a long while, she didn't have to dig to put something on the page, so she pushed herself.

She was startled when Amis touched her shoulder hours later, and she instantly regretted falling asleep over the desk.

"At this rate, you'll burn yourself out by the weekend," Amis said. "Come on. Time for bed."

"What do you think?" Various sheets were spread out under her, and Amis straightened them into a pile.

"You never cease to amaze me, chéri. I love you because, to me, you're perfect, but one of the things I love the most about you is that you never quit." Amis flipped through her work and stopped at the snakeskin sheath dress. She'd drawn a very small print, so she hoped Opal could find something like it in leather. "This is beautiful."

"It's not going to be for everyone, but I like it. We'll leave this one for last because I want it to be perfect." She needed a centerpiece of the show, and so far, this was it. "Think you can handle things here tomorrow? I need one more day, so I'm headed to the zoo again. That should give me enough inspiration to finish."

"You never have to ask, so go to bed and sleep. That might be in short supply in the coming days."

"You know something, though? I'm glad this happened. The loss made me fall in love all over again."

CHAPTER TEN

Charlotte sat in Sawyer's room and looked from her sleeping daughter to the easel with Sawyer's creation in the making. She knew Ellis had put the crude outline on it to show her scale, since Sawyer had only ever drawn in her small pad. The rapt attention Sawyer gave Ellis as she discussed brush techniques was something she didn't see often from her very restless child. It hurt her to think about this job ending, not because of her career but because Sawyer would have to sever her relationship from her new hero.

Wherever they went after this, though, she was glad she'd taken the chance to come. Of course, the job would help open the door to the next position, but mostly for Sawyer's sake. Her parents helped where they could with Sawyer, but it wasn't fair to keep asking them to pay for her mistakes, so she'd tried her best to make it on her own. That meant trying to provide Sawyer with the best possible life she could give her.

In Ellis, Charlotte had found a friend and ally who totally understood not only how her child ticked, but seemed to view the world through the same lens. No matter her first impressions of Ellis, she was a kind and compassionate person who had vast patience for Sawyer.

Ellis Renois, of all people, had given Sawyer another adult who cared about her, and the attention to her child had melted Charlotte's heart. She hadn't planned to spend her life alone, but whoever she let in would have to love Sawyer as their own. That was going to be hard to find, and she wasn't delusional enough to think she'd be lucky or woman enough to make Ellis notice anything about her outside of work.

Her buzzing phone made her jump. It rarely rang, and she wasn't expecting anyone to call her here. A sense of violation washed over her as soon as she saw Kyle's name on the screen. He never called unless she was threatening some kind of legal action.

"Hello," she said as she carefully closed Sawyer's door.

"Where are you?" She hadn't heard his indignant tone since they were dating. Kyle was either trying to schmooze her because the support check was late, or he was borderline angry because she didn't fall for his bullshit. The last time he sounded this put out, they were in high school and he thought she wasn't paying him the attention he deserved and was owed.

"I told you I was applying for an internship, and I got it. What's the problem?" She stepped outside to keep from waking Sawyer.

"I came by to see Sawyer and you weren't there. You can't keep me from her."

"The last time you came by was two years ago. Did you suddenly remember you had a child?" Sawyer was absolutely the best thing in her life, but she'd forever tether her to Kyle. He was an anchor so heavy she wondered if she had the strength to carry it until he was no longer legally responsible for Sawyer. She'd bet money he kept a mental countdown until Sawyer's eighteenth birthday.

"That's not fair." His voice rose, prompting her to pull the phone away slightly. "You can't just take off without telling me."

"Kyle, it's for a couple of months. I'm sorry for not telling you, so forget about the money until we get back." The air outside was as heavy as this conversation, but a sudden cold ball formed in her stomach. She was completely sure this call was coming from somewhere that would benefit Kyle. She'd never seen that about him when she was younger and stupider, but with age came the wisdom to understand his narcissism. For Kyle, the world existed and spun only for him.

"It's not about the money, Charlotte. I'll gladly pay it because Sawyer's my daughter, and I love her. This is about my ability—no, my right to see her."

"Okay." She took a deep breath and scrambled for the best way to handle this situation. Most probably he'd forget about his sudden devotion and celebrate his vacation from child support. "We'll be back before Sawyer starts school, but you're welcome to come see her."

"You need to fly her home."

No fucking way, she screamed in her head. "Kyle, be reasonable. You're working, so she'd have to stay with your mom. Sawyer likes seeing you, but she doesn't like being shut away all day. She's learning to paint, and she's having fun. Please don't take that away from her."

"Where are you?" He wasn't screaming anymore, but his voice contained a controlled rage. "I want to know."

"We're in New Orleans putting together a show for Fashion Week." All that information wasn't necessary, but boring him at times was an effective way to shut him down. "It's not like I took her to war-torn Iraq."

"Where are you staying, and with who?"

"We're staying in Ellis Renois's guesthouse. She's the designer who hired me."

"I know who she is, and from her reputation, that's totally unacceptable. That's not a good place for Sawyer."

"I'm confused, Kyle. Since when do you give a damn as to where Sawyer is or with whom? Do you remember the kitchen incident at all?" She ran through a list as to what was motivating this, and the first hundred things all had the same answer—money.

"That was an accident, and you know it. Mom wasn't feeling well and forgot the burner was on."

"No. She was drunk, and you're lucky Sawyer is as smart as she is. That a seven-year-old had to learn to use a fire extinguisher under stress should have forced me to order a blood-alcohol test, but I didn't because you asked me not to." She put her hand on the back of her neck and squeezed. Her mother always said that it seldom paid to be nice. She'd always considered it a pessimistic view of the world, but now it made sense.

Kyle and his parents, especially his mother, had screwed up so much, and she'd been nice and not acted on any of the incidents for the best of reasons. Through all their problems and disagreements, Kyle was Sawyer's father, so bringing in the authorities at every opportunity wasn't, in her mind, a good thing for Sawyer and Kyle's relationship. She'd thought she had an obligation to keep that connection until Sawyer was truly old enough to make it for herself. Her stupidity was not holding Kyle responsible for anything, especially the times when the offense could've severed his rights to see Sawyer.

"I'm here for a job, and nothing else. It's insulting that you think I'd place Sawyer's welfare in harm's way for a paycheck."

"Yeah, well, I think you're wrapped up in this pipe dream of yours so much that you're not thinking of Sawyer at all."

"I'm not sending her home, so forget that." She squeezed her neck harder to keep herself in check.

"I'll give you a few days to reconsider, so I know you'll do the right thing."

"What's that supposed to mean?" she asked, but Kyle had ended the call.

"Problems?" Ellis asked, her voice coming from the darkness.

Charlotte came close to throwing the phone at her. "You scared me. I'd fuss at you for listening in, but this is your house."

"I'm sorry. It's not a habit, I promise. I was just getting something I forgot in the car, and it was hard not to hear. If you need help with something, though, all you need to do is ask."

Of all the things she didn't want to do, all of a sudden she couldn't hold back. Charlotte started crying because of all the unfairness in her life, and the load made the tears come faster. She loved Sawyer, but she was tired of fighting with the only other person in the world who should've cared about their child as much as she did.

"Oh my God," Charlotte said in a way that made Ellis believe she was both in pain and mortified.

This, though, Ellis had experience with. "Hey, it'll be okay," she said as she put her arms around Charlotte, convinced that the practiced line would calm the hysterics. "It can't be that bad."

The last part got her the stiff arm. "You're such an asshole." Charlotte laughed as she insulted her, but it was still an insult that only Rueben had ever leveled against her.

"That might or might not be true, but whatever it is, I'll try to help you through it if you let me." She thought of taking a step back when Charlotte stepped closer to her and put her arms around her waist, but it wasn't the time to be said asshole. "What's wrong?"

Charlotte started crying again, so she guided her over to one of the outdoor seats for two and let her cry. The act of crying was so ugly, but it was the best release valve when you couldn't stack another emotion onto your mountain. She put her feet on the table and held Charlotte.

Right now, it was the only comfort she could give, so she was glad Charlotte hadn't rejected it.

Slowly and still weepy, Charlotte told her about the call. Sawyer's father sounded like a real peach of a guy, but she agreed that there had to be something behind his sudden interest in parenting.

"You know Sawyer's safe with me, right? I'd never do anything to hurt her."

"I know that. I'm her mom so it's my job to keep her safe, yet I keep letting her go with Kyle when I know he'll just ditch her with his mother. His mother with the very bad drinking problem," Charlotte said and sighed. "Listen to me dumping all this on you like you're my therapist."

"Hey, don't underestimate my couch experience," she said, laughing. "But seriously, the day you came to interview, she snuck back there and didn't seem too fazed by me finding her." Charlotte moved but only to look up at her. "Sawyer reminds me of what I was like growing up. I was a little awkward, and I saw the world differently than anyone else. That makes it hard to fit in."

"What do you mean? And I'm not asking because I disagree with you." Charlotte moved hesitantly but put her hand on her abdomen. "No matter how crappy life is, watching Sawyer grow up makes it all bearable."

"My mom, like you, had me when she was young and in love with a man she never has badmouthed even when she had every right to do so. When I was about Sawyer's age, I asked Uncle Malcom about him since he was there for the entire tableau." Charlotte rested her head on her shoulder so she kept talking. "My father, and I say that even though he was no such thing, never stuck around to hold me or anything that came after. All that makes him really is a sperm donor."

"You've never met him?"

"I know who he is, but I could care less. My mother, Uncle Malcom, and Rueben are my family, and something about Sawyer reminded me of what it was like to be that young and wanting to hone your talent so you could capture the world how you see it. Anyone can learn to draw reasonably well with a little talent, but she's got a good eye as well. You're talented, Charlotte, but Sawyer sealed this deal for you," she said and pulled Charlotte closer.

"If you think I mind that, you're crazy. And speaking of crazy, you do realize she idolizes you, don't you?"

"I do know that, and it's why I'd never do anything to change who Sawyer is or will be. She's good, but she could be great. I also happen to like her a lot."

"Thank you for saying that."

"Makes me less assholey, huh?" That got her another shove. "Now that I've somewhat proved I'm an asshole with a little heart at least, can I do something to help you?"

"Kyle and I are where we are because of crappy but cheap representation. Until I've got a job that leaves a little more at the end of the month, we'll have to make do with that. I'm sure that until then, whatever this is will have slipped his mind."

"You have a job that gives you access to more than a paycheck, so take advantage of it. If you let me, I'll have Rueben get our legal department in touch with you and see what happens." She pulled Charlotte closer and suddenly realized helping her had made her forget Jennifer and Dalton, for a little while anyway. "Maybe they can figure out some way to deal with Kyle that lets you sleep better at night."

"Why would you do that for me? I'm sure everyone who works for you has to hire their own attorney."

Ellis didn't take offense at the question since it sounded like it came from Charlotte's very real outlook on life. Charlotte's reality seemed to be that of a lone soul against the world. When you were that alone, you had to approach any lifeline that showed up with wariness.

"Usually yes, but you won't be the first. I want to do it for you because it's one thing to abandon your child because you don't want to be bothered but want nothing in return. That's been my experience. It's something else, though, when you don't want the responsibility unless there's something in it for you. That's the vibe I get from Kyle." She lifted her arm to give Charlotte the opportunity to move, but she stayed. "You can also tell me to buzz off if I'm wrong."

"Do you mind going inside with me in case Sawyer gets up? We could watch a movie or something."

"Let me go get my stuff, and I'll work while we do whatever."

Charlotte hugged her tightly before she stood up. "Thanks for this, and for offering to help."

"No problem," she said hoping she'd find a way to not let

Charlotte and Sawyer in any more than she had already. No one ever stayed except for her mom, Uncle Malcom, and Rueben, and she was fine with that. She survived with her heart intact by not letting anyone too close. Jennifer and Dalton were lesson enough of what happened when you cared or you trusted blindly.

CHAPTER ELEVEN

Charlotte changed and moved to the sofa, not really expecting Ellis to come back. Her boss didn't seem like the consoler-of-hysterical-women type. "If you believe the tabloids, she's more the maker-of-hysterical-women type," she said to herself.

But she saw Ellis make her way back across the courtyard with a large pad under her arm and knock softly, even though the door was unlocked and she had an invitation. "Come in," Charlotte said, the fear of Kyle's call disappearing when she glanced up at Ellis's smile.

Ellis set up a small work area on one end of the sofa, glancing at the large screen every so often as the old black-and-white movie Charlotte had chosen played. When Ellis's attention returned to her work, Charlotte took the opportunity to peer her way. This laid-back Ellis was much more appealing than the fashion mogul the world was familiar with. Ellis's dark-brown hair and long, dark eyelashes provided a definite contrast to her light-green eyes, but overall Ellis was really attractive.

"Do you need any help?" she asked during a commercial, figuring that doing something would keep her from getting caught ogling.

"Go get the stuff you wanted to show me."

Charlotte forgot all about the movie as Ellis flipped though her work. Her teachers had taken their time with assignments, but nothing like this. Ellis seemed to study every stroke she'd made with an open expression of what seemed to be genuine interest. After Ellis's long examination, she took six sketches out of the book and spread them on the coffee table.

"They're all pretty good, but I really love these." The ones she'd selected were all variations of the business suit and a couple of dresses. "What I'm envisioning for this show will have the over-the-top wow factor everyone is expecting, and these will balance that out nicely."

"In other words, I'm the blah, boring part of the show?" she said, shaking her head.

"Oh, ye of little faith. Do you mind me plagiarizing your stuff for my own evil intent?" Ellis grabbed her pen and very quickly somewhat copied her sketch, then kept going. When she was done, the suit was basically the same, but the model's appearance had completely changed it. Ellis's accessories and wild hair had made her creation fit with the theme. "The average woman will look like your work ninety-nine percent of the time, but for one night we can stretch the imagination with a sexy lion-tamer appearance."

"This is fun," she said, sounding to herself very much like Sawyer.

"You know I was telling my mother the very same thing. For once in a long while, this doesn't seem like work." Ellis got her stuff together and handed Charlotte back her work. "It's late, and I don't want to keep you."

"Are you sure you don't want to finish the movie?" Charlotte knelt on the sofa and pressed her hands together as if subconsciously pleading for Ellis to stay.

The way Charlotte asked her meant she didn't seem to want to be alone, and Ellis understood. Whatever stress Ellis was under, all she could lose was a season, which would be tough, but Charlotte had a daughter on the line. She wanted to go to bed, but her conscience had come out of hibernation at a bad time.

"I'm sorry," Charlotte said, getting up. "I'm sure you're at your limit of whiny stories for the next month."

"That's not remotely true." She put her stuff down and retook her seat on the sofa. "Besides, these classics usually have a happy ending, and I think we could both use that right now."

The movie was indeed one of the sappier ones she'd sat through, so she didn't see any harm in closing her eyes to think about her upcoming load of work. When she opened them again, she grimaced as she stared at Sawyer sitting on the coffee table eating something out of a bowl and watching a nature show. It was light outside, and Charlotte's head was in her lap. The scene was ridiculously domestic and so far out of her comfort zone she had the urge to run.

"Hey," Sawyer said when she moved her feet to the floor. "Are we going to the zoo again?"

Jesus Christ, how did anyone say no to an open and trusting expression like this? "Yes, but not until we get the troops moving and I can feel my feet." They were numb and full of imaginary ants.

"Cool." Sawyer ran from the room like their day had been set.

Now if only she could get up without waking Charlotte so as to not embarrass her or make her uncomfortable. That plan went to hell when she moved her hand out of Charlotte's hair and tensed her legs to move. Now Charlotte would probably retreat to the other side of the very large fence she kept around herself, and Ellis would in turn welcome that move.

"Thanks for letting me take advantage of your generosity last night," Charlotte said, slowly sitting up. "That call really threw me, and you were great about it."

"I meant what I said, even if you don't believe me. My guys are available to you, and they really have done this before. Ruby can give you a list if it'll make you more open to the offer."

"Let's see what Kyle comes up with, and I'll let you know. Like I said, by today he's probably forgotten about it."

"Whatever you want. I'll see you in the ballroom in thirty minutes or so."

"I'm ready." Sawyer ran back in, sounding like she didn't want to be left behind.

"Come on, then. You can help my mother set up while I change."

Ellis needed to meet with everyone before they started in earnest, but she stood with her hands against the tile in her shower and let the water run over her head. The thought of both Brandi and Charlotte made her not want to move from this spot. Life was so odd sometimes, but it'd be nice to have two female friends that weren't a total complication.

The news was playing as she got dressed, so she opted for shorts and another T-shirt when she heard the day's forecast. Starting today, her mom would begin having meals delivered, with Jacqueline's help, but she was skipping the food line and taking Sawyer to the Camellia Grille. It was one of her favorite spots and wasn't too far from the zoo.

"We got the first six pieces roughly cut and in progress, but you'd better approve the material before we get started," Opal said, since she and Amis were waiting for Ellis outside her bedroom when she was done.

"I'll do that before I go. I have a couple more for you, and so does Charlotte. Where's Ruby?"

"He's been holed up in his room working since last night," Amis said. "You've got time, so go check on him before you leave."

She knew by the way her mom said it that he was sulking. They'd been friends for years, but Rueben had a habit of taking blame that was in no way his. "Grab Charlotte's stuff and start deciding on fabric, and I'll be right down."

Rueben didn't answer her knock so she turned the knob and went in. The room was dark, but she could see the scattered sheets all over the floor from the light bleeding though the cypress blinds. Her old friend was passed out on the bed, and the large, empty bottle on the nightstand explained the deep sleep and loud snoring.

"Fuck me, man. It's going to be a long summer," she muttered. After opening the blinds, she ripped the blanket off him, praying he hadn't gotten naked as well as hammered. "What the hell, Ruby?"

Rueben opened his eyes, then quickly covered his face with his hands. "Leave me alone. You're—"

"Better off without me," she said for him. "Give me a break here, pal, and let's skip this shit. I was angry we got robbed, but I didn't blame you. I need you downstairs working and not up here carrying that boulder of guilt up a fucking mountain."

"You don't need me."

"Ruby, get your ass out of that bed, or I swear I'll drag you down there myself and nail you to a chair. I need you to clear your head and get to work." She picked up his sketches, which looked like a drunken, talentless demented person had drawn them. "Before you do that, burn all this shit and take a shower. You've got twenty minutes before Malcom comes up here with his shadows to clean this room. Believe me, you want to be out of bed before he does."

She slammed the door behind her, hoping he felt the vibration all the way to the middle of his skull. She wasn't willing to tolerate dramatics of any kind right now. "Make sure he eats something and actually gets up," she told her mother.

"You were a bit too hard on him, don't you think?" Amis took her arm to go down.

"Hard would've been flinging him out the window into the pool."

"His room doesn't face the pool, chéri."

"There you go. I wasn't that hard on him, was I?" She was aggravated by the time they got to the kitchen, but hearing Sawyer tell one of the staff her ideas for her paintings made her smile. "Come on, Sawyer."

Both Sawyer and Charlotte listened as she reviewed the workload for the day, and they inspected what they'd brought back the night before. Harold Epstein's family had been in business for years for a reason. They carried quality stuff and catered to a clientele that could afford it.

When she was done, she decided to take Charlotte as well, so she grabbed the keys to Malcom's Jeep. "How about an omelet?" she asked, and they both nodded enthusiastically.

These two were like puppies that never said no to playtime, so they stopped to eat first. She couldn't remember the last time she'd played tour guide, but after their meal it was time to get something done. The zoo was more crowded that morning so they walked and looked more than they worked, but she made some notes before they headed for the exit.

"A couple of stops, and then I'll get you back to the pool."

"The pool can wait," Charlotte said as they made it through the hot parking lot. A woman with three kids slowed and stared at Ellis but kept going.

"Damn ad campaign." She drove them to Epstein's and walked the floor and the stockroom with Harold. "How fast can you get something if it's not in stock?"

"Depends on if it's in the States." Harold seemed to grow smaller with age, but the brightness in his eyes never dimmed. "If it's something exotic, and with you it always is, get to those first."

"You're a miracle worker, so bundle up all the bolts I picked and have them delivered. Make sure you go, so my mother can put you in a headlock only to give in. You know she loves the bargaining game as much as you do."

Harold laughed and patted her hand. "Amis, that beauty. I should've married that woman the first day I met her."

"You were already married, old man."

"Ha, and *that* old woman is still giving me a hard time, but with Amis I'd probably be dead by now, so I shouldn't complain."

"You're right about that," she said before she hugged him. "I'll see you later, and I hope you don't mind some overtime."

"Day or night, *liebling*. If I'm sleeping I'll send Madeline," he said of his daughter. "All my customers will be jealous when I tell them at the end where the beautiful clothes you make started. Until then, my lips are sealed."

"Make sure your good suit is pressed. You're getting a front-row seat for the show."

Charlotte looked on as Harold embraced Ellis. It appeared like he truly cared for her, like the people back at the house did. Ellis, it seemed, had the loyalty of those around her, and that didn't happen just because of a sale or a job. That truth made it hard to understand why someone would steal from her.

They left the downtown and headed to the park on the shore of Lake Pontchartrain. It was a quiet afternoon until it started to pour rain, soaking them and some of their sketches. "I guess this is the hint I needed to get home and back to work," Ellis said as they looked out at the sudden summer storm that had created an impressive amount of lightning way offshore.

"Aw, we'll be stuck inside all day," Sawyer said.

"These things seldom last that long, so we might have time for something." Ellis wiped her face and pulled out slowly, since the driving rain was making the wipers almost useless.

It took them an hour to get home, instead of the usual twenty minutes, and they had to make a run for the house when they arrived. It seemed like everyone there, including some new arrivals, was in the ballroom working on something. The mannequins scattered about were clothed, but they had a way to go before the pieces were done. At best, though, the outfits were something tangible instead of trapped in Ellis's imagination.

"It's like a coordinated madhouse," Charlotte said, shivering and bouncing on her feet as she dripped water onto the wood floor.

"I'll have my mother get you something to change in to so you don't have to go back outside."

That was the last of Ellis's attention they got for the rest of the afternoon, but Charlotte was glad to be part of the group. She didn't think she'd be sewing again, but it was hard to complain when Ellis had a needle and thread in hand as well. Ellis might've been a world-class designer, but her stitching rivaled any machine's.

"Any luck on my snake-print leather?" Ellis asked her mother.

"Harold's working on it, and he's waiting on a few samples," Opal answered. "He said he'd call if he gets them late today."

"Do you have anything new?" Rueben asked, and Charlotte glanced up at him and thought he was sick because he appeared so drawn. But the guy was dedicated to still be down here working. "I'll get it cut."

"It needs some salvaging from the rain we got caught in, so take over for me," Ellis said, giving up her seat to him. "Charlotte, grab our stuff."

She gladly relinquished her spot to join Ellis in the study. Her phone was buzzing, but she ignored it when she saw it was Kyle again. She'd deal with him later by threatening to take him back to court for more support. That would definitely get him off her tail.

"Problems?" Ellis asked.

"Not right now," she said and prayed it stayed that way. After all she'd put up with, she deserved a break. "Let's see how bad it is," she said of the sketches.

"Everything's fixable, my friend. You simply have to find a way to get it done."

CHAPTER TWELVE

A mis came to get them when dinner arrived and gladly took four more sketches Charlotte and Ellis had finished. "Harold called and said he might've gotten what you're looking for."

"Good. We'll go after we eat. It's going to be the hardest to put together when it comes to the hems and the zipper, so I hope he got plenty in case we need to do it more than once. Leather doesn't look fabulous when it's folded over." Ellis looked back when Charlotte silenced her buzzing phone again. It had to be the tenth time today.

"That girl Opal hired last year, Katie, is pretty good with leather, so let's see how she does," Amis said.

"I can try if you want," Rueben said, following them to the kitchen. "I had a piece with leather last year, remember?"

"I need you to concentrate on the big picture, Ruby. If we fall behind we're toast."

"Someone has to go back and set up the show as well. What we had planned won't fit with what you're doing now." He put only some mashed potatoes on his plate, with a glass of water. The hangover had to still be kicking his ass. "You want me to take care of that too?"

"I'm more interested in the line than how we're going to display it," she said, putting a piece of bread on his plate and getting him some aspirin. "Once I'm close to finishing the design aspect, I might go up myself and take care of that. I have something in mind but need to think it through."

"So basically, I get to sit around here until you're done being pissed at me?" Rueben held his head as he raised his voice. "Just let me know how to make it up to you, and I'll do it."

Ellis watched him go and sighed.

"Do you want me to talk to him?" Amis asked.

"No. I'll do it. He either has found a new way to manifest whatever guilt he's got over this, or he's lost his mind." She paused when Charlotte touched her forearm as she passed. "Don't worry. It's all part of the business."

"Are you going to be okay?" Sawyer appeared almost frightened, and her voice quivered as she asked the question.

Getting ripped off should've been enough, but the added minefield of emotion all these new and old people in her life came with was exhausting. She couldn't walk out and leave the kid like this, so she bent to Sawyer's level. "Sometimes people sound mad, but really they're only mad at themselves. Mr. Rueben is sad about what happened, and he's trying to make himself feel better."

"By yelling at you? That's not right. My dad does that, and I hate it."

"That's true, but we'll cut him some slack this time." Sawyer hugged her, and the act came close to making her cry. She'd run across so many people who wanted something from her, but Sawyer wasn't after a thing. The kid simply did things like this because that's who she was. "Thanks for that. You made me feel better."

She climbed the stairs and knocked on Rueben's door, with no luck. "Ruby, come on. We need to talk about this."

He opened the door but walked back to the bed and sat down. "Look, I'm sorry for what happened just now. I would've never left the book in my office if I had a clue about all this. All I ask is that you don't lock me out."

"Why the hell would you think that? We've been through so much together, and that alone means I wouldn't ever blame you for this. I haven't blamed you for anything, so I'm not sure where this is coming from." She started to move closer to him but stopped when he put his hands up. "What's wrong? Level with me, because you usually don't come unhinged like that over nothing."

"I just need the night off. I'm being stupid and I don't feel well, so forgive my hysteria. It's been a rough few days."

"I'll send up something for you to eat, so get some sleep after that, and stay away from the bottle. Once this is over, we'll laugh about it, I promise."

He nodded and lay down, closing his eyes.

It was time for a damn drink, she thought as she made her way down. She stopped on the stair landing when she heard Charlotte on the phone. From her demeanor and the way she was pacing, it had to be the ex again.

"Kyle, I told you that's not going to happen. You call with this crap again, and I'll take you up on your offer. Only this time I'll let Sawyer testify to everything. If you don't understand what that means, then think of never seeing her again unless it's a supervised visit. Even if you want to never pay another dime, I'll be okay with that since all I've ever wanted was for Sawyer to know you. I'm tired of this constant fighting, though, so think about the consequences if you don't stop this."

Charlotte listened another minute, then let out a noise like she'd reached the end of her patience as she ended the call.

"Sounds like everyone is having their own version of the same bad night."

"I'm sorry. It's still raining, so the foyer and your office were the only places that were empty. I didn't want to invade your space."

"No need to apologize. Sawyer's dad again?" She sat on the bottom step and patted the spot next to her. Charlotte immediately sat and leaned against her.

"He waited until I started trying to pursue my dreams before making unrealistic demands when it comes to Sawyer. I'm beginning to think he's waiting for me to earn a higher salary so he can ask me to start paying him."

"Why not talk to my guys and see if there's something to make him not only stop making demands, but to get him to stop calling altogether. I don't want to be a pest, but you shouldn't wait."

"Maybe…I don't know. He's never been so interested in Sawyer's welfare, so part of me is shocked, but another part of me is happy. Does that make sense? I mean, she's his kid, so this is how it should've been all along."

"Go with your gut, but keep my offer in mind. Did you eat?"

"Not really." Charlotte held up her phone and smiled. "This killed my appetite."

"Can't have you starve on me. Go get my buddy and let's go out." The rain was still falling but had slacked considerably, so they took

Malcolm's Jeep again. She drove the short distance to Port of Call for some of their famous burgers and loaded baked potatoes.

"This place is cool," Sawyer said as the waiter put down their drinks.

"When you consider the calories per serving, it's the last place in the world you'll find a supermodel, for sure, but I'm glad you like it." She laced her fingers together and decided to enjoy what little she had to be happy about right then.

"Do you think Mr. Epstein will wait for us?" Charlotte asked.

"Harold will no more incur my mother's wrath than he'll set his hair on fire, so he will. If it makes you feel better, I told him to go home and have dinner, and I'd call him when we were done."

Their meal arrived, and like all the other times she'd been here, she didn't finish the entire thing. Charlotte and Sawyer tried their best, but food was still on their plates when they clutched their stomachs and moaned, which made her chuckle. She laughed harder when Charlotte wadded up her napkin and threw it at her head.

"I'm warning you, I bruise easily," she said as Charlotte grabbed Sawyer's napkin.

"I doubt that, and don't you know you're not supposed to make fun of a woman who eats herself into an almost burger coma? Though I doubt any woman you know actually eats anything resembling a burger." Charlotte threw the napkin, only this time she aimed for the middle of her chest.

"Maybe that's what I've been missing all my life. A woman who actually admits food tastes good, which in turn keeps the bitchy to a minimum," she said and winked at Sawyer. "Sorry, kid. I'll try to keep the cursing to a dull roar so your mother doesn't accuse me of being a corrupting influence."

"I don't mind," Sawyer said, smiling.

"The first time anything like that comes out of your mouth, you're grounded," Charlotte said, touching the end of Sawyer's nose gently.

"How about Ellis, Mama?"

"Ellis isn't too big for me to ground as well, if she gets out of hand," Charlotte said, and her snort made Charlotte blush.

"Maybe you were right about red being my favorite color," she said, starting to touch Charlotte's cheek and stopping at the last minute.

Putting her hands on someone uninvited wasn't her style. She liked being with the two Hamners and didn't want to mess things up. "You two ready to go look at some fabric?"

Harold was already at the store when she called, but the material wasn't what she'd envisioned. It wasn't all bad, though, so she knew it gave him another opportunity to visit her mother.

"One more stop and we'll call it a day."

"Where we going?" Sawyer asked.

"It's a surprise, but I'm not sure it's open this late so don't get your hopes up." City Park was out of their way, but Storyland had always been one of her favorite spots when she was a kid.

Sawyer was too old to appreciate it, but no matter your age, everyone enjoyed a carousel. The park had a beautiful one that she visited every year when she came home. It was one of the places she'd taken a few of the interns, and they all pretended to love it because she did. When Sawyer and Charlotte saw it, she saw nothing fake in their reaction.

"It's gorgeous," Charlotte said.

"I've always wanted to do a show here, but it wouldn't accommodate a very big audience." She paid and picked a large black stallion after Sawyer had found what she wanted to ride. Charlotte climbed on a horse next to Sawyer and laughed when the ride started.

"I'd never ridden on one of these," Sawyer said loudly when they came to a stop, so Ellis paid for another go-round. They ended up riding two more times, and the adventure and talking about it put Sawyer to sleep about halfway home.

Ellis didn't think Sawyer was fully awake when Charlotte walked her to her room and led her to the bed. She was sure Amis had done the same thing on many occasions, and as she looked at Sawyer's sleeping face she realized that it vaguely resembled hers at that age. Hell, maybe the excitement of the day was making her crazy tired too.

She left to wait in the other room when Charlotte started with Sawyer's shoes and socks. Charlotte came out and joined her on the sofa and stared up at the ceiling with her. "You're a good mom, and I'm glad you're getting some fun out of this trip as well as working your butt off."

"Thanks for that, but are we taking up too much of your time? I mean, do all your interns get this much attention?" Charlotte seemed to have a shovel in her mouth and was doing a good job of digging the hole she was in deeper with each word.

"That's an interesting shade of red, *Ms.* Hamner." She ran her finger down Charlotte's cheek and smiled. "And to answer your real *unasked* question, this isn't part of my grand seduction plan. The internship was my idea from the first bit of success I enjoyed to give back a little of the luck I've had through the years. I thought of it, and when we began, I figured why do something unless you were actually going to do it. Did that come out as convoluted as I think it did?"

"It didn't, and that's not what I meant." Charlotte turned to face her with an expression of near pain. "I just didn't want to put you behind."

"Hey, take a breath, okay? Usually, well mostly, I don't spend this much time with my interns, but I'm having fun, and you guys are helping me get this done. Do you need me to step back some?" Maybe she'd let the fame go to her head more than she thought, if she'd simply assumed her companionship was welcome just because of the offer she'd given Charlotte. Perhaps the world at large didn't think she was as great as her mother thought she was.

"No. Jeez, I really screwed this up." Charlotte grabbed her bicep and squeezed. "Getting the job was a major win for me, but spending time with you and watching you with Sawyer is a gift. You've been so incredibly kind, so I was trying to be polite. I didn't say it right, but that's all this was, really."

"Thanks, and you only have to keep to yourself if you want to. If you stay, and you think this is a good place for you, we'll talk about making it permanent." Making such an offer should've scared the hell out of her, but she didn't think offering Charlotte a job was a rash decision. "But take your time. We've got plenty of it, so make sure it's a good fit for you before you decide."

Charlotte smiled and nodded. "Eventually, you'll see that I'm not some rude nutcase who doesn't appreciate all this. I'll do my best to prove to you how much it means to me."

"Yeah, yeah. Go to bed and cut all the ass kissing. When you're ready to *literally* kiss my ass, we'll take this up again." She winked and wiggled her eyebrows, making Charlotte's fading blush reignite.

"Not going to happen, so get out of here." Charlotte's words didn't contain a threat since she was smiling as she said them.

"Eventually you'll see what you're missing."

"Maybe, but I'm not that easy, *Ms*. Renois."

❖

"Do you have a print date?"

Jennifer relaxed the hand she was holding the phone with because her fingers hurt. She didn't need this shit on top of everything else she was facing. "Don't harp on that since we all knew it wouldn't be easy." When they'd put their plan in motion, they'd tried to plan for every pitfall and take every precaution. Using names on the phone was their main rule, but these phone calls were as much a pain as trying to get everything done.

"Not what you said at the beginning of all this. Get it done or—"

"Or what?" Jennifer had reached her limit of bullshit, and it wasn't even ten in the morning. "Or else? Is that what you were going to say? Just remember all the steps and leave the rest to me."

"How's Dalton holding up?"

"He isn't, but don't worry about that either. You wanted to keep in the background, so stay there and let me get this done." The ring of the condo's phone interrupted her, but she was glad for the perfect excuse to end the call. "Got to go."

She silenced her cell and answered the call from the doorman. She granted him permission to send up her guest, taking a minute to calm down and compose herself. The ease of everything except printing the book was surprising. At this point she'd have thought they would've had to shell out way more money, but Kyle was Mr. Bargain Basement.

She was glad she'd forced Dalton to go see his wife and kids, so she could take this meeting alone. Whatever Dalton decided about his future with his family might not make a difference when it came to their future. Sometimes if you procrastinated in an effort to avoid the uncomfortable, the feelings of the person who really wanted you cooled. That's what she was experiencing now, since Dalton had put off the unpleasantness of divorce until he had a gun to his head.

"Come in," she said when she opened her door after the soft knock. "Do you want anything to drink?"

"I just want my money."

Kyle Snyder was good-looking in his physical appearance, with his dark hair and green eyes, but he was a complete moron in the brains department. From what she knew of him, Kyle wasn't successful except when it came to using women. He had quite the string of females who would gladly neuter him, if given the chance, as payment for him using them and throwing them to the curb once he was done. If she had to guess, the done-with-them part most probably took less than five minutes.

"We'll get to that," she said, sitting in the middle of the sofa.

"Wrong. We'll get to it now." He stood with his hands on his hips, his legs spread—a classic alpha male pose that wasn't impressing her in the least.

She went to the desk and took out two stacks of hundreds. "This is what you're here for, but let's talk first. Sit down."

He glared at her but took the chair next to her. "Look, I did what you asked for, so hand it over."

"Mr. Snyder, the money's yours, but there's plenty more if you're up to it."

"How much more?" His back came off the chair, and she knew she had him.

"The ten grand I promised you for the phone calls," she dropped the money on the coffee table, "but I could add substantially more."

"How much, and what do you want now?"

"If you want to move forward you've got to be convincing, so think before you agree. You don't have to fool me. You're going to have to do that with people trained to weed out liars. Think you can do that?"

"Believe me, I'll get it done, but it'll cost you fifty grand."

Cheap and easy, she thought as she held her hand out to him since she'd been willing to pay so much more. "We have a deal."

CHAPTER THIRTEEN

Two weeks went by with no more information about the missing bible, and Ellis knew she was on borrowed time if she wanted to capitalize on her misfortune. If she wanted to blunt the fallout of the theft she believed she'd never be able to prove, she'd have to pull her plan off within the week, and it surprised her that she had any time at all.

She'd been up for a couple of hours refining some of the first pieces they'd started, and since early mornings were the only time the house was completely quiet, she was learning to go to bed with the chickens, as Uncle Malcom liked to say. It was the only way not to roll over and forget the alarm when it went off way before sunrise. It was early, but someone was always not only up but didn't mind bothering her, and she usually came with company.

Sawyer got up every morning appearing ready to handle anything, but Charlotte was usually dragging in behind her with one eye closed. This morning was most probably going to be the same, but Ellis had her mind on Rueben. Her oldest friend and business partner had fallen into a pattern that was more of a downward spiral than a routine.

Rueben had started drinking every early afternoon and was totally useless by the time dinner was delivered. She'd tried to talk to him every morning, but nothing she said was penetrating his assumptions of how she felt. It was like everything they'd shared and been through together had disappeared as effectively as his copy of the bible.

There was that problem, and Charlotte was facing an escalating Kyle. She didn't know the guy, but she couldn't understand how Sawyer could be his, or how Charlotte had ever fallen for his bullshit no matter how young she was. Every time Charlotte hung up from one of his calls, she found comfort in Ellis's arms. It was a new and surprising development, but in Charlotte she'd found a friend that she felt she'd known and cared about all her life.

"Thinking deep thoughts this early? That could be trouble," Charlotte said, making Ellis blink rapidly after jerking up. "Sorry. I didn't mean to scare you."

"I see a lot of ripping in your future."

Charlotte snorted and shoved her. With a little time, Charlotte had gotten a lot more comfortable about her as well, and she'd started to unearth some more of Charlotte's talent now that her defenses were down. So far, she'd included six of Charlotte's pieces in the lineup, and Sawyer had finished her first canvas.

"What's on your mind?" Charlotte asked, taking her by the hand and leading her into the kitchen. Charlotte's newfound level of comfort was leagues away from where they'd begun. "And it's got to be something since this is the only time in the day you don't have a huge frown line in the middle of your forehead. If it's made its appearance already, something's off."

"You want honest or the line I'll repeat to the press if they asked me the same thing?"

Charlotte got everything ready to make coffee and shook her head. "The truth first, and I'm curious about the press one, so follow up with that."

"This year's been so strange. It's like everything that's familiar and true just isn't anymore." She rested her hip against the counter and looked Charlotte in the eye, not wanting to say the rest, but when Charlotte moved her hand in a rolling motion to keep her going, she realized it was either lie or refuse. Neither of those options appealed to her when Charlotte smiled at her like that. "Any other year or circumstance would make me think it was slipping away like sand through my fingers, but now it's different."

"Different how?" Charlotte started the coffee and moved to stand a foot from her.

"You're kind of nosy. You know that?"

Charlotte laughed and took her hand again. "Come on. You know you're dying to tell me."

"For one, there's Rueben and how he's handled this." She combed her hair back and sighed. "I go up there every day and pour my heart out, but it's like he's not hearing me. It's weird not having him here almost anticipating my every move and need, but still having him here. It's like looking at a ghost. He's my business partner, but I can't get him past this, and it's bugging the hell out of me."

"What else?" Charlotte tugged on her hand as if challenging her to finish.

"Like I said, this year's different, so as bad as I feel for not being able to reach Ruby, your being here is..." She didn't know how to finish.

"Do you want to know what I think?" Charlotte took her other hand and stepped even closer. "You're having fun, and because he isn't, it's making you feel a little guilty. That's normal, but keep reminding yourself how long it's been since you had a good time. I might be selfish, but I happen to be enjoying this, and Sawyer thinks you're the coolest person alive."

"I am the coolest person alive, but I must not be giving you enough to do if you like me that much," she said, and Charlotte moaned at the bad joke before letting her go and pouring their coffee. She did it even though Ellis had told her repeatedly it wasn't necessary. "But since you seem to adore and idolize me, want to help me with something?"

"We'll have to get you a sling to hold up that big head of yours first, but let's hear it. What do you have in mind?"

"I have someone coming over today from a nationally syndicated morning show, so we have to set up a fashion show in the next couple of days." Sigrid had come through after a few calls they'd shared, so several A-list models were on their way South to pull it off.

"What do you need me to do?"

"The girls should be here late tonight, so in the morning we need you to work with Opal to get all the fittings done," Amis said, coming in to kiss Charlotte's cheek first, then Ellis's. "Where's my favorite artist?"

"She stayed up to tweak her leopard, so she's sleeping in this morning. Do you need me to do anything else?"

"Trust me. You'll be up to your ass in naked women looking for something to wear, so don't ask for anything else to do." Ellis shrugged and spread her hands out when both women groaned. "What?"

"Nothing, chéri." Amis patted her on the stomach, then faced

Charlotte. "You and Opal take care of all the fittings with the team, and I'm going to look for a venue. We worked hard on this line, damn it, so we might as well make something out of it."

"Let's see if you can do with all but a few people, so we can keep working on the new line."

"Charlotte and I will handle it, so get back to work," Amis said, and Ellis noticed the sky was starting to lighten outside.

"Good. Let me go get ready for my meeting." She took her cup and headed for her bedroom and a shower, but stopped first at Rueben's door. His lights were still off, at least she couldn't see any under the door, but she heard the television set on. The room had been quiet when she went down, so she knocked. She needed to talk to him after her conversation with Charlotte.

"Ruby, you awake?" She spoke softly and stepped back when he came to the door. It was a shock to not only see him up but dressed and ready. "Hey, you look great."

"I got tired of feeling sorry for myself." He waved her into the now-neat room she was used to seeing. "So I decided to listen to you in that you don't blame me."

"I don't, and I'm glad you believe me. I missed you."

He smiled as he put his shoes on, then grabbed his book. "Hopefully we're not too far behind because of my being an asshole."

"Charlotte has picked up the slack, so don't worry about it. In fact, she's turned out to be a really good pick, so thanks for choosing her to be one of the finalists." She saw that he was ready so she got out of his way. "She has her list of things to do, so check in, and I'll be down in a bit."

"Check in with the intern, you mean?" he said and laughed.

"We've got some major stuff coming up in the next few days, so yeah. I have a meeting this morning, and we need to get going." She walked out before they ended up right back where they'd been for the last weeks if they had another argument.

Rueben was her best friend and a phenomenal part of her business, but every so often he could act like an infant. She couldn't blame him since she had done so on occasion, but never when they were under the gun like this.

She stepped into the shower after slamming her door and stood in the spray for a long while before she reached for the shampoo. It was a way to calm down and be her best when she met with the anchor from the nationally syndicated show. If she pulled this off, she might be able to bring both lines to market. Doubling down would hopefully make Jennifer and Dalton eat the bible they'd stolen a page at a time because, after this, that'd be all it was good for.

"And if you do, I hope you choke on it, you bastards."

❖

Benson Norwood glanced up from his screen when he heard someone clear their throat. When he saw Jennifer and his publisher standing in his doorway, he wished he'd called in sick since he recognized his boss's expression. Whatever crap Jennifer was giving him, Benson would take the brunt of the blame.

"Just wanted to say hello, Benson, and to wish you good luck on your article," Jennifer said as she waggled her fingers at him before disappearing.

"My article?" he asked.

Raymond Nixon looked more like an old newspaper man than the publisher of a fashion magazine, but his mother had started the business years before and taught him the ropes. Even after all that time the publication still made a good bit of money since it concentrated more on the gossipy part of fashion and its main players than the actual clothes. So Raymond came to work every day in his wrinkled shirts with stained collars and armpits, and his polyester pants. He knew this was no *Vogue*, but he didn't want it to be.

"You still have the entire bible, right?" Raymond asked, dropping into his visitor's chair like someone had shot him.

"I would've given it back by now, but Jennifer refused to take it." He opened the file drawer and dropped it onto the corner of his desk. "If the cops arrive, I'm sure I'll be taking the fall for her and Dalton."

"It's more like you'll be writing the article that'll go with these sketches. We go to print tomorrow and distribution in two days, so drop whatever you're doing and get this done. This will be our largest print to date, so don't let me down." Raymond flipped through the book and stopped on a few pages, nodding as if in approval of what he saw.

"What changed your mind? When I took it to you, you said we couldn't afford the lawsuit." He reached for his notebook and jotted down which sketches Raymond seemed to like the most. His story could start with those.

"You brought it to me because you were afraid of this." Raymond threw a jump drive at him, and it hit him in the chest since he didn't move fast enough to catch it. "She swore that's the original file and there aren't any other copies."

"With all due respect, sir, you must not know that viper very well. There aren't any other copies until she needs another hatchet job done on someone."

"I traded her that for the promise to destroy the video of her and Dalton giving you this." Raymond laid his hand on the bible.

"There isn't a video of that." He glanced around the room in case he'd missed some sort of surveillance equipment.

"That bitch doesn't know a lot of things, but she's easier to deal with if you play along like she's the smartest person you ever met."

"So we're printing it?"

"The whole thing is going in, so write up something about the unnamed source that brought it to you. Just don't mention anything about theft."

Benson wrote that down as well, but something didn't feel right about all this. "What's the pitch then? Someone simply brought us this for no reason?"

Raymond shook his head and frowned. "We got it. Our source wanted to show the disarray within the Renois house, and no one knows if Ellis can recover. The question will be if she can get her shit together so close to Fashion Week."

"If I quote an unnamed source I'm out of the woods if Ellis comes after me? You know how she is. Ellis will beat the crap out of you if you cross her, and she'll do it without ever throwing a punch."

"I haven't always been a good blocker for you, but trust me on this one. Write it and you'll be fine." Raymond slapped his hand on the book and left, taking the stench of cigarettes and coffee with him.

"Yeah, you got my back until the shit starts raining down on us. Then you'll step on me to get somewhere to cover your ass."

CHAPTER FOURTEEN

Ellis put on a light-colored linen suit with a white shirt, wanting to look professional but stay as cool as possible. The producer she was meeting asked her to pick a place, so she'd made reservations at the Piquant's breakfast restaurant, which was outside.

She dropped a small notebook into her jacket pocket, with a pen, in case something popped into her head. All she needed to do was hopefully get three segments so they could show the entire lineup. The knock on her bedroom door made her drop her keys and wallet to answer it, and she smiled when she saw Sawyer.

"I hear you finished your canvas," she said, hugging the little girl. "When I get back we'll go down and take a look, but I'm sure it's wonderful. I'm really proud of you."

"Will you be gone all day?"

"Hopefully not. If I'm nice enough, maybe this woman I'm going to see will give me everything I want right away." She loaded her pockets with everything she needed and put on the vintage watch Amis had given her as a gift after her first show.

"I'll see you later then," Sawyer said with what sounded like a bit of dejection.

"My mom's waiting for you to see if you'll help her out today, and if I didn't have to work, I'd tag along." She placed her hand on Sawyer's shoulder and gently squeezed. "You okay?"

"Think later I can talk to you about something?"

"Sure," she said, thinking that if Jennifer and Dalton could find a way to get Sawyer to ask her to forgive them, she'd do it. "Come find me when I get home."

"Wow, you look great," Charlotte said from the top of the steps, holding her hand out to Sawyer. "And I was wondering where you'd run off to."

"Thank you, and Sawyer's going with Mama, if that's okay with you," Ellis said as she pointed them all down the stairs. "Let me get going before I'm late."

Charlotte and Sawyer wished Ellis luck and stood in the doorway until she pulled out. "Feel like breakfast?" Charlotte asked, her arm around Sawyer's shoulders.

"Sure." Sawyer sounded listless and sad, but Charlotte didn't need to ask why.

Kyle had called again the night before, and she'd thought Sawyer was asleep so she'd closed herself in her bedroom to deal with him. He'd gone from wanting Sawyer brought back to New York to wanting full custody because now his father and mother were back together. Since he still lived with them, it would, in his and his attorney's opinion, provide a more stable environment for Sawyer. That had made her lose it, and she glanced up to find Sawyer in her room looking terrified.

"Let's go back to our place and get some pancakes."

"Miss Amis is waiting for me," Sawyer said, acting almost panicked, as if she'd disappoint or be left behind.

"She wants you to eat something so she's not leaving without you."

When they got back to the guesthouse, Sawyer dropped into one of the stools and rested her chin on her hands. "Just toast is good, Mom. I'm not that hungry."

She put the griddle pan down and stood across from Sawyer at the island counter. "Do you want to talk about it?"

"Do I have to go?" Sawyer's eyes filled with tears that stubbornly wouldn't fall, and the sight caused a real pain in Charlotte's chest. "I know he's my dad and all, but I don't want to go. Grandma says really mean stuff about you, and I think she doesn't like me."

Charlotte quickly came around the counter and put her arms around Sawyer, devastated that she couldn't protect her kid from the people who should love her. "No. You know I'm going to always fight to keep you with me. I love you, and it'll be me and you until you're ready to fly away from me."

"Please, I don't want to go." Sawyer started sobbing so she held her tighter.

Hopefully what Ellis had offered wasn't an empty promise said only to be nice. "You're not going anywhere, I promise, so don't worry about it. All that counts here is what you want."

"I want to stay with you," Sawyer said, almost in a wail.

Charlotte glanced up when the door opened and Amis came in, most probably because she'd heard Sawyer. "What's wrong?"

Amis's question only made Sawyer cry harder, so Amis put her hands on Sawyer's shoulders. She knew that, like Ellis, Amis had genuine affection for Sawyer. "I heard from Kyle again, and Sawyer overheard me."

Ellis had asked if she could tell her mother what was going on, so she knew she didn't have to give a complex explanation. "Go get your things, chéri," Amis said, using the nickname she used for Ellis. "I'd like you to come help me get a surprise for Ellis."

Sawyer left to gather her things, almost dragging her feet, and Charlotte considered keeping her for the day, but she needed to talk to Ellis, preferably alone. "I'm sorry about that. Sawyer's usually so even-keeled, no matter what."

"Don't apologize. Just tell me what happened." Amis faced the direction Sawyer had walked off in, as if watching so as not to subject her to another uncomfortable conversation.

Charlotte gave her the short version of what Kyle had threatened, which was if she didn't bring Sawyer back, then he'd sue her for custody. If she did, he'd drop everything. All he wanted was Sawyer away from Ellis. It was the strangest thing, since Kyle had no idea who anyone outside the sports world was, so she was rather shocked that he was so familiar with Ellis.

"I feel like giving in will only make it worse going forward. Give in once and give in always, my mom likes to say."

"Tonight we'll let Ellis deal with Sawyer, and you and I will share a drink. I'll tell you about Ellis's father. No one can advise you about what's the best step for you, but listening might help you move forward." Amis put her hand up quickly, then opened her arms to Sawyer, who'd just walked in.

"Do I need anything else?" Sawyer held up her sketchbook.

"That's all Ellis was ever interested in bringing, so you're set. Let's go."

"Thank you," Charlotte said, breathing easier now that Sawyer seemed calmer.

"No need for that, darling girl. Sawyer will be fine, but Opal is waiting for you. The girls will be here tonight, and you'll learn the next step after they do. If Ellis closes this deal, we'll have to be ready to go the day after tomorrow." Amis took Sawyer's hand and kissed her forehead.

"Be good, you two."

"Only a little good, Mama," Amis said, and laughed. "Totally good girls never do come to rule the world, do they?"

"Good to know."

❖

"I love this place," Sawyer said when Amis pulled into a parking spot. "Ellis brought us here."

"I'm not surprised. When she was your age we came here all the time. Some of her first sketches were of this carousel. Later on, if we have time, I'll take you to her other favorite spot." Amis held Sawyer's hand and walked around the ride to see where they could set up.

"Mrs. Renois?" A young woman in khaki shorts and a blue shirt that screamed uniform waved from the opposite side they were on. "I'm Wendy, the assistant manager you spoke to on the phone."

"Please, it's Amis, and this is Sawyer," she said after Wendy made her way around.

"Thanks for coming out, and I got all the stuff you asked for earlier."

"Think you can close with no problem?" The fence around the ride was fixed, but at the back they'd have enough room to set up chairs for Ellis and the anchor, as well as the camera people.

"Our manager said whatever you need, since the coverage and the fee we agreed on would be great for business. All I need is a walk-through once we know it's a go."

"Ellis is meeting with the producer now, so by this afternoon, if you're available, I'll come back and tell you what'll need to go where."

She signed the contract Wendy had brought and handed over a

check. Their site was set, but instead of heading back, she decided to do what Ellis would've wanted her to do. The drive wasn't that far, so she headed to the other large park in the city.

"We're going to the zoo?" Sawyer asked, not sounding opposed to the idea.

"Not quite." She turned into the lot across from the zoo and parked at the end by the golf clubhouse. "When Ellis was your age, the golf course here wasn't as nice, but we used to come because of the trees." They headed to the back side of the restaurant to one tree in particular.

The oak was spectacular in size, but the top had a multitude of offshoots that made it stand apart from the grove it stood in. "Thanks for showing it to me," Sawyer said.

"Do you know why I did that?" she asked, and smiled when Sawyer shook her head slowly as if she wasn't sure she should. "I brought you here like I did with Ellis because you remind me of her. Actually, you even look a lot like her when she was your age." Amis combed Sawyer's hair back off her forehead, and the feel and color of it were just like Ellis's.

"I do?"

"You do, so you have to believe that whatever you're worried about will be okay. Ellis told me about you the first day she met you, and I could tell she liked you a lot. That's become truer because of all the time you've spent together, so she's going to help your mother with all this stuff that's got you upset."

"I want to stay here with my mom and you guys, especially Ellis."

"I know, so look at that tree." She pointed to the top. "Doesn't that look like a bunch of arms waving in the air?"

Sawyer finally smiled and nodded. "You think I should draw it?"

"No. I want you to leave your worry here and let the tree carry it. You'll be too busy having fun. This is Ellis's worry tree, as she calls it, and I'm sure she won't mind sharing it. It looks big enough to carry whatever's bothering you both."

"Thank you." Sawyer hugged her, and the gesture seemed somewhat awkward, as if it was something she didn't do often.

"No problem, and now that I've introduced you to this tree, let me know, and we'll come back whenever you like. You're way too young to be worried about so much, so just remember that you and your mom aren't alone in this anymore."

❖

"Did some dog I don't know you have get sick while I was gone?" Ellis asked, since Charlotte was waiting where she parked.

"I need your help," Charlotte said, her arms crossed as if hugging herself for comfort.

"Does this have anything to do with why Sawyer looked so hangdog this morning?" She grabbed her jacket from the passenger seat and waved Charlotte into the house. Once they were there, she found Opal and Rueben waiting to talk to her, but she shook her head and kept walking.

"Ellis, you can't throw this at us and then waste time," Rueben said, causing Opal to take a step away from him as if she wanted to be out of the line of fire.

"I'm not throwing anything at anyone. In case you forgot, this is our job, so get it done. I'll be with you in a minute."

"Good God. This year of all years, you can't control yourself?"

Ellis stopped and stared at him, getting him to break first when he dropped his head and gazed at the floor. "Charlotte, give me a minute, okay," she said, briefly touching Charlotte's shoulder.

"Look," Rueben said once the door to the study closed. "I come down this morning and find out you're planning all this, and I've got no clue about it."

"Shut the fuck up," she said, loud enough for him to snap his mouth closed. "If you ever disrespect anyone on the staff like that again, you're on your way home."

What seemed to be a sudden rush of aggression he'd never displayed before erupted out of him, and he screamed back. "Wait a minute—you get to screw around, we clean up after you, and I'm getting called down for it?"

"Do I need to explain consenting adults to you? And not that I have to explain myself to anyone, especially you, but don't ever talk about Charlotte like that again." She moved toward him, and he shrank away. "Do you understand me? Because if that's not clear, you're done here."

"Don't threaten me, Ellis. I'm as important to the company and as much a part of it as you are."

"You haven't been a part of anything except your affair with Grey Goose since you got here, so get back to work and keep your opinions and observations to yourself. If you don't, I'll personally stitch your mouth shut."

She opened the door and found a mortified-appearing Charlotte outside. Rueben glanced at Charlotte and paused, but kept going. The old house was solidly built, but Ellis could tell Charlotte had overheard their conversation—every word of it.

"Are you sure this is a good time?" Charlotte asked, not moving from her spot outside.

"It's the perfect time," she said, glancing at her watch. "Want to have lunch with me?"

"Are you sure this is a good time?"

"You asked that already. Come on." She left the jacket and opened the door for Charlotte.

She drove them out to the airport on Lake Pontchartrain. The restaurant that spilled out into the lobby of the Terminal Building had been there since the late thirties and was frequented by locals. Ellis enjoyed it for the atmosphere as well as the food. It was like a temple to the art-deco era, surrounded by murals of the great flights in history.

"We're eating at the airport?" Charlotte said, but she was smiling.

"I picked this place especially for you, Miss Vintage." She held her hand out, and Charlotte didn't hesitate to take it. "It's like a time capsule to the era of your favorite clothing."

They took a quick tour, and the manager set them up in their reception room so they'd have some privacy. The only view they had was of some parked planes and the runways, but their surroundings were so nice they could ignore the windows.

"I'm sorry if you overheard me and Rueben."

Charlotte nodded and placed her hands flat on the table. "Can we agree that we've both made some mistakes in our pasts and leave it at that?"

"We could, but I didn't want you to think I'd let anyone on my crew disrespect you like that. I've had some fun with the interns before you, but my problems, the ones I had problems with, came because of the business side and not from anything else."

"Meaning they slept with you to become the next Vera Wang. Is that about it?"

"Don't insult Ms. Wang like that, but that's close to the mark." She exhaled heavily and ran her hands over her face. "Really, only two were a problem, but they made so much noise people think every single one was a pain in the neck, or a victim of my lechery. It's all in how you see it, I guess."

"Can I admit something to you and not have you think I'm crazy?"

"We're here so you can tell me whatever you want, and to keep me from killing my best friend."

"I'm sure Rueben will be fine, or I guess he will be, but I can't blame those women for being attracted to you."

She laughed out of nervousness, or what she thought was nerves. "You don't have to be that nice, Charlotte. I, like you, read all the gossip from my screwups, so before we go down that curvy road, what happened today?"

"Kyle called last night and demanded we go back, or he's going to court to fight for custody."

"What'd you tell him?"

Charlotte stared at her before turning and looking out the large window. "It just occurred to me that this isn't your problem, and it's not fair to dump it on you."

"You don't want my help?"

Charlotte wouldn't look at her. "It's not that, Ellis, and you know it. We've known each other a month, and you're willing to fight for me. I'm telling you that you don't have to."

She exhaled again, not because she was overwhelmed with all this and her business. "Can I admit something to you?" Charlotte nodded. "I never expected all this—this life I've made for myself. I worked hard, granted, but so do a lot of people, and they never climb this far up the ladder. I have everything, but last year I thought about letting it all go."

"Quitting, you mean?" Charlotte's expression was pure surprise.

"The money, the fame, and everything else gets to be the last things that are important when your soul isn't in it anymore. I worked on the show for this year's fall season, and like I said, I was proud of it and convinced myself it was good enough for my finale. You know, something I'd be remembered for, and then I could retreat here and enjoy the rest of my life in peace." She stopped when a server came in with their lunch.

"Wow," Charlotte said, but took her fork when she handed it over. "You were going to just walk away?"

"Not exactly." She squeezed lemon into her iced tea as an excuse to try to gather her thoughts. "I was going to sell—emphasis on going to, so don't peddle that story to the *National Enquirer* because I've changed my mind."

"You can trust me. You know that."

"I'm not worried about that, since this is my summer of enlightenment when it comes to more than work. You never know why or from where you find that spark, or where you'll find someone you know will be a good friend. You know it because it comes from here," she placed her hand over her gut, "and from here." She moved her hand over her heart.

"I understand that last part because you're, in a way, too good to be true," Charlotte reached across to her and grabbed her hand. "Even if you don't help me, I'm tired of being alone."

"Not exactly a ringing endorsement for why you want someone in your life, but I'm getting used to how you put things."

Charlotte laughed before pinching the top of her hand. "I couldn't let anyone in if it was purely for companionship, you idiot, because I have Sawyer to think about."

"Ah, there's the Charlotte I know." She pulled her hands back before Charlotte could pinch her again. "I know what you meant, so let me finish. Getting robbed changed my mind about walking away, but you and Sawyer focused my mind to a way back. I've never offered anyone a job this quick, and it has nothing to do with my libido, so I'm sorry if what Rueben said hurt you."

"I'm not going anywhere, if that's what you're worried about."

"Good, so tell me about Kyle and what makes this guy tick."

Charlotte leaned back and crossed her arms, appearing as if all the good feeling from their talk had bled out of her. "That's easy—money. It certainly isn't me, and it especially isn't Sawyer."

"There's no accounting for stupidity, so let's see if we can't get rid of this guy. Only think it through first."

Charlotte gazed at her as if she'd grown horns. "If I had the power to snap my fingers and make Kyle disappear, I'd have developed a snapping tic by now. Why say that?"

"Because he did one good thing in his life, even if he doesn't see it that way. He made Sawyer possible, and she might be too young to understand why she might need him in her life."

"And if she's old enough to decide?"

"Then one snap is all it'll take. I'm not one for repetitive noises."

CHAPTER FIFTEEN

Charlotte got out of the car, but Ellis left it running when they got back and saw Sawyer waiting outside. When Sawyer got in, she asked to go to the big tree Amis had shown her, and that's all the talking they did until they were standing in front of it.

"My dad wants to make us leave here," she said after Ellis had found them a place to sit among the roots.

"Your mom told me."

"I don't want to leave here. I want to stay with you." Sawyer fell against her in tears, and Ellis wanted to join her because she understood the pain the kid was in. She also understood that seeing either Sawyer or Charlotte in pain was unacceptable at a gut level, so she'd move mountains to help them.

"Listen to me, okay? No one can guarantee much in life. I can't promise we can make a judge do something, because they make decisions without really knowing you."

"Am I going to have to go live with my dad and my grandparents?" Sawyer asked, now crying harder.

"No. It means that I'll keep fighting along with your mom until we find a judge who knows you like I do. You're my friend, Sawyer, and I want you to stay too." She hugged Sawyer, and she practically crawled into her lap.

"You mean it?"

"I do, and now that you know about my favorite tree, you should know everything about it."

"What?" Sawyer wasn't sobbing anymore, but she didn't move from lying across her lap.

"It's a wishing tree, and it's had a great record over the years." She ran her hand along Sawyer's back, trying to calm her. "Give it a shot before we have to head back to our bevy of beauties."

"You sure say funny stuff, Ellis." Sawyer sat up and closed her eyes so tight she looked comical, but Ellis waited by making her own wish.

"I read too much, according to my mother," she said as they stood. "You want to talk some more?"

"I just wanted you to know I don't want to go."

"Good, since I don't want you to go either. We're friends, right?"

"Yeah. You're the only one I've ever shown my stuff to, and I want to keep learning things from you."

"You will, and I promise we'll spend plenty of time together. Actually, you can help me with something if you promise not to tell anyone."

"You want to pinkie swear?" Sawyer held up her little finger, and she told her what she wanted before they swore on it. The fact she'd trusted her with a secret this big made Sawyer practically run back to the car, as if she couldn't wait to start.

The house was full of people, noise, and laughter when they walked back in, and Charlotte stood nearby as the models came to say hello. Ellis thought Charlotte must've been in shock when the top models working in fashion had walked through the front door while she and Sawyer were out.

"Ellis, we're so sorry this happened to you. It pisses me off since this is a beautiful line," Birdie Jones said after kissing both of Ellis's cheeks and then kissed her on the lips. Birdie was at the moment the world's top supermodel, having landed the cover of *Sports Illustrated*'s swimsuit edition and serving as the face for a major makeup company.

"That it is, but tomorrow we're going to show it to the world, so pick something, ladies, but save one for me. It's time to knock the rust off a little and prove I can still walk a runway," Sigrid said when she entered with someone Ellis recognized as one of her top writers.

"What the hell is all this?" Rueben said softly to her.

Ellis completely ignored the question and hugged Sigrid. She came close to laughing since she felt like Sawyer must've earlier, when she found out she had someone on her side. "I'm going to owe you my firstborn for this, Sigrid."

"Nothing so drastic, my darling, but you should remember this when I start making demands for the gala next year."

"I'll sweep up afterward as well as whatever you want, but first let me introduce you to our newest designer, Charlotte Hamner, and her daughter, Sawyer."

"Good to meet you both, and Charlotte, I'd love to see your designs while I'm here. Ellis tells me you're the only other person who loves vintage as much as I do."

"I'd love to, ma'am," Charlotte said in a high-pitched tone.

"And I'd love to see your work, Sawyer. Maybe I can commission something while I'm here and can still afford you."

"Sure," Sawyer said happily, but Ellis figured, unlike her mother, Sawyer had no earthly clue who Sigrid was. She was just a nice lady who wanted to see her art. "But for now, let's go to work."

The models stripped as soon as Sigrid said that, and Charlotte slapped her hand over Sawyer's eyes and led her outside, where Malcom was waiting. "Go on," he told Charlotte. "Sawyer and I are going swimming."

For the rest of the day, Opal gave orders like a field general, and they got their lineup done. They pared it down so that each girl would show three pieces, and Sigrid would wear what was supposed to be that year's finale.

"You know I can't play favorites," Sigrid told Ellis when they were alone in the study. "This thing that happened to you, though, is a story that needs to be told, so please talk to Sierra before we leave tomorrow," Sigrid said, referring to Sierra Madison, her best writer. "I can't force you, but the story needs to come out, and before you complain, I know better than to make you sound the fool. There's that, and you need to say this was a theft. It covers you for when the thieves finally come out with the book."

"I'm kind of shocked they haven't exposed it already." She rocked back in the desk chair and put her feet in the worn divot in the corner. This must've been the owner's favorite position, to have worn the indentation in that spot.

"There's more to this story. You have to know that like I do." Sigrid moved to the pictures on the side of the credenza and bent to look at them. "It has to be so, because I can't find an explanation as to why Jennifer and Dalton would've done this."

"She did it for spite, I guess. It wasn't until she bit me that I figured out how deeply she hates me, and I've got no explanation for that."

"Exactly," Sigrid said, pointing at her. "She could've taken it out of spite, yes, but you never profit from that. You also don't take the chance of substantial prison time for revenge, so we need to keep looking for the why."

"Now we look to work," she said, smiling until the door opened and Rueben came in without knocking. "I guess dinner's ready."

"Actually, Malcom has agreed to drive me to my hotel. These old bones need all the beauty sleep I can get in, if I have to face the cameras tomorrow."

"You're as beautiful as ever," Rueben said, kissing the back of her hand. "And you're an angel for doing all this."

"The world has very few people like Ellis in it, so we do what we can to help where it's needed. Until tomorrow, my darling," she said to Ellis as she caressed her cheek. "And thank you, Rueben."

"I'll come and get you in the morning," Ellis said, walking Sigrid out to the group of models who'd answered her call.

"Don't forget to make time for Sierra."

She leaned against the door and looked at Sawyer sitting on the stairs. "Did you get away from Malcom?"

"We got to watch a movie in your room."

"You didn't eat crackers in there, did you?" She sat next to Sawyer and bumped shoulders with her.

When she was little she and Malcom had spent every afternoon in her room in the matching twin beds Malcom had restored, watching what was called the big movie during the summer. The local channel picked old movies that kids would enjoy and showed them in what they called theme weeks, and they would watch every day and laugh together while eating crackers. Whenever he got up for any reason she'd trade beds with him, and he'd fuss about the crumbs she'd left behind for him. That was as much a part of their tradition as watching the movie together.

Those memories had always been some of her favorites, and she thanked God that she had both her mother and her uncle to give her the kind of foundation that had fueled her imagination well into adulthood. It was the kind of upbringing she wanted to help Charlotte give Sawyer, if she allowed her to be in their lives. Sawyer would never fully come into her own if all she did was worry about things that frightened her into paralysis.

"Want to paint with me?" Sawyer handed over a full box of crackers, since Malcom had probably prepared her for the question he knew she'd ask.

"You've got great ideas, kid."

❖

Charlotte smiled as she listened to Sawyer and Ellis kid around as they worked on the tiger painting Sawyer wanted to tackle next. She'd offered to cook for them, glad to be able to give Ellis a respite from the craziness of the day. However, she didn't think Ellis looked exactly uncomfortable in the middle of all those beautiful women.

The day had started off horribly, yet Ellis had taken the time to ease her worry. But the time she'd taken with Sawyer made her wish that Ellis meant what she said about giving her a place. If she worked for Ellis, then Sawyer would have a place too, and Sawyer would also have someone who cared about her as well. Ellis didn't seem to be faking that.

Ellis was filling the gap that should've belonged to Kyle, and Charlotte was surprised how much that mattered to her. Loving children that much was an attractive trait, and seeing that compassionate side of Ellis made her understand why she never had trouble getting someone into her bed. That wasn't something she'd waste time worrying about, considering the list of women Ellis had been connected to in the tabloids. Hell, Birdie Jones had looked ready to devour her after that greeting.

"I'm losing my mind if that's what I'm thinking about," she said softly as she stirred the beef stew she was making because Amis had told her it was Ellis's second favorite thing.

But if she was totally honest with herself, it'd be okay to admit that she'd had a problem with the way the models had touched Ellis. It seemed way beyond friendship and almost intimate, and that was something she was starting to wonder about as well. Ellis had a way of looking at her that made her feel both naked but beautiful, and it was intoxicating.

Unlike anyone she'd ever known, Ellis had reached deep inside and brought her back to life. That sensation of being in the warmth of Ellis's total attention most probably wouldn't last, and when it ended, the cold sensation of loneliness would replace it.

So she'd enjoy this while it lasted. The memories she'd come away with would hopefully be enough to get her through the nights.

Her ringing phone stopped her descent into that rabbit hole and veered her in another direction when she saw it was Kyle. "Hello."

"When are you coming home?"

"Why are you doing this?" In the numerous conversations they'd had, she'd gotten angry but had never bothered to ask that question.

"I've heard about this bitch so Sawyer's not safe, and she's a bad influence. You need to bring her back where her family is."

His logic would've made sense if he'd given a damn about Sawyer before this, but his insistence still gave her no clue as to his motive. "With you? Is that what you mean?"

"You can insult me all you want, but I'm not backing down."

"I come home, then what?" She turned and stared out the window at the folks sitting around the pool enjoying dinner. "Do I have to resign myself to waiting tables for the rest of my life and chasing you at the end of every month to beg you for the support payment?"

"I've got a few ideas about that, so call me before you head back."

She carefully put the phone down and tried to take deep breaths so she wouldn't cry. That went to hell when Ellis hugged her from behind.

"I know it's hard, but try to keep it together for now, for Sawyer's sake," Ellis whispered.

"This is like a nightmare."

"I know, and there's nothing you can do right now, so try to keep your emotions inside. Sawyer's already freaked out, and we don't need to add to that." Ellis released her and wet a clean kitchen towel to wipe her face. "Let me make a call, and I'll be right back."

"Could you do it from here? I really don't want to be alone right now." Charlotte found comfort by putting her head on Ellis's chest. It was like being wrapped in a warm blanket.

Ellis leaned against the counter and put an arm around Charlotte, so she could call her personal attorney. "Hey, Margie. Could you put me through?" The one thing about Bill Tangren was that he never left the office before eight every night. His recent divorce had tied him to his desk as a way not to go home and think about how much alimony he was paying.

"I was wondering when you'd call," Bill said in his usually booming voice. "Did you find any information on your end to sue the hell out of these people?"

"That's what I've got you for, so keep at it, but I have got something else for you to do." She gave him a rundown of what Charlotte was going through. "How about a small vacation?"

"When do you want me?"

"Tell Margie to pack for you and get you on the ten-thirty flight tonight. I want you working on this so this guy Kyle will take a hike." She rubbed Charlotte's back and glanced down the hall to make sure Sawyer was still engrossed in her painting.

"I'll see you in the morning then."

The call made Ellis feel like she was doing something to help, but it'd be a long string of nights for Charlotte. Relief would only come through resolution, but in this case, she had a feeling that resolution would be slow in coming. "If you want, take the morning off and meet with Bill. With my mom, Opal, and Rueben on the job, we should be fine."

"Can I talk to him afterward? I really want to be there for you tomorrow."

"Whatever you want, but knowing him, he'll be here way before we've got to go. Give him like five minutes and get him started."

"Why are you doing this?" Charlotte asked, moving away so she could stir the stew.

"Because in life you've got to be willing to stand up for your friends and the things you believe in. If I can't do that—I might as well turn into the bitch everyone thinks I am." Ellis started to walk away, but Charlotte stood in front of her. "There's something you need to realize, Charlotte."

"What's that?" She slid her hands into Ellis's and seemed to enjoy the contact.

"I have no ulterior motive except wanting to help you. That's it, so if thinking you owe me something you're not comfortable with is holding you back, know that it's not true." She cupped Charlotte's face and smiled down at her. "You're way too important to me to get anything wrong."

"I've denied myself from letting anyone in for so long, and I've used the excuses of wanting to protect Sawyer and fear of what could happen since Kyle was such a disaster. And now you've made me want things—things I'm almost afraid will be snatched away if I come to think of them as mine."

"Everyone deserves happiness," she said, kissing Charlotte's forehead. "And everyone deserves someone in their corner. I want to be that someone for you if you simply let me."

"You're going to think I'm crazy, but—" Charlotte stood on her toes as if wanting to get closer to her.

Ellis shook her head and let her hand go to press her fingers over lips. "Don't finish that, whatever it is, until you're sure of your words."

She took hold of Ellis's hand again. "You might actually like what I have to say."

"Probably so, but we have all the time we need to get it right. Don't you think?"

"We do, and thank you for that, and for all the rest."

CHAPTER SIXTEEN

You understand how important it is for you to get this done, right?"
Jennifer sat in the back of the deli in Brooklyn and tried not to
squirm at the thought something was crawling up her leg. Kyle had
picked the place, she was sure, to make her crazy, but she refused to
give him the satisfaction. It was hard, though, as she watched him eat
the sloppy sandwich he'd ordered.

"I already laid the threat down, so you need to take a breath. You
need to tell me, and I mean right now, why you're doing this." He left
a blob of mayonnaise on the side of his mouth longer than was good
manners and laughed as he wiped it away with the back of his hand.

"That's not part of our deal, so all you need to worry about is
getting your part right." She couldn't help scratching the top of her
head since she itched everywhere. "I can't tell you how important it is
for you to do what I asked for."

"Not until you answer my question. Don't, you can find someone
else to help you."

She smiled at the threat. Guys like Kyle always assumed they
were holding all the cards simply because they'd been the bully on
the playground from the very beginning. If they threatened, someone
handed over their lunch money—that had most likely been his lifelong
experience.

"If I'm being unfair, then I'll be going, so good luck to you."

"Yeah. Right. Don't try to bullshit someone like me, lady. It's
hilarious." He spoke with his mouth full, which made him even more
disgusting. That he'd had that many women in his past amazed her,

and it proved that some women really didn't have a lot of pride when it came to a pretty face and a cute ass.

She got up and ordered a Lyft, wanting out of this place. They'd have to find some other way to get this done, because she was tired of dealing with Kyle and his stupidity. The car was five minutes away, so she hoped none of the shady-appearing characters milling around outside mugged her before the guy got there. She heard the jingle of bells on the deli door cut through the noise outside but kept her eyes on her phone and the map of where her ride was. At moments like this she wondered why the hell she hadn't taken up smoking.

"Come on, Jennifer. You proved you can pull a bluff. Let's get back inside and finish this," Kyle said as the car she'd ordered pulled up.

Jennifer got in without another word. When they'd come up with this plan, she knew it had too many moving parts. Nothing that depended on people like Kyle Snyder was a sure thing. "Dalton," she said as they neared the bridge that'd take her back downtown. "Where are you?"

Dalton sounded sober, and since it was fairly quiet on his end, he was either at the condo or still at his attorney's office. He'd actually gone to the appointment she'd been after him to make for the past year. Only now that he was in the process of getting a divorce, her interests had cooled.

"I had to meet Kyle this morning, and he flaked out on me, so have we heard from our silent partner?" She rested her head back and closed her eyes. That night months before, when Dalton had told her all the stuff he'd found and how they could take Ellis for everything, it'd seemed way too easy. The excitement of it had made her oblivious to the consequences, but now no matter where she was, she felt like she was dragging one of those old ball and chains. It was like she was guilty and that's all she deserved, to drag around her crime with the menagerie of people she'd invited into her life.

"You know that's dangerous, and we promised we could handle our end. Meet me at the condo, and we'll talk about it."

"No. Meet me at Tao for lunch. I'm tired of being cooped up."

"Okay. I'll be there in less than an hour, and stay off the phone. Whatever happened, we'll figure it out."

The weight of men telling her what to do and not do was starting to smother her, so she dialed the number. "Our slimy little bird just tried to shake me down, so what's next? And if you can't talk, call me back." The person had answered like she was a telemarketer.

"I'm not interested."

The line went dead, so hopefully it wouldn't be too long before she got a call back. She handed over a ten a half an hour later, when they reached the restaurant. All the cloak-and-dagger crap was making her tired, so she stepped inside and walked to the bar. It was early, but drinking seemed to get Dalton through the day, so she was willing to chance it.

"I'll take a beer. Whatever you've got on tap." She dropped her purse at her feet and covered her face with her hands.

"Either I'm rubbing off on you, or you're upset about leaving me behind."

Having someone speak directly into her ear almost knocked her off the stool, and in reflex she struck out, aiming for the throat like she'd learned in all the self-defense classes her father had insisted on. She kept her hands up in a ready position in case she had to go again, but she relaxed when she saw Kyle gasping for air with his hands on his throat.

"What the fuck did you do that for?" Kyle wheezed out, still bent over in obvious pain.

"Did you follow me here?" She dropped her hands but stayed on her feet just in case.

"Do you need me to call the cops?" the bartender asked.

"No. I think my friend will behave. Bring him a beer to soothe his feelings." She sat and took a sip of her drink. "Why are you here? I'm not telling you anything more than I have to, and I thought that was a deal breaker."

"Yeah, I followed you." He glared at her, his voice not back to normal. She had to send her instructors a bottle of wine for the lessons on how to deal with potential attackers. "Do you not have a fucking sense of humor?"

"Considering you haven't said anything remotely humorous, I'm not laughing. I guess we don't find the same things funny. Again, why are you here?"

"I'll do whatever you want, however you want it done. It's not like I give a shit why you're doing all this crap."

"That's good to hear, but now the price is forty."

He took a step toward her, but so did the bartender, so he stopped. "It's fifty."

"It *was* fifty, and then you got ahead of yourself. Now it's forty, and if you don't like it, don't like it, but if you say anything else but that you'll do what I say, the price will keep going down. You don't honestly think you're so important to me that I can't get what I want without you?"

"You seem pretty hot for my help."

"There's always an easy way to do something, and another way to do it. You're the easiest way, but I have other options, so it's either forty or you get the fuck out of here and stop bothering me."

"Okay, forty, but I won't go lower than that."

"Don't worry so much, Kyle. If you do a good job, I won't forget it. You know what I want, so keep your head on straight."

"I called again last night, but she didn't budge. She's taking her job real serious, and she's not about to screw it up." He continued to rub his throat but downed his beer quickly.

"I don't have children, but I hear most women will do pretty much anything to protect their kids. We simply have to remind your ex as many times as it takes what she's got to lose. That alone should soften her up for the next part." She reached down for her bag and dug out a business card. "Give this guy a call, and make an appointment. He's expecting you, so all you need to do is show up and make your next call."

He took it and stared at it like it was written in a foreign language. "What happens if I win this thing?"

"She's your kid, so figure it out." She saw Dalton walk in and looked at him, trying to stop him from coming over. "Is there a problem with that? Once you collect the money, you'll be able to provide for her."

"No, there's no problem, so don't forget our deal."

"You're memorable enough to make that impossible."

Kyle pointed his middle finger at her, and she laughed as she watched him go, prompting Dalton to join her. His smile made her remember a little of what had attracted her to him—he was handsome in that rugged-man sort of way. He seemed overly pleased with himself, and when he held up the magazine he'd brought with him, she could see why. The signature piece of Ellis's show had made the cover of a special addition of *Styles and Trends*, and she wished she could witness Ellis's reaction once it hit the stands.

"Benson and Raymond are two of the biggest assholes I've ever met, but hell if they didn't come through for us," Dalton said, handing it over.

"This should bring them up in the world, while blowing Ellis's all to hell."

"Who gives a shit about anything but that this brings us one step closer to our goals."

"There's plenty left to go, so don't start celebrating yet. Ellis won't just lay down and die, so we have to turn up the heat." She smiled at the bartender when he brought two more glasses. "I've got little Kyle rubbing two sticks together now, and when I'm done it'll be an inferno."

❖

"Do you understand what you need to do?" Bill asked Charlotte while she sat next to Ellis. "I'll do whatever you want, but my goal will be for him to give up his parental rights."

"Can I talk to Sawyer about it first? If she still wants him in her life, I won't deny her that." Charlotte reached for Ellis's hand and gripped it.

"I'm here as long as you need me, so go do whatever you two need to do, and I'll get started on all this."

"Thanks, Bill. We'll call you later, but we've got to get going," Ellis said.

They walked out of the suite Bill had reserved at the Piquant and went down a floor to get Sigrid. The team was already at the park setting up, along with the show's crew. Charlotte stopped her before she knocked on Sigrid's door and put her arms around her.

"We need to get going," Ellis said, but didn't let go.

"I just need a minute to say thanks." Charlotte lifted her head off her chest and smiled. "Aside from my parents, no one has ever gone out of their way for me like this."

Charlotte had an air of wholesomeness, but it had been forever since she'd seen someone with such physical beauty. She'd noticed that the first day they'd met, but Charlotte was more than just a pretty face, as the old saying went. "Give him double the hell he's giving you, and don't settle for anything less than what you want," she said, caressing Charlotte's face gently with her knuckles.

The touch of her fingers made Charlotte close her eyes as if she wanted to savor it, and when she opened them again she couldn't help but lower her head and kiss her. It wasn't a good move, of that she was certain, but Charlotte did something surprising and held her in place and moaned. The last thing she wanted now was to break apart, but this wasn't the best spot for a first kiss.

The door behind them opened, and Ellis raised her head, recognizing the laugh. "Taking it pro, I see," Brandi said as she closed the door on what Ellis assumed was a client.

"Not exactly, but it's nice seeing you again," she said, hoping Brandi would take the hint and go.

"Hi, I'm Charlotte." Charlotte combed Ellis's hair back before holding her hand out.

"Brandi." The two women shook hands as Ellis looked on, afraid the calm of her peaceful morning was about to end. "Nice to meet you, Charlotte, but I have to run. See you soon, I hope, Ellis."

"I'll call you."

Brandi left with a smile and a shake of her head, which Charlotte seemed to notice since she hadn't taken her eyes off her. Charlotte didn't turn to face her until Brandi disappeared around the corner. "Pro?" she asked and laughed. "I never took you for the type, *Ms*. Renois."

"I'm not the type, *Ms*. Hamner, but I'm sure Brandi doesn't mind people knowing she's a pro." She remembered Amis's honesty policy and didn't lie.

Charlotte peered at her like she was dying to ask another question, but she completely surprised her by stepping back into her arms. "When we're finished today, I'd like to talk to you about that kiss and something else."

"Sure, and I'm sorry if I was out of line."

"The tabloids have linked you with enough women for you to know when one doesn't mind being kissed. It wasn't out of line, if you're worried."

"You aren't a summer fling, if that's what *you're* worried about. I'd never do that to you."

"I know, but let's get to work and have this talk somewhere other than this hallway."

Sigrid rode with them to the park, and Ellis introduced Charlotte to the anchor covering the story before they sat down on one of the benches on the carousel for the interview portion. Sierra sat close by, out of camera range, and took notes as Ellis talked about the theft of her entire line. That conversation lasted five minutes, and the woman sent the segment back to New York so they could set up the next one.

The models came down the ramp the park had set up off the carousel and totally wowed the other correspondent that covered the fashion-industry segments for them. After two more breaks, they ended with Sigrid walking down the ramp wearing the white strapless sheath dress with a slit and a small train. The makeup artist had accentuated the dress's simplicity by slicking Sigrid's hair back and doing her lips in a brilliant red.

With Sigrid's height, the dress looked like it'd been made specifically for her, and Ellis stood to take her hand when she joined them on set. The two reporters treated Sigrid like royalty but finished with a few questions for her. They were done and were picking everything up when the producer Ellis had met with came running up.

"Ellis, would you sit for a few more questions?"

"Sure, what's up?"

Charlotte seemed to realize that whatever the woman said next wouldn't be good, so she stood next to her and held her hand as if to take some of the blowup. The other thing she noticed was how Rueben's attention stayed glued to Charlotte.

"We just got an advance copy. *Styles and Trends* is hitting the newsstands later today with a special publication of your line. The entire line, Ellis, and I can't tell you how sorry I am," the producer said, sounding empathetic. "We've been okayed for another five minutes if you're up for it."

"I'll be happy to," she said, knowing that refusing wasn't an option after what these people had done for her. She'd beaten Jennifer and Dalton by only the slimmest of margins, so she'd give her saviors the exclusive.

"Great. We're a go in ten."

"Why in the hell would that bitch give it to those idiots?" Amis said, her face a perfect image of rage. "That damn rag, of all her choices."

"Jennifer got plenty of lessons from Dalton or someone on using the venue that would inflict the most damage to my ego, I guess." She took some deep breaths and tried to bury her own anger.

The fashion reporter joined the interview, and between the two women they reviewed the facts and how Ellis felt about the unfolding events. The show had used their ten-minute lead-up well and had dragged up all the bad blood between her and Benson Norwood and *Styles and Trends*.

"Benson Norwood and Raymond Nixon have both said they were within the law by publishing your book because someone gave it to them anonymously," the anchor said.

"I'm sure everyone on both sides thinks they're within their rights. Only time will tell, but I hope both Norwood and Nixon appreciate the hours and sweat and work that went into the book they hope to cash in on." She leaned forward and put her hand over her copy of the bible. "You need to realize that something done as an apparent shot against me affects everyone who works for me, everyone who'd be hired to make the clothes, the workers who make the fabric, zippers, and so on down the line. In this case, revenge doesn't work in a vacuum. To get to me, you fire one shot, and that's fine, but this cannon blew up the entire landscape. Innocent people will lose out on this, and for what?"

"What happens now?"

"Now isn't the time for cowards, so hopefully I'll see you both on the last night of Fashion Week. The rest will take care of itself, since my mother taught me plenty about karma." Saying the words triggered the fighting spirit in her, which made her look past the anchor's shoulder at Charlotte and Sawyer. Battles were never pleasant, but easier when someone stood next to you.

"So this isn't the end?"

She smiled. "Not by a long shot, ladies."

CHAPTER SEVENTEEN

K yle left the restaurant after sticking around at the front door to see who Jennifer was meeting. He took a picture of the guy and a close-up of the magazine he held up, and whatever it was about, both he and Jennifer seemed to think it was hilarious. He took out the card Jennifer had given him and dialed the number. His supposed lawyer was waiting on his call and was ready to see him.

"You gonna stand there attracting lice or you getting in?" Eglin Snyder asked out the open window of his old Chevy truck.

His father was a long-haul trucker who tried to be out on the road as much as he could, but an injury had sidelined him for now. For the next month, at least, Eglin would have to suffer through the life he was constantly trying to run away from.

Kyle stared at him and wished he had the guts to tell him to fuck off. His dad had stayed only because his mom had gotten it right by having a boy, or at least that's the story Eglin loved to tell when he was drinking. That was the last time Eglin had seemed happy with the situation, or at least that's how he'd been until he'd dropped all that money on the kitchen table after his visit with Jennifer. The stack had made his dad forget his mother's problems, the crap house they lived in, and the lack of food in the fridge.

"If you want, you can take off, and I'll find a way home. I've got an appointment down on Thirty-sixth." He didn't have any reason to disappoint his father any more than he had every day after his birth, and saw no reason to share the wealth with someone who didn't give a shit about him. It'd been Eglin's idea to push Jennifer into giving up the plan and telling him everything, and it'd cost him ten grand.

"Get in and let me know what's going on. You've already fucked up what I told you to do. How the hell you let that woman take that money from you shows me I can't trust you to do this by yourself. I'd swear on a stack that you ain't mine."

"Maybe not, since I ain't anywhere as successful as you," he screamed before jamming his hands in his pockets and walking away in a direction his father couldn't follow him. He hailed a cab and took off, wanting to bleed the anger out before he arrived at Clarence Judd's office.

The building they stopped in front of seemed middle-of-the-road. Clarence wasn't, judging by the façade of the place, the best attorney in town, but he wasn't some ambulance chaser either. Jennifer seemed to have chosen carefully, since the best in town would've been hard to explain on a deliveryman's salary.

He got out and started for the front entrance, and the next minute he was flat on the sidewalk with a woozy head. The punch to the side of his head had totally blindsided him, and the fall had gashed open the opposite side of his face. Before he could get hit again, he rolled and jumped to his feet with his fists up. He wasn't suffering another humiliation like he'd had with Jennifer.

"Next time you want to insult somebody, try somebody that won't kick your ass, boy." Eglin stood in front of him, looking like a rock you'd never make a mark on, much less crack. "You get me?"

"What the hell did you do that for?"

"Because you let me. The day you stop letting people beat you like a little bitch, you might actually make something of yourself. What's in there that's got your panties all wadded up?"

"That Jennifer woman wants me to see an attorney, so thanks for bloodying up my face. Get out of here."

"How much you thinking about getting out of this, really?" Eglin grabbed him by the collar and slammed his back against the brick. "And don't think about repeating that forty-grand number, or I'll really make you bleed."

"I was getting fifty until I listened to you, so now it's forty. That's it. This ain't got nothing to do with you, so let me go before that number goes down again. I'm sorry I even called you to take me into the city."

"You don't think you're going in there alone, do you?"

He brought his hands up and broke his father's hold. "You don't have anything to do with this except trying to take what's mine, so get out of here. You're not messing this up for me."

"Listen. Why would this woman plunk down this kind of money to help you? Have you ever asked yourself that?"

"No. All I care about is getting all I can out of this bitch, and I don't need no help."

"Leave your pride out here, and admit you need someone watching your back." Eglin reached over and straightened his collar. "What can it hurt?"

"Okay, but open your mouth and you're out of here." It was an invitation to show Eglin that he hadn't pulled off some complex deal like he'd bragged about, trying to get him to be proud of him for putting this together. Jennifer had done all the talking from the moment she'd introduced herself, but maybe it wasn't a bad idea to have Eglin come.

"I'm not saying nothing, but I don't want you to leave anything on the table. All I want to do is help you. You're my son."

"Remember what I said." He moved away and saw Eglin's act for what it was. He was here for his share, even though the deal had nothing to do with him. "This time I'm in charge, so keep your mouth shut."

"Don't worry. I know what I'm doing," Eglin said with a controlled tone Kyle knew well. He only spoke that way when he was pissed but trying his best not to strike out.

"So do I, and I'm the one they want. Don't forget that."

❖

Charlotte sat on the side of the pool with her legs in the water. Sawyer had asked to go inside to work on her painting, so she was keeping Ellis company while she swam laps. Her boss had been locked in her study for most of the day, grinding her teeth, from what Charlotte could tell. She'd talked to only Amis and Sigrid, before she left to return to New York.

That the bible had actually been published had driven the

conversation and good humor out of Ellis, but Charlotte didn't need to be entertained. All she needed was to be close to Ellis and try to come down from the high of the morning. She felt a little guilty over her tempered euphoria, but the show and the frenzy to get it done was everything she'd dreamed it to be. Add to that the kiss she and Ellis had shared, and she was still floating.

"You're going to prune," she said when Ellis finally stopped and slapped the water with both hands.

"Mom, can I go to the movies with Mr. Malcom?" Sawyer asked loudly from the door, holding the phone in one hand.

"Sure, but tell him if it's anything scary, he can sit up with you for the next two weeks."

Her answer got Sawyer to drop the phone and run back into the house when she saw Malcom join them by the pool.

"I'm taking a few people, so hopefully it's okay to go out for pizza first. I promise we'll be back no later than nine thirty or so. Amis is out too, with Opal, shopping with Harold for some pieces we haven't found yet. They're tracking down a few leads."

"Thanks. We'll grab a sandwich or something," Ellis said as she hoisted herself out of the water.

The laps had tightened the muscles in her shoulders and upper arms, in Charlotte's opinion, but she guessed her night was about to come to an end. "Thanks for including Sawyer."

"Sawyer's a sweetheart, and Ellis, if you eat a sandwich, I'm going to poison you slowly."

"I'm not in the mood, Uncle Malcom."

"I ordered something from GW Fins, so eat it." He put his hands on his hips and mimicked her pout.

"They don't deliver."

"I told them my niece is the world-famous designer Ellis Renois, and they deliver." He fanned himself, and Charlotte laughed. "The girl who took my order thought this Ellis character was totally sexy."

"Get out of here before I throw you in the pool."

"Here." Malcom handed over a bag and Ellis's sketchbook. "They're delivering to Charlotte's place, so all you'll need is in there. Take a shower, eat, and get to work. Or maybe take the night off and unscrew your head a bit. From where I'm standing, it's twisted on pretty tight."

Sawyer showed Ellis her progress before she left, and Charlotte waited until they were alone to join her in Sawyer's room. "Go ahead and shower, but can I tell you something first?"

"As long as it's not that you're stealing from me," Ellis said, smiling. "Sorry. I'm enjoying my little pity party, but it's time to wrap it up. You can tell me anything."

"Today was totally sucky for you, and I'm sorry for that."

"But you loved it," Ellis said, spreading her arms out. "Well, you loved it until the sucky part, I hope."

"It was amazing, and you were amazing. I know I didn't have anything to do with the original line, but showing it was magical." The way Ellis was looking at her gave her the courage to do what she'd been wanting to do. "Thank you for making me a part of all this."

Ellis stood there and didn't do anything, but Charlotte noticed her expression. She'd been on the receiving end of that kind of pure hunger only a few times, by choice, and this was no different. She wanted Ellis to look at her that way. She wanted her to kiss her like she had that morning. The kiss had surprised her, but it was like Ellis couldn't stop herself, and she was glad that bit of ice had been broken. It made the second one that much easier.

"I'm not imagining things, am I? If I am, we'll still be okay, but tell me if I'm right," Ellis said, tilting her head back. The spark between them was almost visible, Charlotte thought.

"You're not imagining anything." Charlotte was able to catch her breath when Ellis looked away. It didn't really matter, though, because Ellis's proximity was all it took to give her goose bumps.

"This isn't a game, and you've got to know you'll still have your spot no matter what. You don't have to do this." Ellis finally looked at her again, and for once she saw the vulnerability that she'd only glimpsed in Ellis's eyes a few times.

She came within inches of Ellis and put her hands on Ellis's chest. "Today, if it's all I ever get, will be good enough. If sewing for you is how I get to stay this close to you, I'll do it until my fingers bleed." She slid her hands up until they were behind Ellis's neck. "I don't know why anyone else wanted this job, or what they wanted from you—all I want *is* you."

"Don't say that." Ellis tried to pull away, but she held on. "You deserve better than me."

"No. You don't say that. You think you're this empty shell, but you're not. No one who treats my child the way you do and spends so much time with someone like me is empty." She tugged, and Ellis resisted, but she finally gave in and lowered her head.

"Do you have any idea how incredibly beautiful you are?" Ellis spoke softly as she ran her fingers through Charlotte's hair. "I've wanted to do this from the moment you walked into my studio. You're like Sawyer's complete opposite with this corn-silk hair and blue eyes, but you seem to share the same heart. You lost the same genetic lottery my mother did, since Sawyer obviously inherited her dark hair and green eyes from Kyle."

"In your line of work, I find that hard to believe." The way Ellis was touching her was making her body come alive, and she enjoyed it since it'd been forever since anyone had made her feel anything at all.

"The way to see it, in my line of work I know beauty, and I'm seeing it right now." Ellis's mouth was so close and looked so enticing.

Charlotte traced Ellis's lips with the tip of her index finger and smiled when Ellis did. Confident she wouldn't be turned down, she stood on the tips of her toes and kissed Ellis. Her mind went blank, and all she could do was open her mouth slightly to invite Ellis in. When their lips parted, a little self-doubt crept in, since this was the most clichéd of circumstances. An affair with your boss was never a good idea, and an affair with a boss who'd had plenty of them was the worst idea.

"Are you sorry?" she asked Ellis, and the words made Ellis open her eyes.

"No, but—"

"Please don't add a *but anything* to that," she said, and Ellis laughed. "Maybe I should spend the rest of the summer teaching you a little romance. First a hallway and now you follow up with hesitancy? That's losing you points."

"Give me a chance to finish. I'm not sorry, but I want us to take our time with this."

Ellis said the words, but she lowered her head and kissed her again, only this time she held her tighter and teased her with her tongue. It was easy to see that Ellis had a lot more practice than she did, but she didn't care.

"Tell me again how this year is going to be different?" Rueben said, and his words startled her backward. She stayed on her feet only because Ellis still held her. She sure as hell hadn't heard him come in.

"Charlotte, I'm beginning to sound repetitive, but would you excuse me a minute?" Ellis made sure she was okay before letting her go, so she nodded.

"I need to—" Ellis put her hand up as Rueben followed her out of the room. Charlotte watched Ellis walk him to the door and slam it in his face. A minute later someone knocked, and Ellis appeared ready to hit whoever it was until she saw it was the dinner Malcom had ordered.

"You know, if I'm causing you a problem, you can say so," Charlotte said.

"Self-sacrifice sucks. Never forget that, and remember that everyone deserves happiness."

"That's been in short supply in my life."

"No one ever says they have too much happiness, but I have a theory about that. Sit down, let me plate this, and I'll happily educate you." Ellis got everything they needed and put her plate down with some flair. Whatever Malcom had ordered smelled delicious.

"So tell me," she said as Ellis opened a bottle of wine.

"My mother tried love and it didn't work out, and ever since then all she's done is dabble a bit by dating infrequently. Sigrid, though, has been married for life, and by all accounts, she's happy."

"She found the right one, I guess." She cut a small piece of fish and hummed as she chewed. "What is this?"

"Grouper rolled in parmesan panko crumbs."

"It's delicious, but back to our talk."

"My mom always claimed she didn't need anyone because she had me, but I feel guilty that she never tried again. Believe me, I love being the center of her world, but I want her to know love at least once more." Ellis took a big bite, and Charlotte was starting to notice that about her. When it seemed Ellis had divulged too much information, she found some excuse to stop talking.

"You want me to date your mother?"

Ellis had to put her hand up to keep from spitting fish on her, but the joke worked. "I'm sure she'd be thrilled at the prospect, but not what I meant."

"Get on with it then." She pointed her fork at Ellis and snapped the fingers of her other hand.

"Don't make the same mistake and pour all of yourself into Sawyer. Believe me, she'll be fine, so take a chance on getting that happiness you think you're missing."

"That's what I'm trying to do. Only you think I shouldn't take a chance on *you*, right?"

"I wasn't lying when I said you deserve better. All I've known how to do is screw things like this up."

"Maybe we've both picked all the wrong people, but it's a blessing, not a curse." She stood and moved to Ellis's lap.

"How do you figure that?"

"If either of us had found the right person, we wouldn't be here." She put her arms around Ellis's neck and kissed her again. "And I happen to like where I am and who I'm with. Think you can live with that?"

"I'll try my best to muddle through."

The knock at the door stopped them from kissing again, and she got up to answer it, not wanting Ellis upset any more that night. She didn't recognize the guy at the door but opened it anyway, since she wasn't alone. "Can I help you?"

"Depends," the short, pudgy guy said. "Are you Charlotte Hamner?"

The guy's demeanor and smirk made her wary, but she nodded. "I'm Charlotte. What can I do for you?"

"Nothing at all but to take this." He handed over a thick envelope. "You've been served."

CHAPTER EIGHTEEN

The summons was from New York and was Kyle's attempt to get Sawyer away from Charlotte. Ellis had cleared the food away and called Bill, but nothing was breaking through the numbness her fear had brought on. Bill had said all the right things, but nothing in life was a sure bet. Kyle wouldn't be doing this if he didn't have a chance to win—no way would he spend the money on the attorney.

"Charlotte, try to get some rest, and I'll deal with this in the morning," Bill said, taking the paperwork the guy had delivered. "You have my word that Sawyer isn't going anywhere."

"Thank you," she said with no enthusiasm. She was suddenly exhausted, but no way was she getting any sleep.

"Give me a minute, and I'll be right back," Ellis said, but she shook her head.

"Go on and go to bed. I doubt I'll be very good company tonight."

"You think I care about that?" Ellis kissed her forehead and held her, but she stiffened at the contact. She used this survival mechanism when she knew the worst was getting ready to happen. "But if you want to be alone, that's okay too."

"It's not you, and I'll call you if I change my mind or need something."

"I'll have Malcom bring Sawyer up when they get back so she doesn't freak out over this. She can spend the night on the sofa in my room."

"Thanks. You're the best."

The silence boxed her into a bad place as soon as Ellis closed the door, but she was sure it would get worse. Kyle's call twenty minutes later confirmed her intuition. He could never help but gloat whenever he thought he held the advantage.

"Did you get my gift?" Kyle said, and his voice had a strange echo.

"What do you really want, Kyle? What is it, since we both know it's not custody of Sawyer?" She sat on her bed and lowered her head. As much as she loved Sawyer, being trapped in this nightmare of a relationship with Kyle was absolutely draining.

"I know you don't believe me, but I want what's best for Sawyer. I also want to be able to take care of her, so maybe we can work something out. You know—just me and you. There's no reason to get the court involved if we don't have to."

"Like I said, what do you want?"

"I only need one thing from you, and I'll drop all this. Hell, if you want, I'll even sign something that'll keep Sawyer with you."

"Kyle, just spit it out." He started talking, and she was having a hard time comprehending what he was saying. She understood his words but not his motive.

"How do you expect me to pull that off?"

"You'd better think of something, because I've got shit on you that'll give any judge no other choice not only to give the kid to me, but to force you out of her life forever. Think about that before you say no."

"If I do what you're asking, I'll lose custody anyway when I end up in jail."

"Not if you do it right. From what I hear, you're not down there alone, so listen to me." He kept talking but sounded like he was reading from a very comprehensive list. Whoever had put him up to this had put a lot of thought into their demands.

"Does it matter to you at all that I worked really hard to get here? If I do this, I'll never work for anyone in this capacity again."

"Sometimes you have to take your chances, babe. You're the one who left, not me, and you've always known you've been free to come back so we can be a real family. Remember that whenever you're looking for someone to blame."

"You can try to rewrite history, but you left the second I told you I was pregnant. What about that is going to convince a judge to give you a child you never wanted?"

Kyle laughed, and she knew he had that condescending expression on his face that she'd seen every day they'd known each other when he was this pleased with himself. If he could cash in on his ego, he'd be incredibly successful. "If you want to play it like that, I'll give my lawyer the go-ahead to use all the stuff he's got on you."

"Is it illegal now to wait tables and go to school? What the hell else can you have on me, as you put it?"

"Wake up, Charlotte. The guy I hired will make it up as he goes along, if he has to. All I want is to win, and we've known each other long enough that you can tell I'm not bullshitting this time."

"Ask me anything but that."

"You got three days. If you don't cooperate, I'm going to make it so you never see Sawyer again. You can forget joint custody because I'm going for the kill. Don't take too long, or I might do it anyway for all the shit you've put me through."

She pressed the phone to her forehead and started crying. Kyle didn't have any reason to be this cruel, but he'd changed in the short time since they'd seen each other last. Her tears started slowly, but she ended up in the bathroom when the onslaught of emotion made her sick. She heard the door open as she wiped her face, then heard Sawyer and Ellis come in.

"Where's Mom?" Sawyer asked.

"You go get your pajamas, and I'll check on her," Charlotte heard Ellis say, and she sounded close.

Charlotte started brushing her teeth, and she had to hang on not to cry again when she thought about how different her night had turned out. "Hey," she said around her toothbrush.

"What's wrong?" Ellis asked as if she had a special power to see right into her soul.

"I...he wants full custody of Sawyer." It was all she was able to say before her tears started again. She didn't have the courage to tell Ellis about what Kyle had demanded of her, but it was the simplest way out of this. The truth was the key to getting out of this mess, but that would cost her more than she could bear to pay right now with Ellis standing in front of her.

Giving in to Kyle, though, meant the end of any kind of career she'd have in this industry, and while that was important, the hardest thing would be letting go of Ellis. She wanted both Ellis and the career, but would both those things balance out the loss of her child? It wasn't an easy choice, but for her, Sawyer would always win out.

"Let me call Bill," Ellis said, but Charlotte grabbed hold of her.

"I'll call him in the morning. All I want to do now is sleep. This is making me so tired."

"Whatever you say."

"Will you stay with me?" The answer was letting go—just forgetting Ellis and her promises, but having her here made her want to hang on for the little time she had left.

"Finish up in here, and I'll be right back." Ellis placed her hand on Charlotte's neck and smiled. "It'll be okay, I promise."

"If only that were true," she whispered when Ellis walked out.

Ellis waved and kept the smile on her face until her mother had gone into the house with Sawyer. It had taken some convincing to get Sawyer to go after she told her Charlotte wasn't feeling well, but Amis had answered and reassured her about every one of her objections. If she had the same success doing the same for Charlotte, it'd be a good night, but that wouldn't be anywhere as easy.

"Can I ask you something?" Charlotte had turned off the lights in the bedroom but not the bathroom, so she made her way to the chair next to the bed and moved it closer. Being this close, she could hold Charlotte's hand.

"Sure. It's only fair since I ask you stuff all the time." Charlotte sandwiched her hand between hers.

"Why does this guy Kyle only call you at night?" She knew the question was petty and made her sound jealous, but he seemed to have a pattern.

"I'd say it was because of his work schedule, but I think he does it hoping Sawyer's around to see and hear it. I'm sure it doesn't make sense to you, but he's making sure I suffer." Charlotte started to move over but didn't let go of her hand. "It's not what you think, believe me."

"I'm not thinking anything. I'm just curious."

"It's not." Charlotte moved over but didn't let go of her hand. "All of that was over long ago."

The silent offer to join her was one she'd waited and hoped for since they'd started becoming friends, but she didn't crave sex now. "No matter what, I'm going to help get you through this. You can count on me."

"Thank you," Charlotte said, resting her head on her shoulder. "You've been so kind."

"There's always a first time for everything, I guess." She wanted to hear Charlotte laugh again, but she sat up a little so she could look at her.

"Stop it." Charlotte reached up and put her hand over her heart. "Have you let the world define you for so long that you're starting to believe the lies? I know you, Ellis Renois, and I know the truth of you."

She covered Charlotte's hand and gazed down at her. "What truth is that?"

"You're a good person and an even better friend."

"Thank you, and this is going to sound hokey, but thanks for being my friend. It's nice to have someone to talk to that isn't in it for the money." Her compliment made Charlotte close her eyes tight, but that didn't stop the tears from leaking out. "Hey, that was supposed to make you feel better, not cry." She rolled them over so that Charlotte could lie on her chest. In that position, she gently wiped her face while keeping her other arm around her.

Charlotte opened her eyes and put her arms around her to get even closer. Their kiss was full of hunger, and she tried to pull back, only to have Charlotte move with her. This she understood, but it wasn't how she wanted it to be with Charlotte.

"Wait," she said, breaking their kiss.

"I don't want to wait anymore," Charlotte said, lowering her head so she could reach her lips. "For once I want to make myself happy."

"I want to make you happy, but slow down a little," she said as she kissed Charlotte's eyelids before moving to her cheeks and ending at her lips. "I told you we have all the time in the world."

"With everything that's happening, I think I might be out of time." Charlotte peered down at her with an expression of certainty she hadn't seen in many women before her. "I want this…I want you."

It seemed so reasonable since it was something they both seemed to desire, but the small voice of caution in the deep recesses of her skull was starting to grow louder. Charlotte kissed her again before moving away to take her nightgown off, and all her doubts went silent. She'd been with a long list of beautiful women, but she forgot them all when she looked at Charlotte naked and waiting.

The notion that any woman would erase all the ones before her was fucking ludicrous, but here she was. And that's when the reality of this very important situation hit her like a brick to the side of the head. All those women would never be Charlotte because she didn't care to see a future with them. In Charlotte, though, she could see a lifetime stretched out before her like a feast.

"Touch me," Charlotte said, and she lay back down.

She stripped her clothes off after that and almost cried when they met skin to skin for the first time. Charlotte's body was perfection with her curves and softness, so she took her time running her hand from her shoulder to her knees. The trail of her hand puckered Charlotte's nipples to hard, thimble-like points, so she lowered her head and sucked the closest one in.

"Oh yes," Charlotte said in almost a hiss, so she let go and kissed her.

"You're so beautiful," she whispered into Charlotte's ear as she caressed her.

"Please, Ellis, I need you to touch me." Charlotte grabbed her by the wrist and guided her hand between her legs. "I need you."

She moved one of Charlotte's legs over hers and slowly spread her open, smiling at how soaked Charlotte was. Like Charlotte, she didn't want to wait any more, so she wet her finger and gently ran it over her clit. Charlotte took a deep breath and spread her legs wider.

They kissed again as Charlotte's hips moved in sync with her hand, her clit now a hard stone under her fingers, signaling that Charlotte was close to coming. She got a string of yeses when she paused at her opening, and Charlotte's hips came off the bed when she buried her fingers deep. This rhythm of give and take she knew better than most anything else in her life, but she wanted to savor and memorize the moment. There'd been others, yes, but no one had stolen her heart before now. This was the first time she'd made love to a woman she wanted in her life. There'd be no leaving and forgetting her in the morning.

Charlotte held on to her as her back arched higher, and Ellis felt her open up before clutching her fingers inside as the wave of desire seemed to build and crest. She stopped when Charlotte went rigid, then kissed her when she released. This time Charlotte's tears didn't bother her, and the room grew a bit blurry when she joined her.

"That was amazing," Charlotte said as Ellis slipped out of her.

Before she could say anything, Charlotte lay over her and touched every part of her face, paying extra care to the spot where Jennifer had bitten her. It was almost healed, but not quite, so Charlotte kept going.

Since Charlotte's reach wasn't as long as hers, she knelt between Ellis's legs and put her hands on her thighs. She looked like she was about to devour her whole, and Ellis couldn't wait.

"It's been so long," Charlotte said softly before placing her hand where Ellis desperately wanted it.

Charlotte moved her thumb from the bottom to the top of her clit, and Ellis was ready to come like a teenager her first time around. "Harder," she said, and Charlotte pressed down as her fingers went inside and gave her what she wanted…no, what she needed.

"Damn," she said as she crossed the line where she either had to come or die trying. Charlotte had kept up with her and stayed inside, even after the orgasm had rendered her mute. "Thank you," she finally said.

"Believe me, I wanted that as much or more than you did." Charlotte finally moved but kept close by lying half on top of her. "Hopefully I wasn't too out of practice."

"I'd have lost the top of my head if it had been any better."

Charlotte scratched Ellis's abdomen and hummed. "You're only my third, so I'm not the most experienced at this."

"Let's not get into numbers so we don't ruin the night," she said, and Charlotte laughed.

"I guess if beautiful women were falling into my bed all the time like they do with you, I'd have been a little sluttier too."

She swatted Charlotte's butt and laughed with her. "I'm not slutty. I'm lucky. So who were the lucky bastards, if that's not prying?"

"I was young and confused when I met and fell in love with Kyle, so that was my first. But love turned out to be a teenage crush, so I should've waited." Charlotte snuggled closer and kissed the side of her breast. "When I was in design school, though, I met Morgan, and we became study partners. We were both lonely, I guess, so it didn't take long for her to show me why it never felt right with Kyle."

"You don't have to be lonely anymore if you give me a shot."

"Are you sure you want to take on me and my numerous problems?"

"I want all of you," she said, and Charlotte moved so she could see her face. It was like a stake through the heart when she saw the tears again. They were in no way a sign of happiness.

"Oh, God, Ellis." Charlotte fell on her. "I have to tell you."

"Hey, take a breath so you don't make yourself sick again. You know you can tell me anything. What is it?"

What Charlotte had to say was like being stabbed through the gut, then through the middle of her head, and it reminded Ellis why she didn't allow many people into her life like this. It wasn't the time to roll over and show her soft underbelly for the kill shot, so she tried to think quickly.

"When were you planning to tell me?" The act was done, and nothing would make it any easier to try to erase Charlotte from her life.

"I tried earlier, but I couldn't because all I could think of is what I'd lose if I don't do it." Charlotte held on to her like she was afraid she'd throw her on the floor and walk out. "It's not an excuse, but the position I'm in clouded my head."

"This is what you're going to do." When she finished talking, Charlotte was crying harder, but there was no other way. Charlotte had plenty to lose, but then again, so did she.

CHAPTER NINETEEN

You'd better think before you do anything else," Eglin said as they drove home. He'd listened to the script Kyle had read, and all it sounded like to him was a setup. This Jennifer and the people she was working didn't need anybody but a fall guy, and his idiot son was already in over his head.

"Look, just because this is my deal, there's no reason to crap all over it."

Kyle sat with his arms crossed and sported the same pout he'd perfected when he was three. "You think everything I do is a screwup, so maybe you should mind your own business from now on. This ain't got nothing to do with you."

"You can fucking do whatever you want, but you keep doing all this woman's bidding without asking not one damn question, and you're gonna take the fall. Just stop acting like a trained seal and grow a pair." The traffic out of the city was brutal, and all the sitting was making his back ache like someone was twisting his body and legs in opposite directions. Any idea of cutting his recovery short was as questionable as what he'd just witnessed.

"What am I going down for, huh? You're the genius in the family, so explain it to me." The way Kyle threw his insult out meant the kid would never forgive him for the crappy life he'd had and blamed him for. "Let's hear it."

He drummed his fingers on the steering wheel, trying to ignore his discomfort. No matter how many times he'd fucked up or given up and walked away, he'd never been one for reflection. Thinking too hard on your past only led to disaster, so he chose to drink instead. "Listen, do what you want, because you're right. I'm the last man who should be giving you advice. Forget everything I said and handle it however you want. It's your deal."

Kyle turned in his seat and stared at him before laughing. "You think this is going to work? I know you think I'm stupid, but I'm not that dumb."

"What do you want, an apology? Okay, I'm sorry, but look in the mirror before you tell me to fuck off." He took a deep breath, trying to work through the pain, but the only two things that would touch it were a glass of whiskey and a Percocet chaser.

"I'm nothing like you, if that's what you mean."

"Ha," he said as they finally crept out of the tunnel. "Okay, you're your own man, but let me ask you something. You doing all this because you love that kid or for the money? And don't fucking lie."

"You know I need the money, but I'll take her if that's my only way to get it."

"Then you're right again, and we ain't nothing alike. I was gone most of the time because I couldn't stand your mama—still can't. Once upon a time, though, she was crazy about taking care of you, so I let her keep thinking that might finally get her to crawl out of that Jack bottle. It did for a while, but she went right back to it, and with that came the crazy. I can do plenty, but not crazy, so you and me missed out on being together, but she had you, so it never really bothered me none."

"I know you never gave a good fuck about me, but now you're trying to tell me you're a bleeding heart for some kid you never met? Give me a break."

"Forget I said anything, and watch yourself. All this you're messing with is big stuff, and something about it is wrong. Once the law figures out what that something is, you're gonna be the only one holding the bag. That happens, and you're going to get screwed out of more than forty thousand dollars."

"Take all that and stuff it—this isn't your business."

Eglin merged and took the highway home. "You got it. This is all you."

❖

Charlotte woke up alone and lay there for a while longer, enjoying the quiet and the memories of the previous night. If she had the opportunity to live it over, she would have told Ellis what Kyle wanted before they'd slept together. In this case, having no memory of their time together would be easier to handle, since she was familiar with loss and disappointment.

"Hey," Ellis said, and Charlotte felt the bed move right after she spoke.

"I thought you were gone," she said without rolling over, liking the way Ellis felt pressed up against her.

"You honestly think I'd skulk off after last night?" Ellis kissed the side of her neck. "I had to make a few calls this morning, and I didn't want to wake you so I used Sawyer's room."

"You know I'd never hurt you, don't you? If that had been my plan, I would've never said anything." She turned halfway and peered up at Ellis. The initial shock that had been plastered on her face from the night before seemed to have relaxed some.

"For a long time, I thought I'd been blessed with more luck than sense, but maybe fate has something else in mind."

"Am I supposed to know what you're talking about?"

"Not yet, but you're going to give Kyle whatever he wants."

"You're going to just give up? That's not fair." She reached up and caressed Ellis's cheek. "I'll fight him, if that's what it'll take, but I decided last night that if I give in, he'll get more than he's asking for, and my self-worth isn't something I'm willing to throw away so easily. I need to talk to Sawyer and make a decision."

"Compared to what he's asking for and what you've got to lose—I need you to give him what he wants."

She sat up and moved away from Ellis, needing the space between them. "I'm a good mother, so whatever he's got isn't going to lose me custody."

"Okay. How about this? Wait a day and we'll decide together."

"Why can't we do what you said last night?"

"Last night my head was a jumble, after what you had to say. It totally blindsided me because it came from you, but it wasn't totally a surprise. I was expecting a second part to whatever Jennifer and Dalton had planned, but now because it did come from you, I need to be sure if my assumptions are right. I'm willing to gamble on a season of clothes, but not with Sawyer if I'm not absolutely sure." Ellis was dressed but stood up in search of her shoes. "Right now, though, we need to get back to work and act like everything's normal."

"You want me to act normal?" If Kyle was the only thing on her mind, she might've had a chance, but their night together was a game changer.

"You're right. Stay in today and call Bill. I'll make excuses for you. Once I get everyone started, I'll come back and have lunch with you guys."

"I don't understand what you want exactly." Ellis was way too calm for someone who knew what Kyle was asking of her.

"Take a shower, and then meet me in the kitchen. Mama's bringing Sawyer back in twenty minutes, so I'll make toast."

Charlotte smiled after Ellis kissed her and led her to the bathroom door. The terrific shower that usually made her relax didn't hold its usual appeal, so she rushed through it, hoping Ellis gave up some more clues as to what came next. If not, at least they had that much more time alone.

"What'd you tell Sawyer last night?" She ran her hands up Ellis's back while she spread peanut butter on toast, wishing they could stop the rest of the world for a moment.

"I told her you weren't feeling well, but it wasn't anything serious." Ellis turned around and lifted her onto the countertop so she could kiss her again. "I promised I'd take good care of you."

"You did that spectacularly well." They kissed one more time before Ellis moved away to put the food on the table, and then the door opened.

Amis joined them for breakfast, so all three of them listened to Sawyer's recap of her night out with the gang. The way Ellis and the rest of her family had taken Sawyer in was the greatest blessing Charlotte had gotten out of the summer, aside from her time with Ellis.

"Hey, pal, do you want to start working on your new piece while I talk business with your mom and mine?" Ellis asked Sawyer when Bill arrived with a bundle of files. "I'll be in there as soon as we're done."

Sawyer left as if she understood it wasn't going to be a normal workday, so Ellis joined the others at the dining table. "I'm going to ask you to sign a few things, and I don't want you to think it's because

I don't trust you. You've never given me any reason not to, but I was expecting something like the call last night—I just didn't know where it was going to come from."

"Do you have any clue as to how Kyle knows who you are?" Charlotte gazed at her like they were the only two people there. "He has some idea of what I want to do, but that's about it. I doubt seriously if he could name one designer if you put a gun to his head and threatened to blow his pea brain out."

"We'll discuss that, but let Bill get all his stuff out of the way."

"Like Ellis said, this isn't because you've done anything wrong," Bill said, opening the first folder and taking out what looked like a contract. "This is an ironclad nondisclosure contract that carries severe penalties up to jail time if you share any of what we're going to discuss today, as well as disclose anything from the spring line and everything going forward without Ellis's consent."

Charlotte signed without complaint and initialed in all the spots Bill pointed to after he explained what it was and gave her time to read it. The binding legalese would be standard going forward, no matter what her position was within the company.

"I understand all this, but you told me this morning to do the exact opposite."

"Charlotte, we aren't trying to trick you," Amis said as she glanced at Ellis.

"Would you excuse us?" she said, and held her hand out to Charlotte so they could go back to the bedroom. "I don't know this for sure, but I think someone is trying to force me out of business. Like seriously out of business, and that's who Jennifer and Dalton are working with."

"Why would they do that?" Charlotte asked, sitting beside her on the bed.

"Jennifer and Dalton tried to get me to sign what they said was a vendor contract, but in reality it would've given them a majority share of the company. Only an idiot could've thought that would have actually worked, but it did give me the excuse to fire them, so I'm not complaining about their stupidity."

"That's the night they stole the book, right?"

"Yeah, but now I see that it was more an opening act. They

apparently want me to quit so I not only have to sell, but I have to sell cheap. That's not what's happened, though, so they aim to rip my guts out again before I finish the show."

"You're going to just hand it over? Why would you do that?"

"I need you to trust me, and I want you to call Kyle back and ask him how exactly you need to do this. After you do, you're going to follow his directions verbatim."

"He gave me pretty specific instructions last night."

Ellis nodded and flexed her fingers. "Then call him back and ask him to recap to make sure you understand."

"You're going to fire me once I do, aren't you?"

"It's the only way, but you either trust me or you don't."

Kyle sat in his attorney's office staring at his phone and ripping at his hangnails with his teeth. He'd told Eglin that if he said one word, he'd throw him out, so his father sat across from him flipping through a stack of magazines. Eglin had accepted the job of going to get the attorney Jennifer had hired if Charlotte called back.

"This is ridiculous," he said as he glanced at his watch. They'd wasted two hours waiting for something he was sure wasn't coming, because he knew Charlotte.

At first, Charlotte had been flattered by his attention. He'd been a couple of years older, and it hadn't taken him long before he had her flat on her back, and that feat had returned to bite him when the frigid little bitch had gotten pregnant. From the moment Sawyer had arrived, his meek and mousy girlfriend had become a repetitive megaphone for child support.

"Then leave," Eglin said, not making eye contact since he kept flipping through the magazine he was on.

"Yeah. I can see you letting me do that. You can admit that you're here for the money, and that's it. What you can't figure out yet is if I'll share it with you, but you can't take any chances. Can you?"

"Boy, you can do whatever you want. I'm not here for a penny of what you got coming to you, but I do want to make sure it's money you got coming and not a six-by-nine cell."

The flipping of glossy pages was starting to get on Kyle's nerves.

"This is a waste of time, and I told Jennifer that. Charlotte's got oatmeal for brains when it comes to making any kind of score. She ain't giving this up."

"We'll see."

He laughed and slammed his hand on the shiny table. "You barely know me, and you're going to pretend to know Charlotte. I think you've only seen her once, and Sawyer double that."

"You keep telling me that, but people aren't all that different." Eglin cut his eyes up at him without lifting his head.

"Your life must be so boring, always being so right about everything." He wanted to go home to his mother, since in her opinion he was perfect. The ringing phone stopped him from moving.

"Answer it," his attorney said, sounding out of breath, as if he'd sprinted there once he'd heard the phone.

"Took you long enough," he said instead of a greeting.

"This isn't something I take lightly, so know I'm only doing this for Sawyer."

Charlotte sounded tired and subdued, which was the only thing to smile about on this fucking long day. She'd been such a bitch to him ever since Sawyer's birth that he'd enjoy twisting the knife throughout this so she'd fucking hurt. "You're taking the deal then?"

"Tell me how you want to do this, but I want some paperwork from you first. I give you what you want, and you give up your parental rights to Sawyer."

"Like give up the kid forever, you mean?" He stared at his father, but Eglin's face was a mask of indifference.

"No more child support, Kyle, and no more forced visits you've never wanted to begin with. That's my deal."

Severing his ties to Sawyer meant cutting ties with Charlotte as well, and that small flicker that still wanted her made him hesitate. "This thing isn't that valuable to me, so why would I do that?"

"It's valuable to you, and having Sawyer is valuable to me. If you're not sure of what you're asking me to do, let me explain. It's worth a lot of money to someone and plenty of jail time if I'm caught. I'm not handing it over without something in return."

"How much is a lot?"

"Let me put it this way so you'll completely understand. We're talking millions, so I hope you're getting your fair share."

He gripped the phone and couldn't decide what to do. "I'll call you right back, and you'd better answer."

He glanced at Eglin first before giving the attorney his full attention. "Call Jennifer and tell her I need to talk to her."

It took less than five minutes for the phone in the conference room to ring. "She'll do it," he said, trying his best to imitate Eglin's cool façade.

"Then why the hell haven't you sealed the deal?" Jennifer sounded like her usual bitchy self.

"Seventy-five grand and I do," he said in a voice devoid of emotion.

"It's too late for negotiations, so just get it done."

"I'm losing my kid if I do this for you, so seventy-five or nothing. If it's too late to deal, then good luck to you." He hung up and finally made his father smile. "You ready?" he asked Eglin.

"Ready." Eglin got up and pushed the attorney out of the way, putting his hands down when the phone rang again. "Pick it up," Eglin said, as if he could guess who was on the other end.

"Yeah," he said. If he acted like he couldn't care less about what happened, he could squeeze more out of Jennifer, and he had Eglin to thank for that. He glanced at his father as he held the phone, and Elgin nodded.

"Seventy-five, but that's it. Satisfied?" Jennifer asked. "That's all you're getting. We aren't doing this dance every single time you think you're getting screwed."

"We'll see, but I don't have time to talk about it right now. I've got a call to make."

CHAPTER TWENTY

It took two days before a private courier delivered the envelope Ellis had an inkling was coming. She sat in her office and stared at the two sketches that were included, tapping her finger on the bottom right corner. The sight of the theft made the same feelings from the first time bubble to the surface.

She stared at the door when she heard the knock, but hesitated to let anyone in. Whoever it was knocked harder, so she sighed and flattened her hand on the sketch. "Come in."

"Hey, are you hibernating all day or are you working?" Rueben asked when he came in. "What's wrong?" Just looking at her made him ask.

She handed over the copies of their sketches and waited. "I think we're done, so I'm taking the day off, to answer your question."

"Where did these come from?" Rueben held them up and studied both before glancing at her. "You can't give up."

"The first blow came with barely enough time to recover. There's no time even if I wanted to try again. I don't have that much magic left in the tank."

"So we just quit? You know we're done if you don't even try."

"We've got a leak, Ruby, and because we do, any effort will be like some kind of vicious hamster wheel. It's time to get off."

"Who the hell is it? It can't be that hard to find them. It's got to be someone here. These prove that." He held them up again and stared at the spot where she'd been tapping. The small red triangle distinguished his book from hers. A small red ruby had started as a joke between them and had in time become part of his brand.

"You don't think—" He finally looked straight at her. "You can't think I did this."

"I'm tired, Ruby, not judgmental." She rubbed her face and stood up.

"Wait. Your new intern was working late the other night. I'd left my book out to work on the changes we'd decided on. If it was out, and she was alone with it, we've found our leak. It's got to be her."

"Are you sure it's Charlotte? That's a pretty heavy charge to level at her. What motive would she have? There's that, and the fact that she wasn't here the first time this happened."

"The same motive anyone would have, Ellis. It's always all about the money. Someone must have gotten to her, and the deal was too good to pass up. She sold you out. You know what her life was before she got here. If anyone could use the money, it's her. We know everyone else."

"Charlotte," she said into her phone. "Could you come to the office, please?"

"She's not going to admit it, but it's got to be her. I thought she was motivated since she was always staying after everyone else, and I stupidly trusted that all she was after was a job."

"It doesn't hurt to ask before we crucify her." She sat back and closed her eyes while they waited. Charlotte didn't take long and glanced between them as she stopped in front of her desk. "Look what came today."

Rueben handed over the sketches, and Charlotte shrugged. "These two are done," she said, handing them back. "Did you want any changes?"

"You don't understand. They were delivered today with this." She held up a note, and Rueben practically snatched it out of her hand. The enclosed note was another taunt like the first one she'd received. She'd guessed from the wording of the typed note that Jennifer was still having fun at her expense.

"This can't be right," Charlotte said when Rueben held the note in front of her face.

"Oh, it's right," Rueben said, dropping the page along with the sketches on the desk. "And we want to know why you sold us out."

"Me?" Charlotte said, staring at her as if she couldn't believe what she was hearing. "You don't think that, do you?"

"This is from my book, and you were the only one alone with it, so pack it up. You're out of here before you do any more damage." Rueben pointed to the door.

"Ellis?" Charlotte said, but Ellis couldn't look at her. "You know me."

"Just answer him," she said, not taking her eyes off the painting on the wall.

Charlotte stood there silently, but when Ellis wouldn't face her, she ran out crying. The sound of Charlotte's hysteria made her want to go after her, but she stayed put.

"Do you want me to check out her room for any more clues having to do with all this?" Rueben asked.

"Leave it alone, and give me a minute to think."

"What's going on?" Amis asked when she rushed in, obviously having seen Charlotte's exit. "Chéri, answer me."

She told her mom everything and handed over what had been sent. "We're screwed."

"Rueben, would you mind giving us a minute?" Amis patted him on the chest and smiled.

Their talk was short, and Ellis slammed out of the house when they were done. She needed to walk and start to accept the reality of her life now. Whatever sins or wrongs she'd ever done seemed to be coming back in some sort of sick cream pie someone wanted to smash her in the face with. Whoever it was had tried their best to break her and, more importantly, made her question everyone around her but a very few.

"Give it your best shot, because now it's time to fight back," she said to herself.

❖

Amis watched as Charlotte came out of the guesthouse with all her stuff. "You're leaving?" she asked when they started for the front gate, Sawyer appearing upset.

"There's no reason to stay, so it's time to go home. Thanks for everything, and tell Ellis that, even if she doesn't want to hear it."

Sawyer looked at her with the glassy expression of shock.

"Remember the worry tree and how it works," she said as she kissed Sawyer's forehead. "That tree and Ellis will never let you down, *ma petite chéri*."

"It's time to go, Sawyer." Charlotte picked up her bags and waited for Sawyer to grab hold of one of the straps. "Tell her to forget about my last paycheck if she believes I'm a thief."

"Think of it from her perspective."

"I thought I was wrong about my first impression of her, but I wasn't. Ellis Renois is or, should I say, has become a shell made up by her marketing department. There's no heart and soul left in her." Charlotte said it loud enough so that everyone pressed to the windows watching and listening heard every word before she walked away when the cab driver outside blew his horn.

"I can't believe Ellis is just going to let her go," Rueben said once the gate closed.

"It's too late for anything, and you can't simply accuse her," Amis said. "Unless you know for sure she's the one who took your book, you're chancing legal action if you do any more than this. The shame of it is I think Ellis came to really care for this one. The kid got through all those prickly walls of hers, so if she's willing to let it go, so should we."

"It's a weird summer, for sure."

Amis nodded and went back inside. "Call everyone together. We need to have a meeting."

She made a couple of calls from her room on her cell with the door locked. It was ridiculous, but she was starting to become paranoid. Her list took thirty minutes to get through, and she moved her head from side to side to loosen the tension in her body.

Amis stood before the entire group in the ballroom. "I'm sure Rueben has filled you all in on what's happening, so I'm not getting into that again. In time, and after plenty of litigation, I'm sure we'll work through all this, but for now we need to admit we're beaten." She pressed her hands together and took a breath. "Ellis wants to thank you all, but you're free to head back. We'll regroup at the office in a few weeks."

"Is it true that Charlotte stole the book?" one of the seamstresses asked.

"We're not sure, but whoever's involved will be turned over to the police once we have proof. If you don't mind, start packing everything up and clear the house as soon as you can. I'm trying to protect Ellis from the tremendous pain this has caused, and having you all here will be the biggest reminder of all."

The crew got to work cleaning up the ballroom so Amis escaped to the kitchen. She was pouring herself a glass of wine when Rueben joined her. He seemed agitated, and she couldn't blame him. What had begun as a day to start finalizing their line had turned into this.

"Where is she?" Rueben asked, nodding when Amis held up the bottle, so she got another glass.

"I'm going to keep calling her until she answers, but she said she needed space to accept that someone is trying to destroy her. I don't believe she's coming back until she's ready, so there's no need to stay here. She told me she wants you to head back and try to keep everyone from having a breakdown."

"I need to talk to her before I go."

"She's not talking to me, so you might need to wait. I had my assistant make all the plans so everyone has a flight out in the morning. Call me once you get back, especially if something else comes up."

"Are you sure you don't want me to stay?" Rueben appeared to be a lost boy who'd been ripped from his comfortable world.

"Opal will be with me so I'll be okay." She finished her wine and put the glass in the sink. "You've been a good friend to my Ellis, so you know how she is sometimes. She gets kicked and needs to lick her wounds before she comes out swinging."

"Then I hope she finds a target."

"I'm sure she will, and when she does, she'll show them a new meaning to the word ripping."

❖

"Mom, I don't want to leave Ellis," Sawyer said, her bottom lip trembling as she spoke.

"Honey, I need you to believe me that everything's going to be fine." Charlotte put her arm around Sawyer and glanced up when the cab stopped much sooner than she thought. "Grab your stuff, okay?"

Before she could pay the driver, an elderly African American gentleman was standing by the driver's side window with some money in his hand. Once he paid the fare, he took their bags out of the trunk, waving her away.

"Welcome, Ms. Hamner. My name's Wilson Delacour, and I'll show you out back. My employer, Brandi Parrish, is expecting the two of you." He walked her to a solid steel gate that led to a large, well-landscaped yard. "Can I get you anything?"

"No, thank you. We'll just wait." A few women were by the pool, and she couldn't get over how beautiful they were. It was unbelievable that she'd gone from waitressing, to design, to a brothel. Maybe it was time to start questioning her parenting skills, she thought and laughed.

"Hello," the gorgeous brunette Ellis had introduced her to said when they entered the small cottage. "I don't know if you remember me, but I'm Brandi Parrish."

"Of course I remember. You're hard to forget. Thanks for letting us stay the night." She quickly glanced around the room and spotted Ellis's bible. That it was here and not under lock and key made her swallow hard at the thought of Ellis with this woman.

"Ellis said she couldn't chance you staying at a hotel, so it's no problem. Actually, I was looking forward to having you here." Brandi sat and waved for them to do the same.

"Why's that?" She didn't let go of Sawyer, who was doing a good imitation of an oscillating fan but didn't look upset in the least.

"I've known Ellis a long time, and I never thought she'd fall for anything or anyone other than that business, so you must be special." Brandi smiled and glanced at what seemed to be the perfect manicure.

"I'm sure she's just being nice."

"Don't be modest, and don't feel like you have to stay cooped up in here. My girls are all pleasant and well behaved," Brandi said and winked. "Let either Wilson or me know if you need anything, and, Sawyer, it's nice seeing you again."

When they were alone again, Sawyer jumped to her feet and faced her. "If we're at Miss Brandi's, does that mean we're not leaving?"

"We'll get to how you know Miss Brandi in a minute, but I'm sorry I had to keep what was happening a secret. I was trying to help Ellis, and we both had to act as if we were really upset. We both feel bad that we didn't tell you."

"I'm glad we get to stay, no matter what."

"Let's see where we get to sleep for the next few days." There was only one bedroom, from what she could see, but they'd shared before so she didn't mind, yet she couldn't stop thinking about what kind of relationship Ellis had with Brandi Parrish. It was obviously close enough that she'd introduced Brandi to Sawyer, but she wasn't sure why Ellis had done that.

"Hey, Ellis," she heard Sawyer practically scream from the other room.

"Hey, yourself. You doing okay after all the excitement?" Ellis had her arms around Sawyer and seemed both comfortable and thrilled.

"We'll survive," she said as she leaned against the door frame to the bedroom. "How'd it go?"

"Let's eat first, and then we'll talk about business." Ellis held up a large bag with Asian lettering on it. "I got all your favorites."

They sat in the small kitchen and shared the feast Ellis had ordered, and she wanted to relive the night for the rest of her life. It was the first time she'd felt like a part of a family since she'd left her parents' place. Ellis's way with Sawyer was certainly special, and special was the kind of rarity she was attracted to.

"Are you going to be okay out here?" Ellis asked as Sawyer got comfortable on the sofa hours later.

"Thank you for the way you are with her," Charlotte said when Ellis closed the bedroom door.

"I'm sorry I had to treat you like shit today," Ellis said as she came over and took the shirt she was folding out of her hands. They'd had to leave so quickly everything in her bag was in one big wad.

"This is an interesting place to bring us. Though I don't think it's Sawyer's first time." She knew the words were lame, but she couldn't help herself.

"Brandi's a friend I trust, and she's discreet. It's a trait she has to possess in the kind of business she's in. You won't be found here, and neither will I, and right now we need to disappear for a little while."

"Okay." She stretched the word out. She couldn't ask what she really wanted to know, but she almost didn't want to know with Ellis smiling at her the way she was.

"I can see your brain working overtime," Ellis said, tapping gently on her temple. "There's only one way to put this, so I hope you believe me. I'm not going to sugarcoat it by lying about all the women before you, but right now, right here, it's only you and me. That's not something I've ever said to anyone. Right now and going forward, it's only you and me. That's a promise I intend to keep."

She couldn't hold her curiosity back any longer. "And Brandi Parrish?"

"Brandi isn't anyone you ever have to worry about—not anymore. Does that kind of answer your question? I'd like to leave behind everything that belongs in the past. You can trust me not to hurt you by being stupid."

"Yes, trust me. I don't need the grisly details." She stepped into Ellis's arms and sighed when Ellis hugged her. "Today was hard, so please tell me this is almost over."

"Actually, I heard from Bill after you left, and Kyle reneged on your deal before Bill could finalize the paperwork. We knew he had time to change his mind, and he did what we expected."

"Yeah, but he'd never give up that easily, so hopefully Bill will find another way."

Ellis bent a little at the waist and picked her up and laid her on the bed. "Bill thinks Kyle will either try to call you and engage a lot, or he'll clam up. If he calls, Bill wants you to ignore him for now."

"That should be easy." When Ellis joined her, she moved and straddled Ellis at the waist. "You, on the other hand, I don't want to ignore, especially right now. I need you to kiss me and erase this afternoon from my head."

"You know all that was an act, right? When we're done with all this, you can help me make it up to Ruby, but for this to work I had to keep him and everyone else in the dark. It'll have to be that way until I find my leak."

"I'll be happy to, but let's talk about something other than work." She put her hands on the sides of Ellis's head and leaned down and kissed her. Their first night together seemed like an eternity ago, and she was ready to replicate it.

"What would you like to talk about?" Ellis winked at her, so she straightened up and stripped her shirt off, liking the way Ellis's eyes stayed on her.

"I think it'll be better if we don't talk at all." She reached back and undid her bra and dropped it on the floor. Her nipples hardened when

Ellis sat up and kissed her like she was hungry after seeing her half naked. "I need your hands on me."

"Good, because I need to touch you," Ellis said, her hands sliding up her sides to cup her breasts. When Ellis squeezed, her hips bucked forward. "Is it okay with Sawyer right outside?"

The question did something to her, and she opened her eyes and peered into Ellis's. Ellis's open expression showed that she was truly serious about her concern, and it killed any doubt she had about giving Ellis her heart. This didn't seem like a game to Ellis in the least, and she understood that her daughter was important to her.

"Try not to scream, but thank you for asking." She buried her fingers in Ellis's hair and kissed her.

Ellis seemed to slow down and become gentle, but tonight she wanted more than that. "Touch me like you want me," she said, pressing closer.

She only let go when Ellis started taking stuff off before reaching for the buttons on her jeans. Once Ellis had them undone, she didn't wait for Charlotte to get them off before putting her hand between her legs.

"You're so wet," Ellis said as her fingers slid along her wetness, then stopped on her clit, and Charlotte was ready to beg for Ellis to make her come. She bit down on Ellis's shoulder and wanted to yell when Ellis chuckled.

"Not the time to tease." Her voice sounded two octaves higher to her own ears, but she couldn't help it.

"I'm not teasing you," Ellis said softly, moving her fingers just enough to make her crave an orgasm. "I don't have a lot of room in here, so if you want it, take it."

"I—" She didn't know how to finish her thought, and she didn't think she could be what Ellis was used to. She really didn't have the experience, and she considered stopping before she embarrassed herself. Ellis put her other hand on the small of her back and held her in place.

"Look at me," Ellis said after she kissed her. "You're safe with me, so forget about everything and everyone else and remember that this is only about us. It makes me happy that you want me this much." Ellis moved her hand again and ratcheted up her need. "I want you just as much, so do what makes you feel good. There's nothing wrong with taking what you want and need."

Ellis moved her fingers as much as her jeans and underwear allowed her, but it wasn't enough, so with her eyes locked on Ellis's, she decided to take Ellis's advice.

She started to move her hips with her hands on Ellis's shoulders, and for the first time in her life she felt not only beautiful but wanted. It was like what she needed was as important to Ellis as it was to her. Ellis was so different from Kyle, and she wanted to finally put that chapter to rest. It was easy as she clung to Ellis and quickened her pace, and since Ellis had pinched her nipple, the pressure was driving her crazy.

The desire was starting to build, and Ellis didn't let up kissing her when she started to moan. She couldn't control herself anymore, and her movements got jerky, but she wanted more, and if she didn't get it she felt like she'd fracture.

"I need you to go inside," she said, surprised by how desperate she sounded. "Please, baby."

Ellis took her hand back and laid her down so she could take her jeans off. This time, though, Ellis put her mouth on her, and when her hips shot off the bed, Ellis buried her fingers inside. The rush of feeling made her completely come alive, but it all then seemed to concentrate in her groin. They both stopped when she exhaled loudly, then moaned softly.

"You okay?" Ellis asked, looking up at her.

She grabbed the top of Ellis's head and pulled her forward. "No more talking."

Thankfully Ellis got the message and sucked her clit against her tongue, and it was almost too much. She screamed into the pillow she'd put over her head as the orgasm washed through her like a tsunami. Ellis slammed her fingers deep and sucked her until she tugged her head up by the ears.

"I surrender, you win."

"I believe I am the winner here." Ellis moved up and lay flat on her back so she could hold her. "Even though everything else in my life is a pile of crap right now, I got the girl. You may not believe me, but that balances it all out."

"It's what made today excruciating when I faced my boss. Here, you're mine, but I know you still have a business to run."

"Today was hard for me because I didn't want us to get to the point that I'm at right now with practically everyone I know. Someone is evidently working with Jennifer and Dalton to crush me, and the lack of trust in my circle is what hurts the most."

"I can't imagine why anyone would do this to you, but I meant what I told you before. All I want from you is you. That's what's in my heart." She sat up and undid Ellis's pants, moving between her legs to get them off. "No matter what, you're all I want."

Charlotte pulled Ellis's pants off, followed by her underwear. The expression of embarrassed uncertainty on Charlotte's face was finally gone, replaced by the kind of hunger she'd hoped would eventually materialize. Brandi's place was familiar, since that afternoon hadn't been that long ago, but the ache in her chest when she looked at Charlotte was as foreign to her as Greek. She remembered thinking how beautiful Brandi was, but no one in her past compared to Charlotte.

"You're making me nuts, you know that?"

Charlotte ran only her nails very gently up her leg from her feet to right above her knees. "Do you want me to stop?" Charlotte's smile as well as her tone was playful.

"Never, and you should know that no matter what, you're all I want too. I'm beginning to sound like some schmaltzy greeting card, but I want you in my life."

Charlotte lay on top of her and kissed her. The sensation of Charlotte's skin on hers made her want to forget work and everything until she'd memorized every inch of her. She started to move and reverse their positions, but Charlotte held her down.

"Not yet." Charlotte captured her hands above her head. "I want you inside me again, but I want to touch you. Will you let me?" Charlotte went back to kneeling between her legs and used only her thumb to stroke her clit until she was sure it was harder than her teeth. If Charlotte pressed with the same pressure, she'd come because she was so ready, but she wanted to hang on for Charlotte.

"I want to taste you," Charlotte said, and she almost cried from the possibility.

"God, yes."

Charlotte used her flat tongue at first, then only the tip, but throughout she wasn't as gentle as she had been, and she put her hands on the back of Charlotte's head to keep her in place. All she could feel and think about was the building orgasm that rushed through her almost too fast, and she tried to slow down, but she couldn't. She didn't have that kind of control when it came to Charlotte, and she came so hard she thought she'd lose consciousness. When that all-consuming want had burnt through her, leaving her spent, she ended up crying. It was her turn to be embarrassed, and she covered her face with her hand.

"Are you okay?" Charlotte asked, moving quickly to lie over her again.

"Actually, I don't think so," she said, taking a deep breath to stop the tears, but that didn't work.

"Did I hurt you?" Charlotte asked, sounding crushed.

"What I mean is, I never realized I wasn't okay until you came along and gave me what I didn't know I was missing. I'm crying because it feels so good to finally have it."

"I can't believe you even noticed me, much less want me like this."

She took a deep breath and put her arms around Charlotte, rolling them over so she could gaze down at her while holding her. "Babe, you've got to have some idea of what a special woman you are. Someone would have to be blind not to notice you. I'm many things, but blind isn't one of them."

"There have been some who were only interested in the looks aspect, and the sex, but if I was going to hold out for the fantasy, I want it all."

"You're beautiful, there's no denying that, but you're more than that to me. I never committed because everyone I've ever been with has been about the shallowest of connections. Sex is good, but it's only one aspect of a relationship. With you, I want everything, and I'm willing to give you that in return."

"Does that mean you don't mind that Sawyer comes as part of the package? Sawyer and the multitude of problems I seem to have these days. Maybe you should reconsider before you get dragged down with me."

"Remember what I said about honesty earlier?" Charlotte nodded. "Then let me be honest and say I'm glad Sawyer comes with you. That's a settled thing, so you don't have to worry about it. The rest I'll tell you as soon as I set up the end to all this. I'd tell you now, but I don't want to jinx it."

"Can you give me a hint?"

"You'll be the first to know, trust me." She methodically ran her fingers up and down Charlotte's back.

"Can we get back to work, or did what I had to do ruin that too?"

"We're working tomorrow, and we'll start with improving your pillow talk," she said and laughed. "But remember that I asked you to do that little act for a good reason. I totally expected what happened, but the thing I don't get is why tell me about stealing this bible too. I mean, they sent the proof of their theft really quickly."

"I guess they think kicking you while you're down is a good way to knock you completely out."

"That's one way to look at it," she said, stopping her hand for a moment. "We've got an early morning, so do you want me to go? I can stay in the house if you want me to."

"You must be nuts if you think I'm letting you stay in a house full of beautiful women who are all technically available, especially to someone with your bank account," Charlotte said, making air quotes. "No. I've got you all to myself, and I'm perfectly happy with that. You'll be happy to know that I want you for your body and not your money."

"You've got nothing to worry about, and I brought my pajamas just in case. You'll have other stuff to worry about if I stay."

Charlotte lifted her hands so she could reach up and comb her hair back. "What do you mean?"

"That I might have a problem keeping my hands to myself."

"My problem will be if you do."

CHAPTER TWENTY-ONE

It was still dark and quiet when Charlotte woke up to find Ellis still flat on her back fast asleep. The garden lights were bright enough for her to study Ellis's profile, and it was then that she admitted to herself that if she had a wish, it'd be to wake up like this for the rest of her life.

"What are you thinking so hard about?" Ellis said in a whisper without opening her eyes.

"I wasn't thinking. I was looking." She lifted her leg over Ellis's thigh and put her hand on her chest.

Ellis flexed and picked her up and placed her on top of her. "Now this is something to look at." Ellis opened her eyes and caressed her face with her knuckles. "I'm going to have a seriously bad time concentrating from now on when you're close to me, beautiful."

"I'm not sure how I lucked out and got here, but I don't want to leave."

"You're not going anywhere." Ellis ran her hands down to her butt and squeezed hard enough to make her wet. "You make me hungry for more than this, and I want it all."

She nodded as Ellis put one hand between them and pinched her clit between her fingers. "Jesus" was all she could say as she got instantly hard.

"I want you," Ellis said, and moved her fingers up and down.

"Take me. I'm all yours."

"Don't say it if you don't mean it." Ellis slid her fingers up and down again, almost making her come.

"Take what's yours," she repeated, and didn't close her eyes. Having Ellis see a bit of what was in her heart didn't scare her anymore. The way Ellis built the passion in her was amazing, and she put all her concerns aside and let herself go. Now she knew Ellis would be there to catch her when she jumped, no matter the height she climbed to.

"Oh, God," she said louder than she meant, but she couldn't help the loss of control. She jerked her hips and moaned when Ellis didn't let up. "Wait…wait…stop."

"Quietly, baby," Ellis said, removing her hand and putting her arms around her.

"You inspire loud," she said, and laughed until she heard a knock on the door.

"Mom, you up?" Sawyer asked, followed by what sounded like a yawn.

"Yes, but give me a minute, okay?" She scanned the room for something to wear. "Do you really have pajamas?"

"I sure do." Ellis put her hands under her head and smiled up at her.

"You want to put them on?"

"I'd love to, but it would require me to go into the other room to get them out of my bag."

She threw a pillow at Ellis and laughed. It had been ages since she'd been this giddy. "Get up now, and I promise to return the big favor you just did for me."

"Grab my stuff, and I'll jump in the shower first. That is, if I can walk to the bathroom." Ellis got up and walked toward her naked. She was sexy in every way, but this was almost too much. "You can be proud of the fact that I'll be hard as a rock all day, and it's entirely your fault."

"I'd say I feel bad about that, but I'm too busy patting myself on the back."

"I'll remember that," Ellis said, gently pinching her nipples. The rush from sated to ready almost gave her whiplash.

"You're so mean," she said, but Ellis was walking away laughing.

An hour later they were both clean and having breakfast, which was good since Amis and Opal had cooked it while they got dressed before joining them.

"Are we ready?" Amis asked after her usual round of kisses.

"I'm not sure. Opal, are we ready?" Ellis asked, and Opal snorted. "Whoever decides to premiere our line early is in for a surprise."

"What do you mean?" Charlotte asked, her eyes on Ellis.

"When the first bible got stolen, I figured something else was going to happen, so the work at the house was a trap."

"For me, you mean?" Charlotte asked and walked into the bedroom and slammed the door.

"Why would you think that? No. The trap was in no way for you. It just so happened that it turned out you were the pawn, not the mastermind," Ellis said, immediately following her. "I trusted you with all this, and with so much more."

"I don't see that you've trusted me with much."

"Are you kidding? I trusted you with more than the responsibilities of your job, and you know it." The way Ellis put her hands on her shoulders was hesitant, like she wasn't used to all this emotional turmoil.

"Maybe I need to hear you say it." It was probably too fast and way too much to ask of someone like Ellis, but she seemed the kind of person who would respond to boldness.

"I don't know how it happened, but you've captured my heart. You can't believe I didn't tell you everything because I think you did anything wrong. So much was at stake so I only told my mother and Opal. If you acted like you knew what was coming, none of this would have worked. That's the only reason I didn't share everything with you."

"I don't care about that right now. The first part of what you said is where you should've stopped, you idiot."

"I think it's coming back to me how you were able to capture my attention so completely," Ellis said as she turned her around. "You've been giving me what for since we met." Ellis's arms went around her waist, and she smiled. "Who knew what I was missing in my life was someone who isn't intimidated to say what's on her mind, even when it's that I'm an idiot."

"If it makes you feel better, I feel the same way. It might be too early for a lot of things, but you'll never have to worry about me betraying you or leaving."

"I know that, and that's the kind of kid you raised."

"Okay. That sounds like there's a story attached to that statement."

Ellis laughed and nodded. "You were wondering how Sawyer knew Brandi, and neither of us has had the chance to tell you. While I was working on a collection that was almost guaranteed to be stolen, I also worked on the collection we're actually going to be showing. The only way to not make anyone suspicious was with a little help from Sawyer."

Sawyer's sketchbook still had all her work in it, but in the back were the most amazing designs Charlotte had ever seen when Ellis handed them over. "Sawyer knew these were in here?"

"Don't be mad at her. I asked her, and she promised to keep my secret."

"So all those afternoon walks, you were bringing my kid to a brothel?"

"No. We were walking and working, but my mom and Opal weren't shopping all that time with Harold. They worked with a small group of our team that didn't arrive with everyone else, and Wilson was nice enough to lend us his place next door. By taking Sawyer with them when they could, no one was the wiser."

"What's left to do?"

"We need to narrow down the pieces of yours that are going in and take the pictures for our launch. If we can get everything fitted in the next few days, I have Andie Meade coming, so we have to be ready," she said of the best fashion photographer in the business.

"Wait. The models are coming back?" If more supermodels arrived, it would ruin what Ellis was trying to do. "It's not like those guys can fly under the radar."

"I thought about that and found a way around it."

"Are you going to share?"

"If I can't take all the pictures at the carousel like I want, why not use the second most chic spot in the Big Easy? Brandi's throwing open her red doors and letting us use the house and grounds. The girls volunteered to model for us, and considering that they're professionals, I don't think it'll be a problem getting them to follow directions and look sexy." Ellis smiled and kissed her. "I'm told it's why they make a couple grand a date."

"I'm sorry for earlier."

Ellis shook her head before kissing her again. "This will only work if you tell me what you need and want, beautiful, even when what you need is something from your boss. I may not have a lot of experience in long-term relationships, but I want a life with you. I want all that, and I want it to last, so don't ever fear telling me anything."

"Let's get started then."

❖

"What happens now?" one of the seamstresses asked Rueben as the cars left for the airport.

He'd stayed up the night before, but Ellis hadn't come home and Amis hadn't been in a talkative mood, so he was as in the dark as ever. It was like the second blow had imploded Ellis's world, and she'd pushed everyone away. That was understandable, but it had stung that he'd been included on that list of people Ellis had turned her back on.

"Knowing Ellis, she'll be in the city in a few days revved up to work. Whatever this is, I'm sure it's a minor setback."

"I don't know, Rueben. Whoever sent those pictures claims to have the whole book. What I can't believe is that Charlotte sold her out like that. If I didn't know better, I'd say Ellis finally fell hard, and little old Charlotte not only bagged her but tamed her as well. If I had to guess, that's why Ellis isn't going back to work and sent everyone away. She's devastated more from the fact that it was Charlotte than that it happened at all."

"There's no way Ellis is in love with that little twit."

"Are you kidding? Did you see them together? I'm telling you, there's something there. But then again, maybe that's how Charlotte pulled it off. If that's true, talk about cold-hearted bitch."

"How'd you know someone got all the sketches?" He stopped looking at the sights of the French Quarter and concentrated on the young woman's face. Like everyone that worked for them, she seemed eager and was extremely cute, but knew way too much information.

"I overheard it in the house, and since everyone was freaking out, I figured it was true."

"Tell everyone to stay quiet about that. We don't need anything else to go wrong, so keep it to yourself." So maybe Ellis running off wasn't all about the second set of stolen sketches. It had to happen eventually, but what a horrible time for Ellis to go crazy over some cute piece of ass and have a complete mental breakdown. The future could only be salvaged if Ellis managed to pull it together. Hell, he'd been watching Ellis pull success out of her hat for years, and it never ceased to surprise him when she did. She was one of those people that you were lucky to know, much less work for.

It was like seeing her on the morning show a few weeks back. She'd set it up fast enough that she'd turned the tables on disaster, and it'd made him envious of her innate ability to charm, captivate, and win over everyone within sight, including Sigrid. Anyone in the industry would never believe it, since Sigrid had a reputation of being a royal bitch, but with Ellis she always acted like a schoolgirl with a crush.

He'd had no place but on the sidelines of Ellis's world because he could never compete with her thousand-watt personality, but he'd thrived in the niche he'd carved out for himself. There wasn't any animosity between them because their relationship worked. They each had their place, and together they'd conquered their slice of the fashion world. That Ellis hadn't held on to that truth hurt him, but he'd give her the space she needed. Once she was ready, they'd talk and rebuild.

"You okay, Rueben?" the young woman asked, putting her hand over his.

"Yeah, I'm fine. Just thinking about all this is depressing, so let's plan on maybe all going out tonight to keep our spirits up."

"That's a great idea."

"I'm full of them, so stick with me."

CHAPTER TWENTY-TWO

Ｓhe came up with this in that short a period of time?" designer Angelo Bollio asked Jennifer as he flipped through the copies she'd brought with her.

"Ellis can be outstanding when she needs to be. The creative side has never been her problem."

He chuckled and studied the last couple of drawings. They were really good for something Ellis had created while facing the equivalent of a firing squad. Creating a whole new show practically overnight when it was life or death for her company was a total miracle, and damned if she hadn't done it. Ellis's creativity and success had somewhat blunted his own rise, and he'd been waiting for the moment when he could knock her back to earth.

"My deal hasn't changed. If you can convince her to sell, I'll buy and pay top dollar. Once the Renois brand is part of the Bollio house, you and Dalton will come to work for me."

"Now that she knows this collection is compromised, it'll be easier to get her to the table. You might not have to pay as much as you think."

"No matter what, this can't come back on me. Are you sure no one can trace this back to you?" He stared at her, trying to decipher what was going on in her head. Dealing with Jennifer had shredded his rule to not deal in any way with crazy women, but this situation was too good to pass on.

"That question is rather insulting. You didn't act concerned when I pitched you this last year after Ellis basically relegated you to the corner at the Met Gala by upstaging your entrance."

Aside from Fashion Week, the Met Gala chaired by Sigrid was the premier event in the fashion world. It was an opportunity to be seen in the company of every celebrity in attendance, and hopefully a lot of them were wearing your label. The publicity was invaluable, since every major news outlet in both print and television covered the night.

Angelo had arrived with the model that was the face of his line, and the cameras were going nonstop, giving him the kind of exposure he couldn't buy. It took him a long minute to notice they weren't aimed at him and his date, but at Ellis and Birdie Jones. The supposed world's top model had told him on numerous occasions that she was a free agent and would never put one line over the other, so she couldn't work exclusively for him and couldn't date him either. Not dating anyone she worked with was her number-one unbreakable rule.

That night, though, she appeared not only on Ellis's arm, but in a Renois dress that showed plenty of skin. Thinking about Ellis taking it off Birdie after the gala had made him hate Ellis enough to want to ruin her.

"Fuck you," he said, and practically threw the sketches back at Jennifer.

"Don't be mad, and don't back out now."

"I know why I'm doing this, but what's your motive?" He'd never really asked her that. "From what I know, you had a pretty sweet deal with Ellis after you hooked up with Dalton."

"There's sweet, and then there's phenomenal. If I can deliver, the deal I'm expecting from you will be phenomenal."

"It's all about the money?"

"Isn't everything in life?"

Her slight hesitation made him sure she was lying. Whatever Ellis had done, she'd underestimated Jennifer's capacity for cruelty and punishment. "Whatever you say, baby. All I need you to remember is to not lead Ellis to my door unless it's for a fire sale."

Ellis used the large den in Brandi's house to start their fittings. This was usually Ruby's job, but after they'd started, she was sorry she'd ever handed this task off. Sketching and design were important, but getting the clothes to fit was an almost intimate exercise that made all the work real.

"We need to take it in a little in the waist, but the rest is perfect," she said to Charlotte around the pins in her mouth. The suit the woman had on was one of Charlotte's pieces, and the addition of the thigh-high hose with the seam line down the back was sexy as hell. Granted, the camera wouldn't capture the top of the stockings, but the feel of them always seemed to come through in whoever put them on.

"Can I at least keep the stockings and the garter belt?" the woman asked as both she and Charlotte circled her.

"They're all yours, so enjoy them," she said as she finished. Her mom, Opal, and the small team were getting everyone else ready for them, so they moved to the next one. The small leopard print on the material reminded her to send Harold a thank-you note. Her old friend had found everything she'd asked for.

"Hey, I just got into town and don't have a damn thing to wear," Birdie Jones said loudly from Brandi's side. That Birdie had taken the time to come back made her stop and shake her head.

"What, honey? Once I talked to your mother, you didn't think I'd leave you to face all this alone, did you? I know you have some models, but I brought reinforcements with me," Birdie said, moving so the other girls could come in. "If you didn't realize it before, we love you, Ellis."

"Thank you all," Ellis said, putting her arm around Charlotte. The move made everyone smile, but none of them more than Sawyer. She'd been planning to sit with Sawyer that afternoon and talk to her about how close she and Charlotte were getting. Above all else, she wanted to reassure Sawyer that she'd never be left behind.

"You know you're our favorite, Ellis," one of the girls said.

"Enough mush, girls. Let's get dressed," Birdie said as she kicked her shoes off and walked over to Ellis and Charlotte. "Good job, Charlotte."

"Thank you," Charlotte said, with a delighted expression. "And thanks for doing this. It's great to see all of you again."

"You can make it up to me by getting me in one of the designs this one keeps bragging about." Birdie pointed at Ellis and started unbuttoning her blouse.

Ellis almost laughed out loud, thinking about the models' lack of modesty and the reasonable amount of shyness Charlotte still possessed. They got back to work, and she got another idea that she ran by Brandi's girls. Every one of them was on board, so she sent her mother shopping again for items she'd already brought to market.

The fittings went on late into the afternoon, so as Charlotte wrapped up, Ellis took Sawyer back to the cottage. They started the third of Sawyer's paintings, and she took a deep breath, trying to figure out how to begin the conversation she wanted to have.

"Do you like my mom?" Sawyer asked while she was still thinking.

"Yes, I do." She pointed to a spot on the canvas to show where the line Sawyer was drawing had to come to. "You think you'll be okay sharing her?"

"Sure, but do you think we can still do stuff like this? I didn't tell anyone our secret, so you can trust me. I just want to keep having fun with you."

"You bet. I think you and me will do plenty of fun stuff together, and we'll keep at it even after we get back to New York."

"Good, and I'm happy I don't have to go live with my dad."

Her phone rang before she could respond, and since it was Bill she answered it. "Hey, Bill, can you hold on?" She lowered the phone and put her hand on Sawyer's shoulder. "Go ahead and start on the trunk, and I'll be right back." Sawyer nodded and went back to work. "Anything new?" she asked Bill from the other room.

"I heard from our mutual friend, and she'd like to meet tonight if you can."

"She's in town?" It was like her life had become a bad mystery movie instead of the norm.

"Don't worry. She's got everyone still working, but the preliminary report is ready. Think you can meet me here at eight?"

"I'm slammed for time." She looked over the board they'd made of the order they were considering for the show. The clothes were finished, but they had plenty left to do.

"Believe me, Ellis. You're going to want to hear this."

The way he said it made her think that whatever the report was about was the last thing she'd want to know. But if it meant a resolution, then whatever it was would be worth it. She wanted to get back to the way she ran her business so she could concentrate on something other than getting stabbed in the back.

"I'll be there."

❖

Ellis sat in the bar at the Piquant and tried not to make eye contact with anyone. She wanted to get in and out of there as quickly as possible, but Bill had called and was running late coming back from the airport because of traffic.

"Anything else?" the bartender asked, and she shook her head.

She got a text from Bill, so she settled her tab and headed to the elevator. Bill's suite had papers and files covering every surface, which was pretty much what his office in New York looked like, so that didn't faze her too much. He was busy making a space so his investigator Tori Parrington could lay out what she had, so he let her in and pointed her to a chair.

"Hey, Tori. I'm surprised to see you out of the city," she joked as she hugged Tori. They'd met on the few occasions they'd run into each other at Bill's office. He'd been bragging about Tori's skills for as long as she'd known him but never thought she'd ever need the tall woman's services.

"I don't mind a change of scenery if the report's interesting enough."

"Interesting isn't always a good thing, I'm getting."

"No. Interesting is simply bizarre sometimes."

"Sit down, Ellis," Bill said while he poured them all a drink, so this had to be bad if it required this kind of buildup.

"I did what Bill asked, but we also dug into what happened from the beginning. Things like this are usually a puzzle that requires some putting together before you start to see the picture clearly." Tori began showing her the stack of paperwork to back up her story, and she was still having trouble understanding what Tori was saying. Bizarre was too innocuous a word.

"This can't be right," she said, looking at the series of pictures Tori went through. "It's actually impossible. Shit, this is like winning the lottery twenty-five times in a row."

"It's all in there, and we triple-checked everything. We might not be able to prove the first part, but from the day we initialized our investigation until now, all the information in there is verified."

The report was like a weight that made her fall back in her chair from the sheer volume of it. The damn thing landed on her chest, making it hard to breathe. "You don't think it's some colossal coincidence? I mean, it has to be, right?"

"No," Tori said bluntly. "It's in reality a methodical plan that I'm surprised worked because it had so many unpredictable parts. You have to give it to Jennifer Eymard in that she was not only able to uncover everything she did, but utilize it as well as she did."

"Okay." She put everything down and stood up, only to move since she felt like a caged animal.

"How do you want to handle this?" Bill asked.

"I'd like to start by strangling everyone involved. Can you get me off if I go that route?" She laughed at the total absurdity of it all.

"I'm not that kind of attorney, so keep your homicidal fantasies under wraps. Though I think a jury of your peers would clear you since this is so fucked up."

"Thanks for piecing all this together, Tori, but I need a little more time before we do anything. Bill, are you staying a bit longer?"

"Tori's heading back in the morning to personally keep on top of this, and I want to go too and make sure it's handled correctly. They plan to take the company from you, Ellis, so don't think too long. We have enough now to go to the police and press charges."

"Give me a couple more days. I have got a few more things to do, and then I'm going back to shove all this down their throats." The file contained enough to bury Jennifer and Dalton, but they had enough time for that. "Right now, I'm going to finish what they didn't give me credit for."

"The line, you mean?" Bill asked.

"The line and the ability to be as cruel as they are. I'm going to gut them, and I plan to enjoy every single second of it."

CHAPTER TWENTY-THREE

H ey, everything okay?" Charlotte asked as she hemmed one of the dresses.

Ellis had walked back through the French Quarter to try to wrap her head around the truth that was as bizarre as Tori said it was. Bizarre or no, what she'd been shown explained so much and brought everything into focus.

"Let one of the girls finish that and come with me." She took Charlotte's hand and walked to one of the quiet spots in the yard and took a seat in the chaise lounges they found. They sat facing each other, and she hadn't let go of Charlotte's hand.

"What's wrong?" Charlotte combed her hair behind her ear and seemed nervous.

"On Bill's advice, I had him hire his investigator to see if we could find our leak. I know clothes, but I suck at solving this kind of intrigue."

Charlotte smiled and squeezed her hand. "That's good. Does this mean you found something?"

"From the moment I met Sawyer, I had a feeling she was an incredibly special kid."

"Um…thanks. Are you sure you're okay? You seem a little off."

"Let me start from the beginning." She explained again how Jennifer had tried to get her to sign the bogus contract. "It seemed like the stupidest thing at the time, but I think it worked."

"How could it work if you didn't sign it?"

"It worked because it distracted me from the most obvious stuff that came next. The contract and the stolen bible blinded me, but not completely. So I came home and went to work looking for more of the same kind of deception, even when my mother thought I was crazy, and the second set of sketches proved me right."

Charlotte gazed at her and rubbed her hands with hers as if she was trying to warm them. "So you can prove the theft now? That's good news, isn't it?"

"I don't think you understand, darlin'. The theft wasn't the distraction. You are."

"What are you talking about?" Charlotte shrank back and let her go. "Please tell me you're not thinking I had anything to do with this."

"I need you to stop thinking I'm going to blame you for anything when it comes to all this. Hopefully you know me better than that by now." She moved to sit next to Charlotte and laced her fingers together between her legs. "You were a great distraction because you didn't know that was your role to play."

"I still have no idea what you're talking about."

"Trust me, we're in the same boat because I don't understand any of this either, but let me explain. I said that about Sawyer for more than the fact that I believe it." Her head was still a jumble, and she knew she was screwing this up.

"Honey," Charlotte said, standing up. "Lie back."

She did as Charlotte asked and felt better when Charlotte straddled her legs. "Take a deep breath and just tell me."

"I promise I will, but I have one question for you. How did you get to the final round of the interview process?"

"Someone at school had heard about the spot and told me to apply for it. I really didn't know her, but she promised me I'd be perfect for this. I sent my stuff in and got a call back. After that, I talked to some of the team who were coming down here for the summer. Then I eventually got a call from Rueben, and he scheduled for me to meet you. That I got as far as I did was thrilling, and that I got the job at all is unbelievable."

"You never spoke to Jennifer or Dalton?"

"I'm not sure. They could've been in those meetings I had, or on the phone calls I got, but it was the first time I'd met any of those people, and I was so nervous I doubt I could pick them out of a lineup today if forced to do so. Why would you think I was the distraction?"

"Because you came with someone who reminds me a lot of myself at her age. They knew me well enough to realize that Sawyer would hook me with that sketchbook of hers, and they were right."

"So someone, somewhere, had a great conspiracy to find an intern with a kid that likes to draw? That sounds plenty crazy to me."

"I thought so too, but all this time I spent with you, I assumed you and Sawyer shared Kyle's name."

Charlotte put her hands on her cheeks and shook her head. "He got me pregnant, but I never considered marrying him. It wasn't until much later that the state forced him to take a DNA test to prove he was Sawyer's father. He'd denied it until it was proved to him, and that he accused me of sleeping around made me want to kill him, but I got even when he was forced to help me with Sawyer. I never bothered to change her name, and he never forced the issue. That was perfectly okay with me since I don't love him."

She gazed at Charlotte, and deep in her heart she knew the truth of what had happened. Jennifer and Dalton had somehow manipulated the situation to throw Charlotte and Sawyer across her path. Once she noticed Charlotte and got close to her, her ex-employees would use their relationship by using Kyle. Obviously they thought she'd treat Charlotte like all the others by wooing her into bed, but something entirely different had happened.

"His half-sister does though."

"His half-sister does what? Love me?" Charlotte asked and laughed. "Wait—who's his half-sister? Kyle's an only child."

"His mother has only one child, but his father has at least one more."

"Kyle's father isn't around much, and I think I've only seen him a couple of times in my life, so I don't really know that much about him. If he does have another child, I promise I don't know her, so I sincerely doubt she'd be in love with me."

"Charlotte—baby," she said, kissing each of Charlotte's palms. "Eglin Snyder is my biological father."

"What...what? That's not possible. Wait, you love me?" Charlotte started crying, and she couldn't help but join in.

"Forget everything else for right now, and believe only this. I love you because you're everything I never knew existed. You are, to me, perfection."

"Oh, my God." Charlotte covered her mouth with her hands and looked at her with total disbelief. "Is it all right to say that I love you too?"

"I hope so," she said before Charlotte leaned forward and kissed her in a way that felt like sealing a vow. "I'm still in shock by the rest, but right now this is all that matters to me."

"The world's a funny and scary place sometimes, but it certainly makes more sense with you in it." Charlotte lay against her, and they stayed that way for a long while, and everyone seemed to know to leave them alone. The silence was enough to let her work through a few things, but she stayed quiet until Charlotte was ready. "Will you tell me the rest?" Charlotte finally asked.

"Bill's investigation team went to work digging into everyone involved in all this, starting with Kyle Snyder and everything about him. Tori, his investigator, was sending Bill the reports along with pictures. When Kyle took the call from you, he did it from an attorney's office with Eglin Snyder by his side." The resurrection of her father was something she'd never really thought about. She was way younger when she gave up on the dream of him wanting to be a part of her life.

"But your name's not Snyder."

"Like you, my mother was single when she had me, so she gave me her name. He never came back, and she did everything she could do to never make me think I was unwanted, so I've always considered him a sperm donor. He's never been a father to me, and I never missed out since I had Malcom. Until today I had no clue where he was, and he's got no clue who I am, much less where I am and what I do."

"That makes you Sawyer's—"

"Aunt," she said, smiling. That one truth was the only happiness she'd experienced the whole time Tori was talking. "Genetics are an amazing thing, aren't they?" She took a picture from her breast pocket and handed it over. They were different, but the family resemblance between her eight-year-old self and Sawyer was undeniable. "I would've never guessed, but she's a part of me even beyond how I feel her to be a part of me."

"If Kyle finds out any of this, he'll use Sawyer to exploit the situation. I'll never be free of him because he'll continue with these threats, thinking you'll pay to keep Sawyer with us. You don't know him, but I do, and believe me, he'll be here with his hand out as soon as he hears about this."

"I thought about that, and I might have a solution."

Having Charlotte's fingers combing her hair back was soothing, and she wished they were in bed with all this behind them.

"Will you tell me?"

"I will as soon as I find what the meaning of all this is. It's the last missing piece, and my plan won't work without that. Why go through all this elaborate scheme if not for some payout? The why isn't clear yet."

"No hints?"

"To get what we want means facing all the demons from my past. Once I'm free of them, the future for us is clear. And I do know what kind of guy Kyle is, so we might give him what you said he loves most to get what we love most. He'll get a payout and we'll get Sawyer. What we need to do, though, is get him to help us, and if he does, he'll get his reward."

"Love is all we'll need to make our future work." Charlotte kissed the side of her neck before getting up and holding her hand out to her.

"Then we should be fine."

❖

"So what exactly is going on?" Jennifer asked, her speakerphone on and Dalton standing right next to her listening.

"She said the show is off and sent everyone back to New York. The sketches you sent threw her off her game and she disappeared, but not before blaming the new intern for stealing the new line. It was quite the scene, and the gossip about it has already reached epic proportions. Actually, I can't believe that rag you gave the bible to hasn't reported on it yet."

Dalton pointed at her and smiled. They hadn't heard from their mole, who was working with them in New Orleans, in days and were starting to wonder if they'd been discovered. "She sent everyone home?"

"Everyone but Opal and Amis."

"And you didn't think that was strange?" The sensation of losing control of everything she'd methodically planned made her shiver. A cold sensation had blossomed in her stomach and made her nervous enough to cause her palms to sweat.

"It's classic Ellis, so it gets us closer to what we want. Relax and enjoy that we're one step away from cashing in."

She ended the call and sat heavily on one of the kitchen stools. "What's wrong?" Dalton asked, moving to her and putting his arms around her.

"Do you honestly think Ellis gave up and sent everyone except the two people who basically run the shows away? Tell me you're not that stupid."

"Fuck you, Jennifer. You can act like you're carrying water for all of us, but this is as much about me as it is you. Shit, without me we wouldn't be this close to getting this deal done. You and that other fucker wouldn't have thought to use the intern once we found out exactly who she was."

"Take your fucking ego out of this and listen to me. Ellis is up to something, and if we don't figure out what that is, all this is for nothing." They'd set Ellis up for failure, but it suddenly felt like she'd figured that out and was planning the foolproof whammy to bring them down. Dalton and their partner, as well as Angelo, kept thinking Ellis was some simpleton, but an idiot didn't accomplish half of what Ellis had. Failure in this case would come from not having enough time, but not because Ellis simply gave up.

"How about you follow your own advice and ditch the ego. I've known Ellis a lot longer than you, and she's done. The only option now is for her to sell to Angelo, so get with the program." Dalton slammed his hand down on the granite countertop, and the sound made her flinch. "Your problem is you were creaming your panties over her, and she turned you down like you were some stupid groupie not worth her time. I'm not fucking stupid enough to think you would've given me a chance if Ellis hadn't blown you off."

He lifted his hand, and for a moment she honestly thought he was going to hit her, but he just gripped the back of his neck and walked out. The slamming door made her jump, but just as fast she was relieved. She stood and slid the deadbolt and latch into place. She had no desire for Dalton to come back.

She pressed redial on her phone and was glad it was answered right away. "Why did you come back?" she asked, pinching the bridge of her nose while she waited for the answer that could possibly send her running.

"She was gone, so why would I stay? When Ellis runs like this, it might be a while before she resurfaces."

"Do you think she's up to something?"

"All she was up to was trying to fuck the intern. Then she thought the little bitch screwed her, but not in the biblical sense, so she fired her. If you don't believe me, have Kyle call her. She came home a day before us."

She hung up and called Kyle. "I need you to go by Charlotte's place and make sure she's home, and I need you to do it now."

"Why?" Kyle, as always, sounded suspicious.

"Kyle, you realize you've got some money coming to you, so stop asking questions and follow orders."

"Okay. What do you want me to do once I find her?"

"Apologize for blowing her dreams to shit, or whatever else comes to mind. All I care about knowing is if she's here."

"What did you mean about the dream thing?"

It finally hit her that Kyle still wanted Charlotte. The fight for the kid might've had some truth behind it, but only in the sense that he'd get Charlotte back as well. "The thing you asked her to deliver came with some consequences. You had to know someone had to take the fall. Just be glad it wasn't you."

"So that someone had to be Charlotte?"

"Don't fold on me now. Call me as soon as you find her." She hung up and looked around at everything she'd accumulated throughout her life. All the things that had made her happy and had been the trophies of her success would be the things Ellis would most enjoy taking away from her.

"You can either wait for the kill shot or fight," she said, and committed to finishing. "Only I'm going to do it on my own terms."

❖

Amis was reading a book next to the sofa where Sawyer was sleeping. She smiled as Ellis and Charlotte walked in holding hands. "Everything's ready to go for tomorrow, so we'll start around ten," she said softly.

"Thanks, Mama, but you need to get here a lot earlier than that."

"We don't need any more fittings, do we?"

"No. I need to fill you in on what Bill found, but if you don't mind, I can't go through it again tonight."

"Are you okay?" Amis stood and put her hands on both their cheeks.

"We're fine, and we're going to be fine, Amis," Charlotte said, letting Ellis go so she could hug Amis. "As long as we're together we'll always be okay."

"It's a good thing you finally wised up," her mom told her before kissing Charlotte's forehead. "And of course, when I say that, I'm talking to you too, chéri."

"Between the two of you, I'm going to need therapy for my self-esteem," she said, taking Charlotte's hand. "See you in the morning, Mama, and thanks for everything. I love you for always being so good to me."

They changed for bed and had to turn the lamp back on when Charlotte's phone started buzzing. "It's Kyle," Charlotte said, holding it up and showing it to her.

"Let him leave you a message, and we'll forward it to Bill," she said, tired of this guy. She tried not to think about who he was to her, and more importantly, who he was to Charlotte and Sawyer.

"Hey." Charlotte dropped her phone and faced her. "You know he doesn't mean anything to me. Kyle is so far in my personal past I barely remember him, and the only reason he's still in my life is because of Sawyer."

"This really is my summer of enlightenment. Before you, I never knew what jealousy was, much less felt it, so I'm sorry. I don't think you're in love with Kyle, but I can't believe he's not still fixated on you."

"It doesn't matter what Kyle wants or is fixated on. It's beyond too late. Even if I'd never found you, I'd never want a future with him."

"It doesn't freak you out any that he's my half brother?"

"Maybe this is going to sound weird, but if I had to make a big mistake, I'm glad it gave me a path to you. Obviously, I was picked because of who I am and who Sawyer is to you, but what a blessing. I found you, I love you, and Sawyer's a part of you. Once she finds out, she's going to be so excited." Charlotte pressed against her and suddenly appeared terrified. "Is this too fast for you?"

"Actually, you're way late, so see what he wants so we can plan our next step. You and Sawyer are in my heart, and that's settled. Kyle will have to accept that fact, and we'll do whatever it takes to fight him for Sawyer to stay with us. But for now we have to deal with the business side of things. From now until all those clothes become public, we have to stay ahead of Kyle and everyone he's working for."

Charlotte played the message and listened from the circle of her arms.

"Hey, I need to know where you are. I haven't heard from you or Sawyer, so call me when you get this."

"What in the world does he want now?" Charlotte asked. "Usually he's doing his best to ditch my calls since he says all I do is ask for money."

"Nothing about all this makes sense, but it does to someone. I think the most important thing and their goal is to keep us both off balance." The information Tori and Bill had shown her didn't really narrow that part of the scheme down. A piece was still missing, and it was something Jennifer and Dalton had kept well hidden.

Her phone rang next and it was Tori, so she answered it. "Hey, did you find something else?"

"Jennifer met with Angelo Bollio today, so we might've found the person they were dealing with if you end up being forced to sell."

"Hmm," she said as she sat on the bed and lay back. The introduction of Bollio meant the group conniving against her had gone out of their way to find everyone in her life who had in turn gone out of their way to cause her problems in the past. "Is there any way to know what they talked about?"

"No. We could only see who she met with, but not why they met." Ellis heard papers flipping on Tori's end. "The guy we've got on Kyle, though, followed him to Charlotte Hamner's address, and he tried to get in. He pressed that buzzer for half an hour before he gave up and called Charlotte's number."

"He left a message right before you called," she said, and put her arm out so Charlotte could join her on the bed.

"We were able to catch that, and his side of the next call. When he finished with Charlotte, he called Jennifer and reported that he couldn't find her. You might want to keep an eye on Charlotte until all this is resolved."

She tightened her hold on Charlotte and laughed. "That's not going to be a problem." She kissed the top of Charlotte's head. "I wonder why they want to find Charlotte. I'd think her part in all this is done."

"I can't be sure, but from his conversation, Jennifer really needs to know."

"Thanks, Tori, and please keep at it. There's a missing player, and I need you to find them." Her phone buzzed, and she saw it was her mother. "I've got another call, so keep in touch."

"You got it."

She switched to take her mom's call and drew a few deep breaths, knowing her mom wouldn't be calling unless it was important. "Hey, you okay?"

"I hate to bother you, but you got another package and another set of sketches."

"Was there a note?" she asked, closing her mouth harder than she thought, causing her teeth to mash together.

"There sure was. It says, 'No matter what you try, I'll be one step ahead, showing the world what a fraud you are. Think about that the next time you screw someone over.'"

"That's pretty straightforward. Thanks, Mama."

She told Charlotte everything about both calls while Charlotte methodically removed everything she was wearing. Once Charlotte had her naked, she took off her own clothing and joined her. The way Charlotte pressed against her and basically draped herself over her made her anger disappear.

"Do you want me to call Kyle back?"

"Where do your parents live?"

"You ask the strangest questions, but if you need to know, they lived in Jersey until last year, when my dad retired. They moved to upstate New York after that." The way Charlotte circled her finger around her bellybutton as she spoke was making her shiver.

"Good. Call Kyle back and tell him you're visiting your folks. He doesn't have their number, does he?"

"He and my father don't agree on the basics, so no. My dad thinks Kyle should drop dead, and Kyle disagrees with that, so they've barely spoken in ages."

"Give him a call, followed by getting in touch with your parents just in case."

Charlotte moved to what seemed to be her favorite position and straddled Ellis's waist to make the calls. "What do you want, Kyle?" She put it on speaker so Ellis could hear.

"Where are you?"

"Why would you care?" She put the phone on Ellis's chest and moved Ellis's hands to her waist.

"I need to know you're okay," Kyle said softly, as if that tone would make him sound more caring and believable.

"There's no reason in the world I'd want to call you about anything after the last time we talked. I did what you wanted, got fired for it, and then you double-crossed me anyway." Ellis squeezed her and nodded like she agreed with what she was saying. "Once I get back from my parents' place, even if I have to borrow money, I'll see you in court."

"I've got enough money to take care of us now, so we can work it all out. We've got Sawyer to think about, so we should get back together. You want me to come to you and talk about it?"

"What I want, Kyle, and all I want, is you out of my life. I don't want you anywhere near me. You ruined everything for me, so there's no coming back from that." She kissed her fingers and pressed them to Ellis's lips. "Don't call me again. I won't keep Sawyer from you if she wants to talk to you, but I don't want anything else to do with you ever again."

"Wait—"

She ended the call. "One more to go, and then we're done for tonight," she said, dialing her mom's number. Her mother didn't ask too many questions except when she told her she'd met someone.

"I'm so happy for you, sweetheart," Maria Hamner said, making Ellis smile. "When do we get to meet the lucky guy?"

"It's a lucky girl, Mom, and as soon as we're done with Fashion Week, I promise we'll come up with Sawyer."

The pause from Maria's end made Ellis lose her smile. "Does she make you happy?"

"I've never been happier, and Sawyer is just wild about her, so you don't need to worry."

"I'm always going to worry, and I'm always going to be proud of you. That's what moms are for. I want all the details."

"Mom, I promise I'll answer all your questions, but I really am crunched for time. I need you to do me a favor and take the phone off the hook and leave it off until I get in touch again."

"Are you in some kind of trouble?"

"No. This is about Kyle and his kind of trouble."

Maria agreed to everything after she heard Kyle's name.

"Hopefully our life won't always be this exciting," Ellis said, pulling her down so she was lying on her.

"As long as we end up here every night, who cares what life throws at us? I love you, so that's all the excitement I need."

"I still have some surprises in store, so not all excitement is bad."

"You can tell me all about them later." She kissed Ellis and pressed her hips down. "Much, much later."

CHAPTER TWENTY-FOUR

Do you want to shoot the ones here first?" Andie Meade asked Ellis the next morning as they walked the grounds. Her talk with her mom that morning had ended in Amis crying, getting angry, and apologizing for giving her such a loser father.

"Let's do this one first. Then we'll head over to the zoo." She stopped by the pool and nodded at the crew that was setting up. The models were inside in makeup so she was nervous, but that was common. Today was the first step to bringing the line completely home.

"Did you want to do the carousel today?"

"If tonight isn't too much for you, I'd love to finish it all today. That one should be the easiest."

"I'll do whatever you want. You know that."

"Great. I'll leave you to it." She patted Andie on the back and walked back to the cottage to talk to Sawyer. That morning, Charlotte had let Sawyer know what she wanted going forward but hadn't told her she and Ellis were related just yet. That had been her idea, since she didn't want to influence what was really in Sawyer's heart when it came to Kyle and what kind of relationship she wanted to have with him.

She found Sawyer in the garden working on her elephant. The way she used the brush like an old pro made her stop and admire her technique.

"Hey, Ellis." Sawyer stopped and turned around as if sensing her there.

"Hey. Your mom said you guys talked this morning, so I wanted to make sure you were okay."

"Yeah." Sawyer lowered her head and spoke softly.

"I want you to know it's going to be okay no matter what you decide. No one will be upset if you want to see your dad."

"That's not why I feel bad." Sawyer put her brush down and wrapped her arms around her.

"What's wrong?" She sat on a nearby bench and kept her arm around Sawyer. "Do you want to see your dad?"

"No. I feel bad because I don't. I probably should, but I don't. He never really wants to be with me, and his mom says bad stuff about my mom. I never want to go over there, but no one ever asked me if I wanted to skip it."

"If we're not asking you something, you need to remind us. All I want is for you to be happy."

"I am happy here with you and Mama. Do you think my dad will be mad?"

"As long as you're honest and tell him why you feel the way you do, he won't be mad. And whenever you need to talk about it, all you need to do is find me."

"Thanks," Sawyer said as she hugged her. "Are you and Mama working today?"

"We are, but I came over here to see if you wanted to hang out with us. Want to learn the family business? When your mom comes to work with me, you should know a little about it."

The girls came out, and she placed them along with Brandi's girls around the pool. Thankfully it was a sunny day so every outfit popped. They moved to the house and the den that had been the site of so many infamous parties. There, Birdie and Brandi looked to be holding court with some girls lounging around in lingerie. That had been the idea she'd had the day before, and Brandi's girls were willing to model the sexy undergarments that were part of her line. She thought they were a good addition, considering where they were. If you asked the average person, this was probably what they thought the inside of a brothel looked like.

She sat back and watched Charlotte take care of this part. Charlotte, with Amis and Opal's help, went through the steps like an old pro. The zoo was next, and she hung back, not wanting to be noticed with the group. It was dark by the time they returned, and she was waiting, wearing the most business-style suit she owned and holding up a dress for Charlotte.

"What's this for?" Charlotte said, her eyes glued to the black formal dress that had a high collar but the rear cut all the way to the small of her back.

"It's for you and the last pictures of the day. Sawyer and I will wait while the team gets you ready." Her crew took Charlotte, so she sat with Sawyer and talked about the day so far. They stopped when Sigrid's writer Sierra Madison arrived and asked a few questions.

"Thanks for the story, Ellis."

"I'm the one who's in your debt. You guys kept me alive through all this."

The rest of what she was going to say died in her throat when the door opened and Charlotte walked out. She might not have had the height for a modeling career, but her face could carry any launch of any line. She looked incredible.

"Good God, you're beautiful." She stood and took Charlotte's hands. Andie took some pictures and Sierra started taking notes. They left for the carousel and sat on one of the benches for their interview with Sierra, then posed for the pictures Andie would provide for the article.

"So, Charlotte, are you ready for the madness of Fashion Week?" Sierra asked as they moved around the carousel.

"I'd be lost without Ellis and the team, but I'm really looking forward to the opportunity."

They stood next to a white stallion, and she lifted Charlotte onto its side saddle. She stood close to her and liked the way Charlotte put her hands on her shoulders and gazed at her. This would be the picture that cemented their partnership in the eyes of the industry.

"You were right, Ellis," Sierra said once they were done.

"About what?" She held Charlotte's hand and took a few more pictures with first Sawyer and then her mom.

"The article name—it's a great choice."

"You came up with it?" Charlotte asked.

"She sure did," Sierra said and winked. "'Beauty and the Boss' will move some magazines when it hits the stands."

"It's a little long to put on a label, but I'm working on it."

"If you want my opinion, Ellis, the line is absolutely gorgeous," Sierra said.

"Thank you, and thanks for including us in this edition."

"You lucked out with your positioning this year by going last, and the fact that Sigrid happens to love you."

"It's mutual, believe me, but tell her that she's got competition now." She kissed Charlotte before shaking Sierra's hand. "You can be the first to break the news to her that I'm in love."

"And it looks good on both of you."

❖

The photo shoot gave Ellis all she needed for the launch, so she left her mother and Opal in charge of packing so they could head back to New York. Going back was making Charlotte antsy, but not for the reason Ellis first thought. She'd thought Charlotte didn't want to face Kyle and an uncertain future, but Charlotte had finally confessed that being separated from her was starting to worry her.

She had to admit she was going to miss the cottage on Brandi's property and the time they'd spent there. They'd made love and really gotten to know each other between phone calls from Kyle, Bill, and Tori. Kyle continued his quest to win Charlotte back, Bill was helping the police put a case together, and Tori's team was still following all the players they knew about.

Charlotte finally seemed to exhale when she told her they would never part once they got back. They had time to make things permanent between them, but she didn't want to spend another night separated from Charlotte or Sawyer, so they would move to her apartment and decide if that was the best place for them.

Now she needed to get back and finalize the show she'd started working on after the designs were finished. She didn't have that much time left and just had to keep everything under wraps, because a leak now would be devastating. The small team with her was ready to go, so she walked back to the house to pick up what she needed for the early morning flight.

"Congratulations, sweet pea," Malcom said when she came in through the kitchen door. "Your mom showed me some of the proofs and the marketing layout, and you've outdone yourself. I'm glad you got back to what made you—showing the world what's in your heart and, more importantly, the passion that defines you."

"I love everything about you, but I love you most for always having my back."

He followed her upstairs, and she saw he'd already packed her things except for two books he'd left on the bed. "You're all set, and I thought you might want to give these to Sawyer."

The sketchbooks were hers, and she saw he'd dated them on the back corner with only the year. "She's way better than me at the same age," she said, sitting and flipping through them. "Mama told you what Bill found?"

"Life's a weird bitch sometimes, isn't it?" He sat next to her and put his hand on her knee. "Can your old meddling uncle give you some advice?"

"You know you can."

"I think before you get what you want, you're going to have to deal with Eglin. If you do, please don't fall for his bullshit. You don't need that in your life, and neither does your mother. Eglin was the only thing that almost broke her."

"Eglin Snyder has no place in any of our lives. Like I told Charlotte, he was a sperm donor, and you're the only father I've ever known. You and Mama are my family, so you don't have to worry." She turned and hugged him, enjoying the smell of the cologne he'd worn forever.

"Thank you, and I'm happy you've finally found the one who'll always love you. Take care of her and that little girl. Sawyer proves to me that Eglin's lineage is worth anything only when you mix it with a beautiful, smart woman."

"It shocked the hell out of me, and I'm going to do whatever I can to give them a future that's free and clear of the Snyders. Hopefully they'll want to spend it with me, if I can come through for them." She stood and put the two books in her old leather messenger bag.

"How are you planning to do that?"

"I'm going to start with the carrot first. Writing a check is sometimes the easiest way to get what you want."

"If Kyle doesn't bite at the carrot, then what?"

"Then I have a bag of sticks I'm going to beat him with until his life will never remotely be the same again. I'm a Renois, so I know how to bruise you," she said, and smiled. Her mom and uncle had taught her how to expand her creativity, but they'd also taught her how to take care of herself.

"Good. I'll see you in a few days. Make sure you have groceries in the house before I get there. Diet drinks and coffee don't count."

"You know I won't let you starve. Kiss me so I can head back. Like always, you made the summer wonderful, so thanks for everything. What are you planning to do when I retire and am in your hair all the time?"

"I'll be too busy running around after your kids to be worried about you."

She laughed and handed over her car keys. Her driving was done for a while since she was walking back to Brandi's. Malcom would take care of her bags so she didn't intend to try to argue with him about that, considering she lost that fight every single summer.

She returned a few calls while she walked, since the appointments she needed to make would help her win at the game someone had pulled her into. To get that part done, she'd trusted only one other person, aside from those with her now, to set her schedule for the coming days.

"Hey, Boss," her assistant Liam Keller said in the same upbeat tone he always used. He'd only been with her for two years, but she'd met his partner and his entire family and eaten at his mother's house. They'd become friends even though she wasn't in the office very often.

"The building hasn't burned to the ground, has it?"

"Just the phone, so you might need to replace at least mine when you get back. I have, though, been offered enough bribes for your whereabouts and what's happening that I could've retired ten times over."

She laughed, wondering why anyone would care what she was up to and where she was doing it. "If you sold out, then enjoy yourself before I get back and fling you out the window."

"Are you kidding? My mother would beat you to it if I cut off her direct line to free clothes. Give that woman a blouse, and she's yours for life."

"Funny," she said and went through the back gate at Brandi's and headed to the big house. "Have you heard from anyone more than normal?"

"Just Ruby, but all he wants to know is if you're okay. You might want to call him and put the poor thing out of his misery."

"Ruby has no poker face, so I need a few more days of total silence on all this. He'll be pissed, but the investigation isn't done yet. How about anyone else?"

"Everyone here is nervous as hell about their jobs, so it's been pretty somber. The only ones I hear from most often are the media, especially that Benson Norwood guy from that rag."

"Okay. I'll deal with him soon enough. Take care, and I'll see you soon." She hung up and went inside, and Wilson pointed her to the office. Brandi was dressed casually but appeared at home behind the big desk.

"I'm going to miss you and your little family, handsome."

"You're a good friend, and I'll never forget everything you did. It's not much, but here." She handed over a VIP invitation to the showing.

"Are you sure?" Brandi ran her index finger over the raised print.

"Ms. Parrish, seeing you there would be my honor. The benefits part of our relationship might be done, but I'd love to keep the friendship part." She kissed Brandi's cheek and hugged her.

"I'd say I'd give you a great birthday present every year, but Charlotte would rip my spleen out if I tried, so you're right. Get out of here, and I'll see you in the city for your big night."

"Bring your pen," she said, smiling. "After that photo shoot, you're going to be more famous than you are already."

"Get out of here with all that."

"I will, but know that I'll always be back."

CHAPTER TWENTY-FIVE

W ow," Sawyer said when they pulled to the front of Ellis's building. The doorman got their bags, then, after Ellis's tip, promised to completely lose his memory about seeing them. "Wow," Sawyer said again when they got upstairs.

"Glad you like the place, or hopefully that's what all the wows are for." Ellis glanced around the main room and noticed just how unwelcoming and the opposite of homey it was. She'd had the apartment professionally decorated, but now she planned to let Charlotte and Sawyer have the run of the place. Maybe they could make it feel like she did in the house in New Orleans. "Let's see where you want to sleep."

"I can sleep in here," Sawyer said, sitting on the large sectional couch. "Like I did at Miss Brandi's."

"I think you might be here longer than that, so go ahead and pick a room so you can avoid Uncle Malcom's early morning baking sessions." They took a tour, and Sawyer chose the room with the most windows. She and Charlotte helped Sawyer set up her easel and unpack all her supplies, so she was happy.

"What's this?" Sawyer asked when Ellis handed over the two sketchbooks Malcom had given her.

"These were mine when I was your age, so you have proof of how much better you are than I was. It's a gift from Uncle Malcom and his way of telling you how great he thinks you are."

"Thanks." Sawyer held them against her chest like they were a valuable treasure.

"Can I talk to you and your mom for a bit? Then you can paint if you want." They walked to the kitchen, and she laughed when she didn't have anything to offer them but soft drinks and coffee. "First, I know we talked about your dad before, and you know that he wants to fight your mom so you'll go live with him."

"Please. I don't want to go. I don't want to see him."

"You're not going anywhere, neither of you, if I have anything to say about it." She put her arm around Sawyer and smiled at Charlotte. "I just want you to take your time making a decision, and remember that both your mom and I will be okay and support whatever you decide." She held Sawyer tight for another moment, then let go so as not to influence what she was going to say.

Sawyer stared at both of them for a long pause before taking a deep breath. "It's always been just me and Mom, and she takes care of me. That's all I want, but no one ever asked me what I want except you. I like drawing, and I liked spending time with you this summer."

"Thanks, and I'm always going to be honest with you and ask what you want. I might not be able to give it to you, but I'll try my hardest. Now I have a question for your mom." She took Charlotte's hand and held the other one out for Sawyer. "I was serious about wanting a future with both of you, and even though this will sound really fast, how about you and Sawyer move in here with me and help me put some stuff on the walls? This place looks too much like a mausoleum."

"Are you kidding?" Charlotte and Sawyer said together.

"If you want to go home, you can, but at least think about it."

"I don't know about Mom, but I'm staying," Sawyer yelled.

"Good." She glanced at her phone and saw it was Liam. "Sorry, guys, but I've got to answer this one. Hey, what's up?"

"Your first appointment is waiting for you at the deli down the street. Do you want me to go? I might break a nail if there's a fight, but I'm there if you need me."

She laughed. "I appreciate it, but I'll be okay." Charlotte and Sawyer had their heads together, so she grabbed her wallet and told them she wouldn't be long. "Mama should be here in about an hour so tell her not to worry about dinner. I'll pick something up."

"Are you going to be okay?" Charlotte asked.

"You need to stay here for this one, but I do need you to do one thing while I'm gone."

"Whatever you want."

She put her hand on the back of Charlotte's neck and brought her closer so she could kiss her. "Pick a room too, but make sure it's the last one down the hall that has the big bed and balcony in it."

"I think you're trying to distract me, so tell me where you're going."

She kissed Charlotte again and shook her head. "I'm getting you a birthday present."

"My birthday's months away."

"I'm a planner, baby, so stay home and don't worry about anything."

"That's my job now when it comes to you, so live with it."

"I'm counting on that too, so thanks."

❖

Ellis waved to her regular waiter and pointed Bill toward the table in back. When Liam had invited Kyle here, he'd obviously told him lunch was included, she guessed, when she saw how many plates he had in front of him. She hesitated when the reality of the fact that this guy was her half brother hit her right in the heart. That wasn't something her brain had fully computed yet, and it was still such a wacky concept she hadn't even said the words out loud, because once she did it would be all too real.

"You ready?" Bill asked.

"Yeah. If you tell me I'm the better-looking one in the family," she said jokingly.

"Hello," she said, sitting across from Kyle and startling him enough that he came close to spitting a mouth full of pickle at her. "Thanks for coming."

"Who the fuck are you?"

"Sorry. I'm Ellis Renois. I believe you forced Charlotte Hamner into stealing from me. Does that sound at all familiar?"

"I didn't do nothing, so I don't have to listen to this," Kyle said with his mouth still full.

"You probably did better with picture books in school, so let me help you out." She started putting all the pictures that Tori's people had taken in front of him, slamming her finger down each time. "This is my favorite."

The picture was of him accepting an envelope of money from Jennifer in exchange for something small. "The flash drive you handed her had my entire portfolio of sketches on it, so how much was it worth to her?"

"You can't prove nothing."

"You're right. I can't prove *anything*. I am, though, going to turn all this over to the guys in drab-gray suits investigating the theft. The only thing you've got to look forward to is the interest your money will be making when you spend years in jail."

"What's the deal then, since you didn't go to the cops first?" He was good at acting cool since he went back to eating, but he was way out of his depth.

"How much did she give you?"

"Seventy-five grand."

"You should've asked for at least double that." She handed the pictures back to Bill and rested her hands on her knees. "That's what I'm willing to give you if you tell the cops that's what Jennifer paid you to do."

"You're going to give me double for doing that?"

"You give a statement today, and I sure will." He gave her the creeps, but she kept smiling. They might've shared half their DNA, but they were nothing alike. It made her wonder what his mother was like.

"I never liked that bitch anyway, so sure." He laughed as he shoved a wad of corned beef in his mouth with his fingers. "Wait, this is a setup, isn't it?" Kyle looked directly over her shoulder toward the door, and she didn't need to turn around to see who was there.

"Do you need to ask him?" she said while Bill glanced between them. She'd promised Malcom not to drag Eglin into their lives, but she was curious about him. He had to be halfway charming to have interested Amis all those years ago. "You can. I'm not in a rush."

Eglin Snyder appeared next to her, or she thought it was him since she refused to look up. He sat and shrugged at Kyle. "What the hell is this?"

"I offered your son a hundred and fifty thousand dollars to give a statement about the deal he made for the theft of my intellectual property." She slowly turned her head and, on first impression, found Eglin handsome. His hair still held some of the original color at the top, but the sides had the white that came with age. It was strange seeing such a strong resemblance to her own face in a man she didn't know at all.

"Does he look stupid?"

Her smile widened, which made Bill put his hand over his mouth, she was sure to muffle his laughter. "Do you really want me to answer that?"

"Who the hell is this bitch?" Eglin asked, and she wondered what aside from a pretty face her mother had ever seen in this guy.

"I'm the bitch you and the genius stole from, and I'm here to say that I really didn't appreciate it."

"You don't know shit," Eglin said, and Kyle made a slashing motion at his throat with his hand. "You didn't say anything, did you?" he asked Kyle, pointing his finger about an inch from his face.

"He doesn't need to. I've got it all, including your part in this, on all these glossies showing you stealing my shit, as you so eloquently put it. Now the choice is the money I'm offering or court."

"It's obviously worth it to you for him to talk." His smile appeared cruel, but it did bring out the family resemblance even more. Did he not see how much alike they looked?

"My philosophy is, there's the easy way or the hard way."

"What do you know about the hard way?" Eglin laughed, and for the first time in her life she wanted to hit someone until they bled.

"This is my attorney, Bill Tangren." She waved at her friend. "Bill," she said, cuing him.

"I've had an investigative team following all the major players from the beginning of this scam. You don't take this deal, and we'll turn all the information over to the police. Then I'll see you in court again for the civil suit I'll be filing. If the time and effort it'll take to defend yourself doesn't break you, losing every one of your assets will." Bill took another couple of sheets out and handed them over.

"I don't care about your crappy cars, the semi, the house, and the very little money, but I'm going to treat all of it like you treated my property." She wanted this over, so she spoke in the kind of terms people like Eglin and Kyle understood. Her boot was on their throat, so if they wanted any kind of mercy, they'd come to see things her way.

"So he confesses and you're not going to prosecute?" Eglin peered up at her briefly but didn't seem to be able to take his eyes off the paper he held.

"You're either with me with your pockets full of money, or you're against me with not one shitty thing to your name."

"I'll do whatever you need me to do," Kyle said.

"Half now and the other half after you give your statement."

"Where do I need to go?"

"That's one reason Bill's here." Bill put a paper in front of him and handed over a pen.

"What the hell is this?" Kyle asked.

"It's a little insurance that you don't take my money and then not give a statement. Jennifer might've trusted you, but I don't." She tapped the line where he had to sign.

"This is sounding hinkier by the second," Eglin said, loud enough to attract attention.

"Okay. Don't sign it," she said, standing up.

"I still get the money?" Kyle sounded completely serious.

"You get to go to jail, and I'll call in every favor I'm owed to make sure you end up with a large roommate who'll develop the hots for you. If all this money seemed way too good and way too easy to make—it was. You stole from more than just me, Mr. Snyder, and your actions would have driven a lot of people out of work. You have to pay the consequences, and I'm never going to stop trying to collect. In terms you understand, it's simple. You fucked with the wrong bitch."

"Let's go, Ellis. The detectives are waiting on us," Bill said.

"Wait, just wait. The boy said he'd do it," Eglin said, his hands up and out. "I fucking told you this was bad news," he said to Kyle.

"Sign it," she said, and Kyle did, followed by Eglin.

"That's it?" Kyle asked as he accepted the envelope she handed over. "I want cash," he said when he saw the check.

"And I want all the time I wasted creating a new line this summer back, but that's not likely."

"Okay already." He shoved the check into his pocket. "Is that it besides talking to the cops?"

"One more thing, but this one is for a friend." She let Bill lay out all the necessary paperwork before she started making her case. "Charlotte requested something from you in exchange for what you asked for, but you changed your mind about that too. I'm asking you to give her what she wants."

"You fucking fired her, so why would you care?" He wasn't as loud as Eglin, but his tone carried menace.

"I reacted to what happened, but I understand now what you threatened her with. You told her you were going to take her daughter away. Whose idea was that?"

Kyle glared at her but just as fast looked away. "Jennifer needed Charlotte to think I would and panic. She had me calling all the time so she'd be worried about losing Sawyer, but I wasn't going to do that. I just needed to make it so she'd give me what I wanted to make it stop."

"Think about Sawyer now and sign the papers. You'll be released from your obligation but not necessarily lose Sawyer."

"What do you mean?"

"Your daughter talked to me this summer, Mr. Snyder. She's too young to completely understand what cutting you totally out of her life means, but she doesn't want to have to come with you only to be dumped at your mom's."

"You don't know my kid." This time he yelled.

"I know her because I took the time to get to know her, and more importantly, I asked her what she wants. She's a good kid who doesn't want to spend time with people who bad-mouth her mother. Sign it." She picked up the pen and held it out to him. "You know it's the right thing to do."

Kyle took it and put it to the page, and she was shocked until he stopped. "What's this worth to you?" That question didn't shock her. She'd expected it.

"This is what it's worth to me." She took a bankbook out of her pocket and handed it over. She'd made the deposit before they'd flown home.

"Fuck," Kyle whispered, his facial expression registering so much shock that Eglin snatched it from his hand and stared at it.

"My name will stay on the account until this becomes legally binding. You have the right to change your mind, but think of that as your reward for doing the right thing."

"Do I know you?" Eglin asked, squinting his eyes.

"No, you don't. Not at all." The irony of that truth was both sad and hilarious.

"Are you sure? You look so familiar."

"You and your son are memorable, so I'm sure I'd remember if we'd met."

With the bankbook in hand, Kyle signed the papers everywhere Bill pointed as fast as he could manage, as if he thought she'd change her mind. "Thirty days, right?" he asked.

"I'm sure all that money will gain interest by then, so it's a win-win." She offered him her hand and sealed the deal. "Bill will take it from here, so I'll see you in a month in family court. We'll take a trip to the bank after that."

She almost shivered from the sense that all this was totally slimy, but she started walking, glad it had been that easy. It was like she was buying Sawyer, but in the end her girls would get what they wanted—freedom from these guys. She heard a chair scrape behind her, but she was determined to leave.

"Wait a minute. Who's your mother?" Eglin yelled.

"Amis Renois." She put her fists on her hips and looked right at him. "She's someone who might remember you, because I sure as hell don't."

"You're Amis's kid?" His voice died away to nothing, and he grabbed the back of his chair.

"Yes, but that's of no importance to you. Maybe now you know why I understand your granddaughter so well. Children are something precious that need time and affection."

"What's she talking about?" Kyle asked.

"This is my bastard," Eglin said, laughing. "Man. I should've stuck around."

"She's your kid? Like my sister kind of kid?" Kyle glanced between them, appearing to have trouble keeping up.

"Well, fuck me," Eglin said, coming closer. "This is why you're trying to take my grandkid? You think money is all she's missing? Maybe Kyle needs to do what he threatened. Maybe that little kid needs to be fought over."

"The money's so important that I'm giving your son a lot of it. What Sawyer needs is people who love her and want her in their lives. She's tired of being a burden to Kyle, so you're right."

"About what?"

"If you want something, you should fight for it. The money was the easy way out, but I'm willing to wait and do this in a way I can be proud of."

She walked over to Kyle and gave him back the papers he'd signed for Sawyer. No matter that she wanted a clean start for Charlotte and Sawyer, but she wouldn't do it by stooping to Kyle and Eglin's level.

"I'd like for you to make the statement, but after that we're done," she said to Kyle.

"I don't know if I want to do another damn thing for you. Thanks for lunch and the money." Kyle patted his pocket and laughed.

"Bill," she said, wondering how this guy managed not to play in traffic during the course of the day.

"On it," Bill said, getting his phone out and calling the bank and stopping payment on the check.

"Mr. Snyder, I can almost predict your next move, so think about it before your stupidity gets you deeper in the hole you're already in."

"Don't pretend to know me," Kyle said, appearing ready to hit something.

"The media card is your next play, but selling your story will come back to bite you—hard. I may not know much about kids, but dealing with the media is one of my specialties."

"You're a lot like Amis, and I'm betting she ended up alone," Eglin said, smirking. "How is old Amis?"

"She's the president of a multimillion-dollar fashion house. She finished slumming a long time ago."

"Fuck you," Eglin said.

"You're both getting ready to learn the literal meaning of that expression, dear old Dad."

❖

Ellis spent the rest of the afternoon running last-minute errands for the show. It took a few hours before her head stopped hurting from the anger the meeting with Kyle and Eglin had built up. When she stopped to pick up dinner, she'd started thinking of a way to explain it to Charlotte.

"Come see, Ellis," Sawyer said when she put the bags down and hugged Charlotte and Amis.

The room Sawyer had settled into appeared like a completely

different space. All the canvases Sawyer had finished had obviously arrived and were leaning against the wall, and most of her clothes were out of her bag and on the desk for some reason. Sawyer had also taped some of her sketches on the windows, and that's where she was pulling her toward.

"Sorry about the mess," Sawyer said.

"What's all this?" There were only a few sketches, but Sawyer had tried to imitate her style as closely as possible.

"I wanted to help you because of everything that happened, so I designed these."

The models in Sawyer's work were all kids, and each one had a different message on the T-shirts they wore. She looked at each one and wanted to cry at how sweet and thoughtful this kid was. Charlotte came in and leaned against her. "This is the nicest thing anyone's ever done for me. Thank you, and I think they're great."

"Can they be in the show?"

"Let's see what we can do, but next year for sure you're going to have your own section, if you come up with more designs."

"Thanks for teaching me stuff," Sawyer said and hugged her, pressing her face into her chest as if she couldn't look at her for the next part. "I love you."

"I love you too, and I'm going to love having you here so we can learn stuff together." Sawyer pressed closer with all the strength she seemed to possess, which finally made Ellis cry. She glanced at Charlotte, who seemed to read her mind when she opened her mouth. It was time to tell Sawyer what they'd kept from her.

"Come here a minute, Sawyer," Charlotte said, sitting on the bed. "We found out a few things recently, and it's time for you to know."

"So you're related to me?" Sawyer asked Ellis when Charlotte finished talking.

"It's probably weird, but I'm your aunt. Your dad and I have the same father, so yeah, we're related." She'd had no real way to gauge what Sawyer's reaction would be, but having her almost tackle her to the floor laughing wasn't what she was expecting.

"Then I don't have to go back. We can live here with you and be happy. We can do that, right?" Sawyer was speaking so fast she barely understood her, but this was the most animated the kid had ever been around her.

"That's what I want. Let's start with dinner, and we can plan."

They had a pleasant evening, and she helped Charlotte get Sawyer ready for bed, leaving her door open in case she needed to find them in the night. Once they made it to the master bedroom, she spent a long moment holding Charlotte as she leaned against the door.

"Do you want to talk about it? And the right answer here would be, you'd love to talk about it," Charlotte said, putting her finger in the middle of her chest.

"I met with Kyle today and, as a bonus, got to meet my father. One of these days I've got to talk to my mother about her taste in men."

"Everyone makes mistakes, baby. I'm living proof of that. Like me, though, she rebounded well." Charlotte kissed her chin and tugged her toward the bed.

"How do you figure? My mom barely dates."

"I doubt Opal would agree with you, but we'll talk about that later. Right now I want to know what's up with you."

She told Charlotte everything about her meeting and how it had turned out. When she was done, Charlotte moved away from her, and she figured she'd get an earful for going off on her own.

"How much did you offer him?" Charlotte asked, but it was hard to guess how she was feeling.

"For which thing?"

Charlotte smiled and crossed her arms over her chest. "To sign the custody papers?"

"A million dollars."

Charlotte's arms fell lifelessly to her sides. "And for his statement?"

"A hundred and fifty thousand. One was more important than the other, but I'm sorry I tried it without talking to you first."

"You're an adorable idiot, you know that? You want to make a deal with me?"

"I'll make any deal you want," she said, smiling.

"From this moment going forward, you and me are a team. However we get what we want—we do it together. Think you can do that?"

"You've got my word."

"Good, but this second I'm more interested in getting your pants. Hand them over."

CHAPTER TWENTY-SIX

Fashion Week started five days later, and Ellis took Charlotte and Sawyer to a couple of the shows so they'd get a sense of the hype. The music, lights, and endless strings of models never got old to Ellis, and the styles, though beautiful, weren't anything close to what they had in store.

They were leaving a bistro close to her place when she noticed Eglin across the street. She left Sawyer with Charlotte and promised not to be long. "Are you stalking us, or do you need something?"

"I thought I'd turn the tables and watch you for a change."

"Okay. I didn't realize I was that interesting."

"At least now I know why that pretty little bitch ain't interested in my boy. She fell in love with the money right quick."

"Considering who you are, I can see how you'd think that, but don't ever talk about Charlotte like that again. I may design clothes for a living, but I'll hurt you."

"Cool it. I only want to talk to you about the kid. You still want Kyle to sign those papers?" She nodded. "Double the offer, give me half, and I can get him to do it."

"That's a lot of money so I'll have to think about it."

"Try not to take too long." He jammed his hands into his pockets and didn't move. "You tell Kyle any of this, and the deal's off. Actually, I'll do whatever it takes to get him not to do it if you double-cross me."

"Got it." They walked home after she was sure Eglin had left. Tori met them at the door and shook her hand. "You got all of it?"

"Loud and clear. We'll get Kyle alone tomorrow and show him the video. It might not change his mind, but we can hope."

"Did she get it?" Charlotte asked when they got upstairs.

"She's going to show it to Kyle like we planned. Eglin was so busy watching us, he never bothered to look around him. If it works out, we'll hear from Kyle next." The room was dark, but she could still see the outline of Charlotte's body when she undressed.

"You're not nervous at all?"

"About Eglin, you mean?" she asked.

"No. About the show."

"Day after tomorrow I'll be puking, but right now, I'm not nervous at all."

"That's what I love about you, baby. You're always good to go." Charlotte dropped to her knees and unbuckled her belt so she could get her pants off. "It's very flattering in a sexy sort of way."

"I can't help that I crave your touch. You've been making me insane since I met you."

"That's because I've wanted you from the beginning, but I couldn't admit it to myself since you were also aggravating as hell." Charlotte got her pants and underwear around her ankles and used her thumbs to spread her open. "You make me wet and hungry, but I need to touch you first. I need that and for you to come in my mouth." Charlotte looked up at her, and her gaze along with her words made her hard. Thankfully she hadn't made it much past the door, so she used it to keep herself upright as Charlotte sucked her clit in and didn't let up. She came so fast, it was like they hadn't touched each other in months, but she couldn't hold back.

"You make me totally nuts." She helped Charlotte to her feet and kicked her clothes off.

"Hang those up. I'm not cleaning up after two of you." Charlotte smiled and slapped her on the ass.

"You're going to stand there naked and expect me to hang my pants up?"

Charlotte glanced at her over her shoulder and nodded. "It might teach you some patience, baby." Before Charlotte could say anything else, she dropped her pants and threw her over her shoulder.

"Let's test your patience, beautiful." She placed Charlotte on the bed and stood over her. "My God, you're gorgeous, and I finally realize what my mother meant."

"About what?" Charlotte sat up and inched toward her on her knees again.

"She always said to wait for and fall for the one who's more beautiful in here." She placed her hand on Charlotte's chest and kissed her. "Thank you for sharing your heart with me, and for bringing joy and fun back into my life."

"We learned how to do that together, baby." Charlotte kissed her and pulled her down on top of her. "Make love to me." She began to kiss her way down, but Charlotte held her in place. "No. I want to see how you feel while you touch me. I love you, but I want you to make me yours."

"You are mine," she said, moving only enough to maneuver her hand between Charlotte's legs. "And I'll do whatever it takes to keep you." She wet her fingers by slowly dragging them up and over Charlotte's clit, and she moaned. That one sound made her hard again, but there was time enough for that.

"Baby, I love you, but I need you to fuck me. Put your fingers inside me now." Charlotte's hips came off the bed, and she pulled the hair at the back of Ellis's head. "I've been wet for you all day, and I'm tired of waiting."

She slid two fingers in until her thumb pressed against Charlotte's clit, and she didn't move as she looked down at Charlotte. It didn't matter where they were; this was now her home. Charlotte would be the very last woman in her bed and the first to claim her heart.

"You are mine," she said as she pulled out and slammed her fingers back inside.

"All yours, baby," Charlotte said and tugged her hair harder.

"Then let me hear you," she said as she started their dance and gave Charlotte what she wanted.

"Yes," Charlotte said as she spread her legs wider and lowered her hands down to her ass and squeezed as if encouraging her to go faster and deeper. She stopped when Charlotte screamed and went rigid. Watching her come for her was one of the most beautiful sights she'd ever witnessed.

"I love you, but maybe now you'd like to stake your claim as well," she said, chuckling.

"Oh, believe me, I'm planning to do just that for the rest of my life, if you let me." Charlotte's hand slid between her legs as she spoke, and the touch made her believe in happily ever after.

"I'm all yours, and only yours."

❖

"What's on tap for today?" Charlotte asked the next morning while Ellis packed her briefcase.

"Today we rejoin the land of the living, and the living go to the office."

"We? Are you sure you want me there?" She looked down at what she was wearing just in case Ellis was serious. "Everyone there thinks I stole from you."

"Everyone there thinks that because that's what we led them to believe. Today they'll hear the truth. If they don't like it, they're gone, but we've come as far as we can on our own. I need people working on this so it comes off like I want it to."

"I guess it's too late in the game for anyone to steal it now," Charlotte said, heading back to the bedroom to change. She'd already met some of Ellis's people, but she wanted to make a good impression.

"That's wishful thinking, babe. Until those girls are on the runway, I'm not going to relax. I'm usually not this paranoid, but someone's trying to fuck me, and they're in the building."

She moved to Ellis, sat in her lap in her underwear, and gave her a quick kiss. "There is someone in the building who's trying to fuck you, sweetheart, but I promise it's only because I find you incredibly sexy." The tease was meant to ease Ellis's tension, and it seemed to do that because she laughed.

"You're a riot, but get dressed, funny lady." The phone ringing got Ellis to help her up so she could answer it. From the conversation, someone was at the door. "This should be good."

"Who is it?" She held up an outfit and Ellis nodded.

"The god of fashion, if you ask him. We're being graced with a visit from Angelo Bollio." The doorbell made Ellis smile in a way that made her think she was looking forward to this. "Come out when you're ready." Ellis kissed her and rubbed her back.

The bell rang again, and Ellis chuckled. Angelo wasn't used to being kept waiting, or maybe he was slightly panicked. "Angelo," Ellis said, opening the door. "What a surprise. I'd thought you would've been up to your ass in sequins and gold lamé by now."

"Fuck you, Ellis." Angelo walked in and stopped in the middle of the room with his hands over his head. "The police just left my office and think I have something to do with what happened to you. If you fucking sent them to my place, I'm going to sue your ass."

"You don't get to come to my house and curse, Angelo. I didn't send anyone anywhere, so cool it or get out." Ellis slammed the door and walked close enough to him that he backed up. "The question you should be curious about is why the cops would show up at all. Why is that?"

"How the hell would I know?" Angelo's voice was almost a nervous squeal.

"Get out of my house and pray they don't pin any of this on you. If they can, prison is the least of your worries, because I'll bury you." She got close to him again and jabbed her finger into the middle of his chest. It was the only way to keep from punching his perfectly lotion-slathered and perfumed face.

"Look." He backed off again. "I've always thought you were an asshole, so I wasn't exactly torn up about what happened to you. That doesn't mean I had anything to do with it."

What sounded like her cell rang and stopped, so she figured Charlotte had answered it. "Hey," Charlotte said, handing the phone over. She listened to whoever it was and hung up.

"You tell me right now how you got involved, and I'll tell them to cut you some slack. I also promise not to sue you for everything but your toothbrush."

"I didn't do anything," he said in a whine so long she came close to offering him some cheese to go with it.

"Not what I heard, and the only thing to remember through all this is the most important thing of all. If you don't, I can pretty much guarantee it's all you'll be thinking about when you're sitting in the gutter wondering where exactly it all went wrong."

"What's so important that I won't be able to forget, except counting my money when I sue you for defamation?"

"You wanted me on my knees so you could pick at my bones like the vulture you are, but you need to consider who you struck your bargain with. Jennifer and Dalton are your partners in crime. Ask yourself if you think either of them will lie to protect you, or if they'll pin it on you to save their asses?"

"You're so fucking smug."

"No, I'm right, and you know it." She opened the door and waved him out. "Now get the hell out of my house."

"Was that really Angelo Bollio?" Charlotte asked.

"If you tell me he's one of your favorite designers, you're fired," she said, squinting at Charlotte.

"I'm a blonde, so I'd never look good in all that gold," Charlotte said, sticking her tongue out at her. "What did Bill tell you, if you can share?"

"To bait that idiot with his pals to see what happened. Hopefully it works, but I don't have time to think about it." The ride to the office took thirty minutes, so the place was buzzing with people talking about what was basically their championship week. Everyone should've been on edge about one thing, but they didn't have a line to fuss over, so gossip was keeping everyone busy.

Pretty much every person they met smiled at her and did a double take because of who she was with. The gossip that Charlotte and Sawyer were in the building must've spread fast since Rueben was waiting in her office. His face was the perfect mask of nothing, as if he didn't know what to feel about what he was seeing.

"Where have you been hiding?" he finally said, after shaking himself as if he had a chill.

"Not hiding, Ruby, working." She was going to hug him, but if he'd been a porcupine all his quills would be up and ready to strike, so she stopped midstride. "Let me get Charlotte settled, and I'll meet you in your office."

"*Why* is Charlotte with you at all? Did you somehow manage to forget that she totally ripped us off?"

"My mom didn't do anything wrong, so don't talk about her like that," Sawyer said loudly, so she went over and put her arms around the rigid little girl.

"Rueben, I'll meet you in your office." Thankfully he took the hint and left so she could deal with Sawyer, who was now crying. "It's okay, and I'm proud of you for taking up for your mom like that."

"Why doesn't he like us?"

"You know what my mom always tells me whenever I ask that? She says the only thing that matters is having people who love you. Those are the people who'll always stand by your side because they know the truth of you by knowing your heart. I love you, and I love your mom. You just beat me into standing up for her, but I promise to do that for the both of you."

"I'm sorry I yelled."

"I'm not. Your mom's important, so in this case, yelling was okay."

"Come with me, chéri," Amis said, opening her arms to Sawyer. "I have a visitor who needs to talk to Ellis and your mama, so let's take a tour so I can show you off."

"Who's our visitor?" she asked, not really needing another set of surprises.

"Do you remember the detective from that first night?"

"I do, and I'll be happy to speak to him as long as he's not here to pin it on me."

Amis's office was actually a bigger space than hers, and they found the detective standing in front of a large framed picture they'd used in their marketing campaign that year. The black-and-white photo of her and three models had a throwback feel to it, which maybe was a sign that she loved vintage even before Charlotte came into her life.

"Hello, Detective," she said, holding Charlotte's hand. "Hopefully you have some good news for us."

"Hi, I'm Charlotte," Charlotte said, gently hitting her on the arm.

"Nice to meet you, and yes, I think I've got good news. After talking to you this morning, Angelo went running to save his skin, only this time we were listening in, not that we didn't appreciate Tori's help. From the conversation we heard, we were able to pick up Jennifer and Dalton for theft."

"You arrested them?" The reality that it had gotten this far was totally insane.

"Not only that, but they haven't been able to post bond yet. A night in that hellhole they're in will seem like an eternity to both of them."

She had to sit down and was glad for Charlotte's support. "Did they say anything?"

"Dalton hasn't opened his mouth, but Jennifer asked to see you. I told her I doubted I could get that, but I'd ask." He sat across from them and tapped on his notebook with his pen. "It's a weird situation when the woman appears unfazed but the guy's scared shitless, but that's the dynamic between these two."

"If I see her, can you hold what she says against her?"

"I can't force you, but if you go it might provide us a better picture. I've got evidence they did it, but the jury always wants to know why. She might give that up to you if you feed her enough rope."

"The bitch almost took a chunk out of my lip for no reason, so I doubt she's interested in giving me anything if she thinks it'll help me."

"You'll never know unless you try."

"And if she says anything, it'll bring you one step closer," Charlotte said.

"When do you want me to do this?" She felt Charlotte tighten her hold on her hand so she relaxed and smiled.

"Now is okay with me, if you're available."

"That's fine, but I'd like to talk to Dalton first."

"If you don't mind his attorney being there, and he agrees to it, sure. He has some fantasy that we've got nothing on him so if he stays quiet he's going home. He hasn't budged, so don't get your hopes up."

"Dalton had the perfect life before this, but I doubt his wife will let him come within a thousand yards of the house. There won't be any going home in any fantasy."

"Maybe a meeting with you will get him talking. His cellmate's been busy, from what I hear, getting his mind off the rest of the world, and the only way to stop that budding romance is if he raises some cash fast."

She snorted. "He always claimed he's irresistible. I guess his charm didn't come in handy now. Add to that his fear of urinating in front of anyone, and this is rather entertaining."

"Can't blame him on that one," the detective said and handed over a card with the address of where she needed to go. "I'll meet you there."

"Thanks for all the attention to this, Detective." He shook hands with her and nodded.

"I have a wife who loves your stuff, but I'm a cop, you know. This is as close as she'll ever get to you and your clothing line. I'll tell her all about it later on tonight," he said, and laughed.

"The show's in a couple of days, so we'll set her up, but let's see if I can design something in bright orange for my old friends."

❖

Television and movies were as close as Ellis had ever been to the inside of an official interview room having to do with the police. She sat in the hard chair, wondering how long the drab Formica-topped table had been in there and how many people had spilled their guts on it. Confession might've been good for the soul, but she doubted it came easy in this place.

The door opened, and she tried to keep her expression passive. Dalton appeared drawn and lost in the oversized prison garb, and the large white bandage across his forehead wasn't helping. He dropped heavily into the chair across from her with the help of a guard. She didn't recognize the other guy in the nice suit, so he must've been the attorney the detective mentioned.

"Aren't you going to gloat?" Dalton asked as he held his hands up so the guard could remove his cuffs.

"Hostile isn't perhaps the way to go here, Dalton," she said, crossing her legs and putting her hands in her lap in an effort not to touch anything. "I didn't put you here. I'm the idiot who paid you a lot of money to work for me."

"You can't be shocked, can you?" Dalton leaned forward, and the guy in the suit put his hand on his forearm.

"This might make me sound stupid, but actually I am shocked. I've thought about this for days, and I still don't get it."

"I'm not admitting to anything, but you've never learned to look around you, Ellis. You were too busy being blinded by the limelight that never seems to dim when it comes to you. You never really noticed how those closest to you were left out, and you weren't about to let us in."

"Okay." She sighed, still not understanding how this guy felt so entitled. "All I was looking for here was an apology. You don't owe me anything but that. I'm not exactly after vengeance, Dalton, but I'm not going to throw you a lifeline either." She stood up and knocked on the door like the detective told her when she was done.

"Wait. Don't you want to know why?" Dalton yelled.

"That's the last thing you're going to tell me, so good luck to you. I'm through wasting my time here, because in reality it's really simple. It's the money and maybe the fame, but that's all it is. You were a manager and nothing more. If you wanted the limelight you should've gone in to some other line of business." The detective was waiting outside, and they both ignored Dalton's screams. The only one who seemed interested was Jennifer, who was being led into the next room with another guy in a suit.

"So," she said once she sat across from Jennifer. This was actually the only person she was interested in talking to. Dalton was a coward and Angelo an opportunist. Together they needed a brain to pull this off, and that was Jennifer. "Why are we here?"

"You had me arrested. Are you kidding with this?"

"I'm so glad you believe I'm so powerful that I can arrest people at random with no cause at all. You did this, so own it. It was a gamble, and it didn't work out. One of the things I didn't understand was that contract you tried to get me to sign. Why that farce?"

"Think of all the time and effort you would've saved yourself if you'd signed it. What is it you always love saying? There's an easy way to do things and a hard way."

"Jennifer, I have to say again what a bad idea this is," the lawyer with her said.

"And I told you to shut up. Ellis is never going to press charges because she cares more about the why than in seeing us go down." Jennifer locked eyes with her and smiled. "But what Ellis really wants to find out is who else. How many other people right under her nose will make her life a living hell? She knows I'm right, but that answer only comes with her dropping the charges."

"The one other person involved, you mean? Come on, now. I'm not that stupid. I just want to know why drag Charlotte and Sawyer into this? I've already figured out why you were involved." She smiled, and Jennifer seemed to become enraged.

"You don't know shit," Jennifer screamed at her as her entire body physically shook.

"I talked to the weaker link first, sweetheart," she said, laughing, "so you know I do. To think that I could've avoided all this by a pity fuck makes me want to kick myself. The thought of touching you makes me want to throw up, but you're right. Think of all the trouble it would've saved me."

"What?" Jennifer spoke softly this time, but Ellis heard the rage loud and clear. "You can't believe that. You're not exactly that delusional, are you?"

"I remember that night too, so there's no reason to be embarrassed about it now. You did everything but lie across my desk naked and beg me to put my hands on you. I guess you were under the impression that I'd fuck anything that walks, but even I have my standards."

"Oh, my fucking God. All I wanted out of this was to bring you down so I could cut a better deal. It's not my fault the stars aligned in our favor to make it easy."

"Jennifer, you need to shut this down now," the attorney said more forcibly.

"I'd listen to this guy," she said, her smile growing wider. "You're going to need all the help you can get when Dalton and the others dump all this on you to get out of this place. Whatever is coming will snowball until you can't stop it, and what's sad is that you know it. You started it, and now you can't stop it."

Jennifer appeared ready to kill her, given the chance, until the last thing she said. That for some reason made her laugh. "You don't know anything." Jennifer laughed harder. "And because you don't, I'm going to walk out of here. We're done, so good luck, Ellis. You're standing on quicksand, and that, you bitch, is a cesspool of your making."

Jennifer got up and knocked to leave. She left without saying another word, but Ellis couldn't help but think about what Jennifer had ended with. That this was something she'd started didn't make any sense.

"It wasn't enough to convict, but it was still damning," the detective said when they were alone. "Thanks for coming down here, and I'll keep you updated."

"I appreciate everything you and the others have done, and I'll be in touch about your wife's tickets."

She decided to take the subway back to the office and used the extra time to think about everything Jennifer had said. The only two things from their conversation that seemed important were the stars aligning and that it was something she herself made. She knew that was where the answer lay, but Jennifer wasn't giving it up that easily.

The receptionist welcomed her back and relayed the message that her mom and the rest of her group were waiting in Amis's office. She let her head drop back on the wall of the elevator on the way up. The only people waiting for her were Amis, Opal, Charlotte, and Sawyer—no Rueben. It was as if he'd completely disappeared from her life by choice, and that was one more mystery on her shoulders.

"How'd it go?" Charlotte asked, since she'd walked in and not said anything.

Her rundown on her meetings wasn't very long, because neither conversation with Dalton or Jennifer had taken much time. The take-away was supposed to be that they'd done it for the money.

"That's all she said?" Amis asked, and she nodded.

"How do people think they're going to get away with dumb shit like this?" Opal asked. "This was both the most elaborate yet stupid plan in the history of business."

Opal was right, and she glanced at both Charlotte and Sawyer. They were the key to the success of what Jennifer and the others had set into motion, and she hadn't seen it until right at that moment. Every conspiracy needed bait at its center, so it made sense that hers would depend on a beautiful woman for its success. They'd thrown Charlotte into her path, and she'd acted accordingly.

"Because they understood better than anyone alive, aside from my mother and you, how I tick. After all, every web is only as enticing as the spider makes it. In this case, it was a beautiful spider, wasn't it?" Her eyes never left Charlotte's, and what she was saying seemed to finally register on Charlotte's face.

"Ellis, you can't think—"

She raised her hand to stop whatever Charlotte was going to say. "It's exactly what I think," she said and walked out.

CHAPTER TWENTY-SEVEN

Rueben stood up when Ellis entered his office. His expression was somewhat unreadable, but if she had to guess it was a mixture of shock and some trepidation. She closed the door gently behind her and leaned against it.

"Are you ready to talk now? You keep running off on me, so I'm wondering if you're trying to avoid me," he said, sitting down slowly as if wanting the desk between them. "Where'd you run off to?"

"I got to visit Jennifer and Dalton in jail for a chat," she said, moving from the door.

"It's hard to believe you'd actually go, after everything they did." It sounded as if every ounce of energy in his body had bled onto the nice carpet.

"My only question is why?"

"Why what?"

"Don't...just don't," she said, with an urge to run out of the building. "I told Jennifer it was a gamble that didn't work out, but don't fucking deny it. Now all I need...no, want to know, is why."

"You can't take their word over mine," he said, his eyes filling with tears as if he could summon them at will. "You can't."

"What I could never figure out after reading Tori's report that surprisingly contained my father and a brother I know nothing about was how they were found. Eglin Snyder's name isn't on my birth certificate. It's not something I've ever made public." She pushed away from the door and leaned over the desk. "Only a very few people know my entire life story, so from what you're saying, the traitor is either my mother or Opal. Is that what you're asking me to believe?"

"Ellis, you know me. We've worked together from the very beginning. Eglin would've been easy enough to find if you were looking for him." His tears were flowing freely now, and he pressed his hands together in a praying position.

"How'd you find Charlotte and Sawyer?" None of his dramatics cut through the hurt. "Answer me," she screamed, letting some of the anger out before it ruptured something she wouldn't be able to put back together deep inside.

"I attended her graduation on behalf of the company and noticed Sawyer. The kid looks like every picture I've seen of you when you were her age. It was almost funny to think she was your bastard, but a little digging led me to Kyle and Eglin. Jennifer and Dalton took care of the rest."

"That answers that, but not the why. Why'd you do this?" She finally had to sit or fall down. He'd kneecapped her, and it had blindsided her. The only way the betrayal could be any deeper was if it had been her mother.

"When were you going to tell me you were selling the company? The day someone put me out on the street? I've dedicated my life to you, and hearing you were going to cut me out hurt me. It's like all my loyalty meant nothing to you, so I had to fend for myself. Angelo Bollio understood that, so if you wanted out, that's great, but I wanted to leave on my own terms."

"I looked over an offer, you bastard, and I rejected it. An offer that never left my office, so we'll get to how you saw it since I don't appreciate anyone going through my desk." She'd loved Rueben from the very beginning, and that hadn't disappeared overnight. The contempt she felt for him, though, was making it hard to feel anything at all for him. "Why would you ever think I'd throw you to the curb, even if I'd considered it?"

"Maybe you should ask yourself why you didn't even think it was important to see if that's what I wanted. It's like I'm your fucking slave who has to bow and scrape to stay in your presence, and you reward that loyalty by including a couple of my pieces in the show." He started crying hard and grabbed the hair at the sides of his head and pulled. "I'm so goddamn tired of getting overlooked by every pretty bauble that gets naked for you. It's why I knew Charlotte would work so easily in keeping you in the dark."

"You've been right where you've wanted to be, and I've never overlooked you. I loved you enough to make you part of my family, but this? I'll never get over it, and I'll never forgive it. Get out of my sight—we're done."

He shook his head and screamed like an animal. "It's not that easy, Ellis. You owe me. I've been here too long for you to simply put me out."

"You stupid fucker. Your contract with this company is no different than mine, and sharing designs breaks the first, most important rule. I'm sure my mother will agree with firing your ass, so pack your shit and get out of my sight."

"What does Amis have to do with anything?"

"You were so busy trying to screw me that you missed one important thing in all this. You and those bastards you colluded with to destroy me figured I'm some power and fame hog, but all I've ever wanted in my life is to design. That's it, so my mother is important here because she owns the fucking company. That's how I set it up. We both work for her."

"No, you—"

"No, you and the rest of the world think that, but legally it's hers because I gave it to her. Even if I'd been dumb enough to sign the contract Jennifer had drawn up, it wouldn't have meant shit." She stared at him and couldn't believe she'd missed all the signs of his betrayal. "Do you honestly think I would've left my mother out after everything she'd done for me? I admit I loved you, but you don't know me at all, so leave. Get out, or I'll have security drag you out. If you don't believe that, fucking try me."

"Ellis, please, let's talk about this. We can start over, and I promise I'll make it up to you."

"Make it up to me? How do you think that's possible? Not only did you give those bastards the first bible, but you tried to set Charlotte up to take the fall for the second theft. You're done here, and you're done with me."

"No," he cried, and she shook her head at the mess of tears and snot on his face.

She walked out and found her mother and two security guards. "Make sure you inventory everything he's taking," she said to the guards. "And lock him out of everything as of right now."

"Already done, ma'am."

"I'll take care of this, so get back into my office and peel Charlotte and Sawyer off the ceiling. Later, we'll all discuss your habit of leaving a room before you clear the air first," Amis said, pointing her in the right direction.

"Call Bill too when you're done, please."

"Ma chéri, I'll take care of it all, so you take care of what's most important now."

"You're right about that. Those two and you are the most important people in my life. We'll talk about Opal tonight so I can add her to that list."

❖

"My mother's already taken me to the woodshed, but that's not why I owe you a huge apology," Ellis said, dropping to her knees in front of Charlotte and Sawyer. She'd found the two scrunched together on Amis's couch looking totally unhappy.

"It's not?" Charlotte asked as she rubbed Sawyer's head, since Sawyer appeared really upset.

"I've been mostly alone in my heart and in my head for most of my adult life. With the exception of my mother and a few others, I've never let anyone in. She and those few know how I am and work around it, but I want to change that behavior. I'm not alone anymore, so I promise to not run off like that again, especially when it gives you the wrong impression." She reached for their hands and smiled when they didn't reject her need to be close to them. "I'm sorry, and no matter what, I never believed you had anything to do with this."

"It's okay. I could see how it'd be easy to think that," Charlotte said.

"I would've forgiven you even if you were involved."

"We love you too much to ever betray you like that." The way Charlotte said it made any barriers between them disappear.

"I love you both too, and thankfully, this is finally over. You two want to help me finish out Fashion Week?"

Charlotte and Sawyer both hugged her, and Amis and Opal joined in when they walked in. "Enough mush," Opal said gruffly, but she wiped happy tears from her eyes. "The girls are here and ready to see if we have to make any tweaks."

The next day and the following until their premiere, Charlotte and Sawyer never left her side as she did a multitude of interviews, and she had to admire how quickly Charlotte grew used to the attention and how fast the camera fell in love with her. The only one who got the exclusive of the entire story, which included the loss of Rueben from her life and business, was Sierra.

She'd told that part with a seeming detachment that had been necessary to keep herself together. After Rueben had left, she thought about his part in all this, and it had sliced right through her soul. They'd been family, but he'd thrown that away over some petty sense of entitlement and had spent the summer locked away from her because he'd known the effort would be wasted. While she worked to set things right, he was waiting to give it all away for some promise of fame.

"Everything's in place so we're good to go," Amis said as Ellis checked each model to see if anything needed to be adjusted.

She'd filled the inside of the tent with a multitude of large plants and a fog machine set to low. The interior appeared jungle-like, with all the lighting pointed at the runway. This show, more than any other, would be a production from beginning to end, so hopefully it'd be memorable. Her nerves had calmed some when Amis had let Brandi and Jacqueline backstage to say hello. It was a great reminder that even with Rueben's betrayal, there were still people in the world who had her back and loved her.

"Let's see if our safari guide is ready," she said, kissing Amis's cheeks.

They'd found Sawyer a safari outfit like the ones in the old black-and-white movies, and she'd been surprised that the somewhat-shy kid had agreed to volunteer. "You ready?" She hugged Sawyer before handing over the pith helmet.

"I think so."

"This might make you feel better about it." She pointed to the monitor, and the big screens at each side of the stage had Sawyer's paintings scrolling on them. "They're going to love you, almost as much as I love you, but no one but your mom is ever going to love you that much."

Sawyer walked out and said her lines hesitantly at first, but gained confidence as Birdie and the others kissed her cheeks when they reached her. The clothes received enthusiastic applause after each round, and the audience quieted when the lights dimmed for the last piece. Ellis took Charlotte's hand and waited for the grand finale.

"There aren't enough words in my vocabulary to thank you," she said to Sigrid as she joined them right behind the divider.

"You're one of the good ones, Ellis, and you survived. Going forward, though, your designs will only exceed this because you've found your better half, and that, my friend, will only fuel your imagination. I wish you both more happiness than I've found in mine, and that's a lot."

The spotlight stayed on Sigrid as she stepped out in the long, black vintage-appearing gown from Charlotte's portfolio. The crew had again slicked Sigrid's hair back and added a stunning cat-faced diamond brooch to her right shoulder. Her appearance alone was a sign of her stamp of approval for the collection, but also a sign of her friendship with Ellis. It was her old friend's first walk down the catwalk in years, and Ellis would have a hard time repaying the favor.

Sigrid held her hands up when she was done, and Ellis and Charlotte came out to a standing ovation. They made room for Sawyer between them and simply enjoyed the hard-fought-for moment. Despite the torpedoes to the hull they'd taken, they'd made it.

"Wow," Sawyer said, blinking through all the camera flashes.

"Welcome to the family business, buddy," Ellis said, making Sawyer laugh.

They enjoyed the night's celebration with the staff at the office. The gossip about Rueben and the others had run through the place like wildfire through a dry field, but had just as quickly burned out. The sense of relief that everything was over had brought back the excitement of the next year and beyond that nights like this usually included.

"You guys ready to head home?" Ellis asked after a couple of hours. She was tired enough to sleep for a week.

"Yeah, I'm beat," Charlotte said, following her back to her office. They both stopped short when they spotted the security guard waiting with Kyle.

Ellis had sent him a ticket, along with the surveillance tape of Eglin, and she wondered if he'd done anything with both items that should've changed his perspective, or at least his outlook. He stared at her with an expression of a man unhappy with his life, but she couldn't really blame him. They'd both been screwed with Eglin as a father, but at least she'd had Amis. Kyle's mother didn't sound like she'd invested a lot in his future. She'd also won Charlotte's love, and that most probably was the hardest thing to overcome when it came to where he stood.

"I want to talk to Charlotte alone," he said, making her look at Charlotte, who nodded.

"Use my office, and we'll hang out next door in case you need anything," she said, taking Sawyer's hand.

"Don't leave, okay, Sawyer? I want to talk to you too, if that's all right," Kyle asked, and Sawyer nodded as well, so she watched Kyle follow Charlotte in and close the door.

Her sense of jealousy made her want to run in there and tell him to stay the hell away from Charlotte, but she had faith in what they shared. It frankly sucked, though, to be an adult, but baby steps, she thought, and smiled.

"It's okay. She loves you," Sawyer said, as if reading her mind.

"Thanks, kid, and you're right."

❖

"I didn't know what it was you wanted to do until tonight," Kyle said, glancing around the space.

"How'd you figure it out?" Charlotte sat down, folding her legs under her. She and Kyle had been through plenty, but all they had in common now was Sawyer.

"Ellis invited me to the show, so I went." He sat down on the edge of one of the leather chairs and put the envelope he'd brought next to his feet. "I didn't know Sawyer could draw like that."

"She's really good, and Ellis helped her transfer that to canvases this summer for the show tonight. She even sold one, so we started a college fund."

"That's good," he said loudly. "She's a good kid, so she deserves that."

"She is, so we can both be proud." She watched him look everywhere except at her. "Did you need something?"

"You and me had some good times, huh?" He sounded wistful and hopeful at the same time, so she was confused.

"That was a long time ago, and I was too young to really know that maybe it wasn't all that much fun. I'll never regret having Sawyer, but raising her by myself has been hard. My parents helped a lot, but it was difficult because Sawyer wasn't their responsibility—she was ours, but you've never wanted anything to do with her. Don't try to gloss over that now."

"You and her are together, aren't you?"

"If you mean Ellis, yes, we are, and if you think you're going to use that—"

"Wait, just wait. It's only a question. I know I screwed up and there's no going back. I should've done better with Sawyer and you, but I can't change that." He combed his hair out of his eyes and shook his head. "You don't think it's weird she's my sister?"

"No, because I doubt Ellis sees you that way, and nothing would change between us even if she did. I love her and so does Sawyer, so I hope you can accept that. Ellis isn't going anywhere."

"I always hoped we'd be a family, but I know I fucked that up. I haven't been great with her, but I love her, you know. She's my kid."

"I know she is." It was becoming clear that he wouldn't be giving in so easily. "I hope you'll be okay with Ellis in her life. You may not like her, but Sawyer idolizes her, and for good reason. She loves spending time with her, and Sawyer opened up and flourished under that attention. Ellis managed to get her to share her art with her after the first five minutes of knowing her. Up to then I was the only one who knew she liked to draw and was that good."

"Ouch," he said, holding his hands over his chest. "I deserved that, but I signed the papers." He picked up the envelope and handed it over. "I don't want the money, but I'd still like to see her. Maybe we could start over if I promise she'll actually spend time with me and only me."

"Sawyer would love that."

"And if things don't work out, you can call me, okay?"

She smiled at the offer and was glad to let go of old hurts. "Thanks, but I'm not planning to let her go."

"Make sure she never forgets how lucky she is."

Charlotte stood and hugged him, kissing his cheek for his generosity. "Thank you."

She walked him next door, where he talked to Sawyer about what came next and told her not to worry. There would be no court and no fight over her. He finished by shaking hands with Ellis and apologizing for his part in the scheme against her. That had been a surprise, considering his attitude, but Ellis had graciously accepted.

"See you soon, Sawyer," he said, standing to go.

"You'll see her next Saturday, actually," Ellis said, handing over a sheet of paper. "You and Sawyer are starting art classes at ten, and you have reservations for lunch at one. Don't be late."

"How do you know I can draw anything?" he said, not refusing what she'd handed over.

"Call it a hunch on my part," Ellis said, and winked at him. "It's all in the genes."

CHAPTER TWENTY-EIGHT

"Can you believe it?" Charlotte said after they were finally alone in their room.

"Which part? The show was fabulous, but knowing that we can move forward together with Kyle's blessing was the best part of tonight." Ellis slowly took her suit off, circling Charlotte and pressing against her back. "You and Sawyer are going to be the centerpiece of my life. I love you, and you'll never doubt my devotion for you."

"I know that, my love, and I'm looking forward to whatever comes next, because no matter what it is, we'll be together."

"I've got one more surprise for you tonight," Ellis said, turning her to face the wall that had a sheet-draped something leaning against it. "It's the first of many, I'm guessing."

"What do mean?" Whatever it was didn't excite her as much as Ellis lowering her zipper and putting her hands inside her dress. "Do you know something, baby?"

"What's that?" Ellis used her fingers to push the dress off her shoulders so it would drop to the ground. The anticipation of Ellis's touch made her nipples so hard against the lace of her bra it was almost painful.

"You make me hungry for you," she said, turning around and kissing her. "That's never happened to me, but when you're this close, I can't help but want you."

"The feeling is mutual, and I want to show you how much I love you."

"Then touch me," she said, impatiently tugging on Ellis's shirt to get it off.

"In a minute, but let's look at your surprise first." Ellis moved them closer to the sheet and handed her a corner so she could pull it down. "For you, my love."

When she tugged, the canvas came into view, and she knew immediately where it would hang, which made her cry. Ellis's wall up the stairs in New Orleans would for the first time have a face to go with the dress that was the centerpiece of that year's collection, and it was hers.

"From the minute I met you, I thought you had the face that could launch any line, and I was right. You're beautiful, sweetheart, and you're mine. I'm one lucky bastard."

"It's beautiful, and I'm the lucky one in that you see me like this." She stood in the circle of Ellis's arms and stared at her likeness in disbelief. "When did you paint this?"

"This summer when I was working on the line that we showed tonight. Sigrid is right in that you'll be the muse that fuels my imagination from this night on."

"Thank you," she said, turning around and raising her head so Ellis would kiss her. "Make love to me."

"Gladly," Ellis said, and carried her to the bed.

They took their time making love that night, along with plans far into their future together. "Do you fly down to New Orleans any time aside from the summer?" Charlotte asked as she lay next to Ellis.

"Mama and I actually head down for the holidays so Uncle Malcom can fatten us up, as he likes to say, but I'm sure he can cook here."

"No. I'm looking forward to making traditions with you."

"You're a gift, Charlotte, and I love you. I didn't think it was possible to be this happy."

"You haven't seen anything yet, Boss."

"I'm looking forward to every minute of it, beautiful."

Sixteen years later

"So that's the whole story," Sawyer said to the *Vogue* reporter. Her solo show was the next day, but she'd made time for the recounting of her family's history. Her mom Ellis had always preached that the clothes were important, but the hype was part of the package.

"And Rueben, Jennifer, and Dalton? Why did they seem to get away with what they did? From what the police told me, they all could've done a lot more time for what they stole."

"The angle you should write about is not that they got away with it, but my mother's capacity for forgiveness. She forgave them the crime, and they paid with what they tried to take from her."

"Which was what?"

"In a word—everything. The civil lawsuit left the three of them with very little, and Angelo Bollio was exposed for his part in their plan. His business suffered just like the magazine *Styles and Trends* did."

"Hardly anyone remembers that poor excuse for a publication." The woman closed her notebook so Sawyer guessed that wasn't making it into the article.

"Off the record," she said, and the woman nodded, "the same could be said of Angelo Bollio's clothes."

"True, but the same can't be said of your stuff. Sigrid has always said you were a prodigy."

"Hardly. My mom claims it's all in the genes."

Like Ellis had promised, her T-shirt line had debuted the year after Rueben had been fired. It had become a good seller, and both Charlotte and Ellis had helped her grow as a designer and develop her own style, which had been introduced into the Renois line through the years. This year, though, her mothers had gifted her with her own label.

"Lucky break, being one of Ellis Renois's kids," the woman said with a smile.

"Ha," she said, laughing. "My parents were forever nicknamed beauty and the boss, but they're not known for letting anyone skate, especially me and my brother Malcom. They made us work for everything, but they've both shown us what true love really is. That was our lucky break, not having Renois for a last name."

"Don't worry. I'm not putting that in the article. Your brother is young and sweet, but he's as tough as Amis and Opal when it comes to taking up for you and your mothers."

Sawyer's phone rang, and she apologized for answering it. "Hey,

Mama." She listened as Charlotte reminded her of a long list of things she'd already done. "Got it covered, so tell Mom not to stress over it anymore. I promise to do you both proud."

The way Charlotte laughed never failed to make her smile. Her mother's laughter had been so fleeting before Ellis came into her life, since she had constantly worried about what came next and how she'd take care of them both. Ellis had given them both a secure foundation to fly from and the fairy tale Charlotte had always dreamed of.

Their life had totally changed when they came to live with Ellis in New York and New Orleans, but no matter where they were, they were at home with Ellis, Amis, Opal, and Malcom. They were a family, and their love and support gave her a sense of fearlessness to climb as high as she could dream, and they gave her a relationship with her father she didn't think possible.

Those art lessons had been the beginning of her and Kyle getting to know each other, and he'd come to be the type of parent she'd never dreamed he could be. Eglin had predictably disappeared once he knew none of the Renois money would be coming his way, but Kyle and Ellis had become friends in the years that followed. Ellis had even helped him get a job in the art department at *Vogue*, and he'd gone on to remarry. That chance meeting with Ellis had brought them all that happy ending they didn't think possible.

Their happiness only grew when Ellis adopted her, and then they welcomed her baby brother Malcom a few years later.

"If that's it, I've got to run," she said when she ended the call.

"Everything okay?"

"Perfect, but as my mothers love to say, the story continues, and plenty of happiness is still to come."

About the Author

Ali Vali is originally from Cuba and has frequently used many of her family's traditions and language in her stories. Having her father read adventure stories and poetry before bed as a child infused her with a love of reading, which is even stronger today. In 2000, Ali decided to embark on a new path and started writing.

Ali lives in the suburbs of New Orleans with her partner of thirty-one years, and finds that residing in such a historically rich area provides plenty of material to draw from in creating her novels and short stories. Mixing imagination with different life experiences makes it easier to create the slew of characters that are engaging to the reader on many levels. Ali states that "The feedback from readers encourages me to continue to hone my skills as a writer."

Books Available From Bold Strokes Books

Beauty and the Boss by Ali Vali. Ellis Renois is at the top of the fashion world, but she never expects her summer assistant Charlotte Hamner to tear her heart and her business apart like sharp scissors through cheap material. (978-162639-919-8)

Fury's Choice by Brey Willows. When gods walk amongst humans, can two women find a balance between love and faith? (978-162639-869-6)

Lessons in Desire by MJ Williamz. Can a summer love stand a four-month hiatus and still burn hot? (978-163555-019-1)

Lightning Chasers by Cass Sellars. For Sydney and Parker, being a couple was never what they had planned. Now they have to fight corruption, murder, and enemies hiding in plain sight just to hold on to each other. Lightning Series, Book Two. (978-162639-965-5)

Summer Fling by Jean Copeland. Still jaded from a breakup years earlier, Kate struggles to trust falling in love again when a summer fling with sexy young singer Jordan rocks her off her feet. (978-162639-981-5)

Take Me There by Julie Cannon. Adrienne and Sloan know it would be career suicide to mix business with pleasure, however tempting it is. But what's the harm? They're both consenting adults. Who would know? (978-162639-917-4)

Unchained Memories by Dena Blake. Can a woman give herself completely when she's left a piece of herself behind? (978-162639-993-8)

Walking Through Shadows by Sheri Lewis Wohl. All Molly wanted to do was go backpacking…in her own century. (978-162639-968-6)

A Lamentation of Swans by Valerie Bronwen. Ariel Montgomery returns to Sea Oats to try to save her broken marriage but soon finds herself also fighting to save her own life and catch a murderer. (978-1-62639-828-3)

Freedom to Love by Ronica Black. What happens when the woman who spent her life worrying about caring for her family finally finds the freedom to love without borders? (978-1-63555-001-6)

House of Fate by Barbara Ann Wright. Two women must throw off the lives they've known as a guardian and an assassin and save two rival houses before their secrets tear the galaxy apart. (978-1-62639-780-4)

Planning for Love by Erin Dutton. Could true love be the one thing that wedding coordinator Faith McKenna didn't plan for? (978-1-62639-954-9)

Sidebar by Carsen Taite. Judge Camille Avery and her clerk, attorney West Fallon, agree on little except their mutual attraction, but can their relationship and their careers survive a headline-grabbing case? (978-1-62639-752-1)

Sweet Boy and Wild One by T. L. Hayes. When Rachel Cole meets soulful singer Bobby Layton at an open mic, she is immediately in thrall. What she soon discovers will rock her world in ways she never imagined. (978-1-62639-963-1)

To Be Determined by Mardi Alexander and Laurie Eichler. Charlie Dickerson escapes her life in the US to rescue Australian wildlife with Pip Atkins, but can they save each other? (978-1-62639-946-4)

True Colors by Yolanda Wallace. Blogger Robby Rawlins plans to use First Daughter Taylor Crenshaw to get ahead, but she never planned on falling in love with her in the process. (978-1-62639-927-3)

Heart Stop by Radclyffe. Two women, one with a damaged body, the other a damaged spirit, challenge each other to dare to live again. (978-1-62639-899-3)

Undercover Affairs by Julie Blair. Searching for stolen documents crucial to U.S. security, CIA agent Rett Spenser confronts lies, deceit, and unexpected romance as she investigates art gallery owner Shannon Kent. (978-1-62639-905-1)

Taking Sides by Kathleen Knowles. When passion and politics collide, can love survive? (978-1-62639-876-4)

Unexpected by Jenny Frame. When Dale McGuire falls for Rebecca Harper, the mother of the son she never knew she had, will Rebecca's troubled past stop them from making the family they both truly crave? (978-1-62639-942-6)

Canvas for Love by Charlotte Greene. When ghosts from Amelia's past threaten to undermine their relationship, Chloé must navigate the greatest romance of her life without losing sight of who she is. (978-1-62639-944-0)

Repercussions by Jessica L. Webb. Someone planted information in Edie Black's brain and now they want it back, but with the protection of shy former soldier Skye Kenny, Edie has a chance at life and love. (978-1-62639-925-9)

Spark by Catherine Friend. Jamie's life is turned upside down when her consciousness travels back to 1560 and lands in the body of one of Queen Elizabeth I's ladies-in-waiting…or has she totally lost her grip on reality? (978-1-62639-930-3)

Thorns of the Past by Gun Brooke. Former cop Darcy Flynn's heart broke when her career on the force ended in disgrace, but perhaps saving Sabrina Hawk's life will mend it in more ways than one. (978-1-62639-857-3)

You Make Me Tremble by Karis Walsh. Seismologist Casey Radnor comes to the San Juan Islands to study an earthquake but finds her heart shaken by passion when she meets animal rescuer Iris Mallery. (978-1-62639-901-3)

Girls Next Door, edited by Sandy Lowe and Stacia Seaman. Best-selling romance authors tell it from the heart—sexy, romantic stories of falling for the girls next door. (978-1-62639-916-7)

Complications by MJ Williamz. Two women battle for the heart of one. (978-1-62639-769-9)

Crossing the Wide Forever by Missouri Vaun. As Cody Walsh and Lillie Ellis face the perils of the untamed West, they discover that love's uncharted frontier isn't for the weak in spirit or the faint of heart. (978-1-62639-851-1)

Fake It till You Make It by M. Ullrich. Lies will lead to trouble, but can they lead to love? (978-1-62639-923-5)

Pursuit by Jackie D. The pursuit of the most dangerous terrorist in America will crack the lines of friendship and love, and not everyone will make it out from under the weight of duty and service. (978-1-62639-903-7)

The Practitioner by Ronica Black. Sometimes love comes calling whether you're ready for it or not. (978-1-62639-948-8)

Unlikely Match by Fiona Riley. When an ambitious PR exec and her super-rich coding geek-girl client fall in love, they learn that giving something up may be the only way to have everything. (978-1-62639-891-7)

Where Love Leads by Erin McKenzie. A high school counselor and the mom of her new student bond in support of the troubled girl, never expecting deeper feelings to emerge, testing the boundaries of their relationship. (978-1-62639-991-4)

Forsaken Trust by Meredith Doench. When four women are murdered, Agent Luce Hansen must regain trust in her most valuable investigative tool—herself—to catch the killer. (978-1-62639-737-8)

Letter of the Law by Carsen Taite. Will federal prosecutor Bianca Cruz take a chance at love with horse breeder Jade Vargas, whose dark family ties threaten everything Bianca has worked to protect—including her child? (978-1-62639-750-7)

New Life by Jan Gayle. Trigena and Karrie are having a baby, but the stress of becoming a mother and the impact on their relationship might be too much for Trigena. (978-1-62639-878-8)

Soul Survivor by I. Beacham. Sam and Joey have given up on hope, but when fate brings them together it gives them a chance to change each other's life and make dreams come true. (978-1-62639-882-5)

Unbroken by Donna K. Ford. When Kayla and Jackie, two women with every reason to reject Happily Ever After, fall in love, will they have the courage to overcome their pasts and rewrite their stories? (978-1-62639-921-1)